T0117047

Jersey Devil

R. Wayne Emerson

iUniverse, Inc.
Bloomington

Jersey Devil

iUniverse books may be ordered through booksellers or by contacting:

iUniverse
1663 Liberty Drive
Bloomington, IN 47403
www.iuniverse.com
1-800-Authors (1-800-288-4677)

ISBN: 978-1-4502-9126-2 (sc)
ISBN: 978-1-4502-9128-6 (dj)
ISBN: 978-1-4502-9127-9 (ebk)

Printed in the United States of America

iUniverse rev. date: 3/18/2011

PROLOGUE

On the evening of October 31, 1735, Mrs. Deborah Leeds and her husband held an ancient ritual of evil, a ritual that would forever affect their lives. Once, they had been a prominent and high-class couple, but through a series of bad investments, they had lost everything. Turning away from God, the Leeds had begun to dabble in the occult, and soon they had begun to worship the Dark One himself. They were not alone, and others who were like-minded sought them out, joining them in their worship of evil.

There were thirteen in all, seated around the table that night. Wearing masks portraying foul beings, seven men and six women made up the coven of evil. Surrounded by the others and lying in the center of the table was Deborah Leeds. She rested, stark naked on a cloth of black satin, awaiting the birth of the child who would change everything for her and her family.

While the vessel lay in heavy labor, the worshipers of the dark god began to chant and praise him. Believing that through their ritual they were going to bring the Antichrist into the world, the coven of evil prayed to Satan, begging the Devil, pleading that the child of destiny might be born of the woman on the table. Promising Satan the obedience of their child, the Leeds opened up their souls to the Master of Lies, allowing him to corrupt that of the unborn child within Deborah.

The invitation was such that Satan could not refuse the offer, and indeed, he did taint the soul of the child, removing any spark of kindness or goodness in the unborn baby. Though he had taken the offer, Satan had no intention of granting the Leeds and the pitiful coven surrounding them the birth of the Antichrist. The details of the birth of such a child had been written in scripture; there could be no deviating from the words of the prophets. Instead, the Supreme Liar and Deliverer of Darkness called upon another of his kind, one that gladly accepted the invitation to pervert that which should have been holy. Angered by the deception of Samuel Leeds, the unnamed demon caused the baby to be born deformed, unclean, and with no semblance of humanity.

The demon that accepted the offer had come to Satan some days before the ritual. Boasting that he had tempted the man into such a foolish act, the demon had set a plan in motion, a plan that it had been waiting a thousand years to see to fruition. As was the way of the Evil One, Satan answered the prayers of the Leeds, but not without a price, not without some cruel joke, and not before sending his minion to taint the child before it could be born.

The labor Deborah Leeds suffered through was awful, and the child split her terribly as it was born into the world. Through it all, she boasted that it was a small price to pay to bring the Antichrist into the world of men.

One of the coven members was a midwife, and she was seated directly between the legs of Deborah. She above any of the others in the room, felt singularly blessed. To bring the son of Satan into the world was a great honor, an honor she was prepared for, or so she thought.

The first part of the baby that showed was the head. Confused and momentarily frightened by what she saw, the midwife turned to Samuel Leeds as if expecting some explanation. The smile on the face of Samuel only served to confuse the midwife more. She was scared stiff. Having delivered many babies, the midwife had never seen anything like that which was in front of her now. Red coarse hair showed before the crowning of the head, a head that was shaped like none that she had ever seen before.

With another push from Deborah, the sides of the head came free, and the midwife let out a gasp. The wiry hair on the head of the creature being born to Deborah was all wrong, it wasn't human. When she saw the small, monkey-like ears, she nearly fainted.

Faith in the Dark Prince was all that kept her from fleeing in fear, and she steeled herself against what she might see next. The Dark Master worked in his own way and if what was being born in the house of the Leeds that night was the will of the master, the midwife would endure it.

Tucked in against the chest of the baby was its face, a face that was elongated and resembled that of a horse.

Along with the shoulders came the wings, tiny wings like those of a bat.

Unable to control herself, the midwife screamed at the horror she was witnessing being born that night.

Hearing the scream of the midwife, the coven discontinued its chanting and gathered around the child, which now lay sprawled out on the black satin fabric that had served as a swaddling cloth for its birth. Down to a one, they were all aghast at what they saw that night.

Lying on the table, writhing as if in pain, was not the Antichrist. Instead, it was an abomination, a child of the Devil that could never have a place in the world of men.

Weak, pitiful, and deformed so that it resembled a human not at all, the child let out its first cry. The steely bark of the creature was loud, breaking the windows of the house. Unlike anything they had ever heard before, the shrill cry of the beast caused the men to grind their teeth and the women to cry out for mercy. It was both painful and pitiful to hear.

Covering their ears against the inhuman scream of the child, the men and women of the coven prayed that they might never hear the unholy voice again. Panic ran through all who were standing around the foul child. They knew that something had gone horribly wrong. Cries of despair rang out, and those gathered cursed themselves for fools. What they had brought into the world was not the Antichrist but a foul being of ugliness. Somehow they had offended the Dark One, and they were ashamed.

Frightened and unsure of what to do, Samuel scooped the baby up in the swaddling cloth of black satin that had been set off to the side. Intended to be the royal robe of the Antichrist, the cloth became a shameful cloak that would hide the deformed child of Samuel and Deborah Leeds.

Rushing to the front door, Samuel Leeds pushed through without a thought of putting on a coat or hat. In his arms, the pitiful creature writhed and squirmed to be free of its covering. The corners of leathery wings and the sharp edges of hooves that were still covered in amniotic fluid smeared across the arms and chest of the man who was supposed to be the proud father of the beast.

Daring to take another peek at the abomination he held in his arms, Samuel cringed, nearly crying out in disgust. The lovely child with the wicked heart that should have been born to him and his wife was a monstrosity, a mixture of animals; it couldn't possibly be alive, yet it was. He could see its large nostrils flaring as it continued its struggle to be free of the satin swaddling cloth.

Running with a speed born of desperation, Samuel soon found himself on the rickety bridge that led into the town proper.

Out of breath and out of sanity, he was desperate. Frantic to be rid of the disfigured child that had been born to his wife, Samuel cast the baby off of the bridge and into the cold waters of the river below.

In what felt like slow motion, the baby fell. Not a sound came from the devil child as it was tossed away like a heap of unwanted rags, before it splashed into the icy waters of the swiftly flowing river.

Staring over the edge of the bridge in disbelief at what he'd just done, Samuel began to cry. He hadn't asked for the deformed child, and there was no way that the world would accept the baby. Had he kept the child and tried to raise it, it would have had to be raised in secret. In the end, he knew that there would have been no way to keep the child. May the Devil have mercy on its misbegotten soul.

Returning to the house, Samuel ordered everyone to leave and never speak of what they had witnessed in his home that night. Obedient to both the man and the evil that he worshiped, the coven left, never to rejoin again. The midwife had already sewn up Deborah, and soon there would be no indication that she had ever been pregnant.

When Samuel and Deborah were asked what had happened to the baby, they would say that it had died in birth and had been buried in the cemetery by the old Whitmore Chapel. Stillbirths were a fact of life in the seventeen hundreds, and the story would be believed.

Try as they might, the Leeds could not conceive any more, which left them unable to bargain with the Devil again.

Within three years, Deborah died of influenza and Samuel died of smallpox. The legend of the deformed baby should have died with them, but it didn't.

1

October 31, 1984

A chill wind was blowing through the town of Burlington, New Jersey, on the last day of October. For the children of Burlington, Halloween was almost as magical as Christmas. What could be better than sprinting from door to door, screaming, "TRICK or TREAT," at the top of your lungs so that someone might toss a bite-size Snickers bar or a pack of candy corn into your Halloween basket?

It was unnaturally cold in New Jersey that Halloween, but you could feel the excitement in the air. Every school kid, from kindergarten to the twelfth grade, was anxiously waiting for the final school bell to ring. Not only was it Halloween, but it was Friday as well, and that meant a full night of fun without the worry of getting up for class the next morning.

Children weren't the only ones excited by Halloween; the adults loved it too. It was a day to relive their childhoods. Who didn't like the idea of ghosts and goblins knocking on their door, smiling when they were rewarded for the costumes that they wore?

Of course, there were always some, like Ms. Beverly Ann Anderson, who found Halloween to be insufferable. Anderson was the old lady who lived at the top of the hill on Thirty-Sixth Avenue with her dog, Charlie. The house she lived in was like all the others on the block with the exception being that it was run down and in dire need of repair. The roof sagged in places, and a brown shutter hung at an odd angle, having come loose from its hinges on the right side of an upstairs window. The house was white, but time and the elements had stripped much of the paint from it, giving it the look of a cow or a harlequin-colored dog. In the front yard were the termite-infested remains of a warped picket fence. One spoke in three was missing or broken, and it hadn't seen paint in ten years. The backyard was surrounded by a rusty, chain-link fence. Intertwined with vines and falling apart, it did little more than keep Charlie confined.

Charlie was one of those dogs that barked at everything and everybody who walked by the fence. On a daily basis, neighborhood children walked by, teasing the dog and shouting wicked things about the woman who lived inside the house, a house that nobody dared ring the doorbell of on Halloween. The cut-through path that led from Thirty-Fifth Avenue to Thirty-Sixth Avenue, went right by old lady Anderson's yard and gave Charlie plenty of excitement.

If a child was unlucky enough to lose a ball in the yard, it was forfeited. Charlie was a biter, as several of the neighborhood children could attest to. The small, brown terrier mix loved nothing more than to chase children up and down the fence line. If he found himself outside of the fence, or if someone was foolish enough to try to retrieve a ball from his yard, the dog couldn't pass up the chance to attach his jaws to the children. The dog had been there for as long as anyone could remember, and some of the children, who had limited knowledge of the occult and witchcraft, claimed that Charlie was old lady Anderson's familiar, which was a pet that watched over things for a witch or a sorcerer. In some tomes of the occult, it was said that a witch who kept a familiar, usually a black cat, could gain even more power through the use of such an animal.

The woman in the house was mysterious and sightings of her only happened every so often. The neighbors knew she was there, because they could hear her yelling at Charlie from inside of the house. On the rare occasions when you did see the eighty-one-year-old woman, she was usually wearing her housecoat and slippers and was dragging her trash can to the front of her house, where it remained on the side of her front steps.

Never once did someone see the old woman when she didn't have a sneer on her wrinkled, leather-skinned face. Her messy gray hair and her gnarled fingers only helped to verify that she was involved in witchcraft and the occult. All that was missing was a pointy hat and a broomstick. To see her with either would have been proof of her communion with darkness.

Just like in every other town in America, the Crystal Springs subdivision of Burlington, New Jersey, was full of myths and misunderstandings. Both kids and adults alike made up wild tales about the woman. Some said she had killed her husband and kept him in a freezer in the basement. Some said that she snatched up little children, who made the mistake of walking the path by her house late at night.

None of it was true. The reality of it was that Beverly Ann Anderson was an old maid who had never married and had kept to herself.

In 1972, she had had a stroke, which accounted for the permanent scowl on her face. With no family left in the world, Beverly Ann Anderson was just an old woman who would have loved the company of children or the kind greeting of an adult, though she received neither.

There was no misunderstanding the troubled teen who jumped the guardrail at the end of Thirty-Seventh Avenue and entered the old Whitmore Cemetery. Just another kid who fit in nowhere, the young man fought authority at every level. Conrad Beyer had been a delinquent for most of his life. From age nine to seventeen, he had been suspended from school more times than anyone could count, and he had had three extended stays in the juvenile detention center in Camden. Upon turning eighteen he had stolen a car, for which he did six months in the county jail.

A short walk through a small patch of woods led Conrad to the edge of the cemetery. The ground under his feet was hard, and the leaves and acorns from trees crunched loudly under his shoes as he walked. No fence surrounded the cemetery, and even if one did, Conrad Beyer would have climbed over it to gain entry. The grass around the gravesites was tall, and many of the headstones were covered in mold or badly cracked. Some of them were missing altogether.

As the short, greasy-haired youth walked through the graveyard, he ardently searched for one grave in particular. For two hours, the troubled young man wandered the cemetery, looking at headstones and grave markers for the name of the one who might be able to assist him with his conjuring. It was said in many of the occult tomes he had read that the dead, those who were particularly evil in life, could aid the living with conjurations.

Squatting down over a crumbling headstone, which was covered in filth, Conrad discovered what he was looking for. The headstone read, *"Samuel Leeds, may the Devil take him."*

Clearing the debris away from the headstone, Conrad sat where he thought the man's coffin might be lying in the ground. He closed his eyes and prayed. Removing a small, leather-bound book from the inside of his jacket, the teen took off the rubber band that was wound around it, and opened it to a page that had been earmarked for the occasion.

He had stolen the book from a small antiquities shop just the year before, and ever since he had begun reading its contents, he had been hooked. *Groban's Tome of Demons and Devils* was well-known to those in the world of the occult, and the copy he had was invaluable. Inside of the book were notes made by a man who had understood evil and believed in the powers of Satan. Inscribed on the inside cover of the small book was the name *"Samuel Leeds,"* the name of the man who was buried in the very grave on which the teen was sitting.

Studying the tome, the teen had come to understand the hidden meanings in the words. If one wanted to know the true meanings behind the words, he had to study them with an open mind. For a long time, the meanings behind the words in the leather-bound book had remained outside of Conrad's ability to understand them. But out of nowhere, a change had come over him and he could then understand those words, words that promised great powers to anyone who was willing to give himself over and open his soul to the Dark Prince.

A willing soldier, Conrad had made promises to the Father of Lies, promises that, for the first time in his life, he meant to keep. Though the Dark One never answered him directly, somehow he knew that his prayers were heard and that his sacrifice would be acceptable.

The teen reached into a hidden pocket in his jacket, but this time it was no book that he pulled out. Instead of a book, what Conrad Beyer removed from his jacket was a crucifix that was made of pure gold and adorned with glimmering rubies and diamonds. The crucifix was just as invaluable as the book in his hands, and stealing it from the rectory of Saint Mark's Church in Pennsauken had been difficult. More than one person had seen his face as he had fled from the rectory. It wouldn't be long before the police identified him. His time was limited. If he wanted to feel the power of evil and brush up against greatness, it was now or never.

The crucifix in his hands was said to be a great force for good in the world. Rumor had it that the cross had been used in the exorcism that had taken place in Mount Rainier, Maryland, in 1949. A movie had been made of the event; the devil was portrayed as the weaker of the wills that had battled for the soul of the child. If not for divine intervention from God himself, the devil might have taken the soul of the priest, along with that of the child. The exorcist who managed to remove the demon from the child in Maryland was among those who Satan hated above all. Most didn't know that it was a boy and not a girl who had been possessed in that house, and the devil who had taken possession of him had never planned on relinquishing his prize. If not for the interference of a holy man from Africa and the favor that that man held with God, the demon would have succeeded in claiming the boy, heart and soul.

Placing the crucifix face-down on the cold ground, Conrad removed a piece of dark cloth from his pocket and covered the relic. He examined his work carefully, trying to be sure not to let any of the metal from the crucifix show through the dark covering. The next thing the teen did was cut his wrist with a switchblade knife, allowing the blood that fell from the wound to cover the cloth over the crucifix. Unzipping his pants, the would-be sorcerer urinated on top of the blood-covered cloth, further soiling the holy relic. Bile from his throat and dirt from the bottom of his shoe followed the urine. Then Conrad felt that he was finally ready.

Opening *Groban's Tome of Demons and Devils*, Beyer began to chant the words that had been written in Latin, a language that he didn't know, a language that had been revealed to him by his dark master. It had taken weeks to learn the meaning of the words and how to properly pronounce them. For long minutes, Conrad recited the words of evil power. A feeling of impending doom came over the young man and the flesh on his arms pimpled with goose bumps. As he continued his chanting, the teen could feel the wind around him pick up speed. The air was growing colder still. Uncanny warmth protected him from the cold and he was barely conscious of it.

Completing the opening of the ritual, Conrad moved to the next phase of the rite he had to perform. Though he shouted, no one heard the words that flowed from the mouth of the teen. The words were ancient and privy only to those who had faith in the Prince of Darkness. Dark and foreboding, the words played off the lips of the teen, like the blood that dripped from his wrist, which he had never bandaged.

No smile came to his face as the cloth-covered crucifix burst into flames and melted on the cold, hard ground over the grave of Samuel Leeds. All business, the teen was wondering why he didn't feel power coursing through him yet. Clearing his thoughts so that the Dark One would not be offended, Conrad knew that the power would come. The promise had been made, the bargain struck. The power would be his.

Satisfied with his work, Conrad slowly began to back out of the verses he was yelling. Though he consciously tried to end the spell casting, he couldn't stop his lips from speaking the words. Horror and shock came over the teen when he realized that he was still yelling the words of doom and despair from the book. Trying to break off the ritualistic chanting, he found that he was unable. Struggling was futile.

A power … something with a will stronger than his own had taken control of his body, and he couldn't stop. His eyes opened wide with fright and he looked frantically from side to side for help as his lips continued to form the words of the ritual. As far as his eyes could see there was no one to help him. Only he and the one he prayed to could hear the words. There would be no interruption.

A sweat broke out on his forehead, and tears fell from the corners of the boy's eyes, but he couldn't stop chanting. What had started out as warmth was now growing uncomfortably hot, and when he looked down at his legs, Conrad saw that they were on fire. Stark fear and panic took over; he begged to be released from his chanting.

His pleas went unanswered, and his mouth, which was now dry, continued to shout out the words of power. The fire on his legs spread to his waist and stomach, and his mind screamed out with the pain that his throat refused to voice. All the while, his lips parted and the words of summoning poured from them.

Within minutes, the unholy fire had consumed the teen, and all that was left of him was bits of burnt bones and clothing.

The ground where he had once stood was blackened, and the air smelled of seared flesh and hair. Lying next to the black spot on the grave was *Groban's Tome of Demons and Devils*, and though everything around it had been charred, the book remained unharmed. No fire had touched its cover or pages.

The teen had only been dead for seconds when the earth around the grave began to shake; the most dreadful scream came from the ground around the headstone. The scream was like the bark of a hoarse dog, only it was ominous and had a steely quality to it. For those who heard it, the scream was unlike anything their ears had ever born witness to. They were spooked by the noise; it frightened them so badly that they closed the curtains around their windows and checked the locks on their doors before going back to their soap operas.

2

At one second after 6:00 p.m., the front door to every house in the Crystal Springs subdivision burst open. Children whooped and hollered with glee as they raced for the first houses on their carefully laid out maps of the neighborhood.

Karen and Bruce Cheek watched from the open doorway of their two-story, three-bedroom house on Thirty-Fifth Avenue. They had no fear for their children as the two girls, Deidre and Wendy, raced up the hill toward the end of the street. Burlington and the Crystal Springs subdivision were virtually free of drugs and crime. They could leave the door to their house unlocked, if they were going away for a few hours, without fear of someone stealing from them.

Every one of the modest homes in the neighborhood was the same, from the three steps that led to the tiny front porches, to the lunch-box sized front yards, they were all the same. The only thing that individualized the houses was the color of the paint on the siding and the type of fence that surrounded the yard, if the owners could afford one. Some had had the money to finish off the basements of their homes, but for most that was a dream that would have to wait.

Deidre and Wendy Cheek were fourteen and ten years old, respectively, and this was the first year that they would trick or treat in the new subdivision that their parents had moved them to. Dressed as Wonder Woman, Deidre was perturbed that she had been forced to wear a coat over her costume. At every door she knocked on, the residents there called her a princess; her headband was the only part of her costume that wasn't covered by the goose-down jacket she wore. The girl couldn't remember a colder Halloween, but she wasn't about to complain. She loved her new house and her new friends.

Wendy Cheek was dressed as a tiger, with her long, striped tail hanging down from the back of her suede jacket. The cowl of the costume had pointed, striped ears on its top, and it kept the sides of her face warm as she ran.

From the beginning, the pickings had been good, and the girls smiled at every candy bar or goody bag that hit the bottoms of their baskets. There were a few people who insisted on giving out popcorn balls or candy apples, but they needn't have bothered. The Cheeks had parents who were overly attentive, and any homemade candy was thrown away for fear of poison or razor blades being hidden inside. Urban legends died hard in the 1980s, and very few were the parents who took chances with Halloween candy.

Though it was dark and there were no streetlights in the neighborhood, the lights over the doors on the houses lit the way and made the children feel safe. The shadows that grew under trees and on sides of the houses were spooky, adding to the event, but the shadows weren't enough to keep the children from the candy that awaited them.

When it came time to cross to Thirty-Sixth Avenue, the girls avoided the cut-through next to Ms. Anderson's house. The light over her door was on, but no one was ringing her bell, at least no one who valued his or her skin.

As the night grew darker and the girls tired, they headed home with baskets full of candy. Because Halloween had fallen on a weekend this year, the fun was far from over for Wendy and Deidre. Their tour ended on Thirty-Sixth Avenue, and Deidre had a little bit of mischief left in her.

Turning to Wendy, Deidre said, "I'll bet you six candy bars that you won't use the cut-through next to old lady Anderson's yard."

Staring at her older sister, the fear registering clearly in her eyes, Wendy said, "Screw you. I'm not going down there for anything."

"That's 'cause you're a fraidy cat," chided her sister.

"Am not," Wendy shouted as she began to walk away from the foot of the path. "It's just that I'm not stupid," she said to her older sibling.

"Stupid? I'll show you stupid," Deidre said, stepping onto the bare ground that formed the path between the two avenues.

Seeing her sister step on the path, Wendy cried, "No, don't do it."

Every child in the Crystal Springs subdivision knew better than to cross that path after dark, especially on Halloween.

"Now you have to give me three candy bars … or else I'm gonna do it," Deidre said, her mind already made up.

Wendy knew it was a trick, but Deidre looked serious. Three candy bars was a lot to ask for. Not every home gave them out. Wendy didn't want to part with the candy, but she didn't want Deidre to go down the path in the dark either. Deciding that she liked her sister better than the candy, she gave in.

"All right, I'll give you two, but we have to go home now."

Realizing that she wasn't going to get a better offer, Deidre said, "It's a deal."

Accepting the Baby Ruth and Three Musketeers bars that her sister offered her, Deidre dropped them into her basket with a smile on her face.

The trick or treating that night might have been the best trick or treating that the pair had ever done, and the girl dressed as Wonder Woman would never forget it.

Her parents had checked her candy and they were satisfied that what they had left her with was safe. Deidre munched on a Kit-Kat bar while flipping through the *TV Guide*. Finding what she wanted on channel six, the fourteen-year-old smiled. A *Nightmare on Elm Street* was playing at nine.

For years, she had begged her parents to watch the film, and every time they had shot her down. She was fourteen now and it was a weekend night; what did she have to lose? Asking her parents for the forbidden fruit wasn't an easy thing; it usually led to dejection. A teenager's ego was a fragile thing and the last thing she wanted to hear, after getting her hopes up for weeks, was no.

Acting casual as she entered the kitchen and tossed her empty wrappers into the trash can, she tried not to show how nervous she was. Her mom and dad were in a good mood; now was the time.

"Um, mom, dad, can I watch *A Nightmare on Elm Street* tonight?"

The question startled the married pair, and Bruce set his coffee down, not sure of how to answer his daughter. He could see the hope in her eyes. He didn't want to disappoint her, but was she ready?

Turning to his wife, who looked about as ready for the question as her husband, he asked, "Well, what do you think? She is fourteen now."

The woman was clearly uncomfortable with the question, but it had to be addressed at some point, didn't it? Shifting in her seat, Karen began to open her mouth, but she hesitated. She would have liked to say no, but Deidre was a good girl, and this was something that she had wanted to do for a long time.

"All right, you can watch it, but Wendy has to go to bed first."

"Yes!" the teen shouted as she pumped her fist into the air. Victory was sweet. Things were finally going her way.

It didn't take long before Deidre's father chased Wendy to bed, but there had been moments when the young girl thought she might miss the beginning of the movie. Wendy was known for her ability to prolong the inevitable and tonight, above all other nights, Deidre didn't find it funny.

Settling down in front of the television, Deidre and her father watched the televised version of the movie. Though there were times when the girl was startled or she had to hide her face behind a pillow, nothing happened that would disturb her long-term.

The night had been a total success. Trick or treating and *A Nightmare on Elm Street* meant that her friend Cheryl was going to be so jealous.

After climbing the stairs to her room, Deidre turned on the lights and got into her pajamas. With the lights on, the teen checked inside her closet and under her bed. It was better to be safe than sorry.

A bit unnerved by the movie, the girl who could never confess to her father that she was spooked, snuck into Wendy's room to steal her night-light. With the night-light plugged in, she drew the covers up to her neck and drifted off to sleep. No bad dreams came to her as she slept.

It was a noise on the roof that woke her, and she sat up, staring at the alarm clock next to her bed. *Three o' clock in the morning*, she thought to herself as her eyes focused on the clock. *Who in their right mind pulls pranks at three in the morning?*

As she sat there, the sound on the roof over her bedroom came again. It was a strange sound, almost as if someone had put a horse on top of her house. The more she heard it, the more she was certain that those were hoofbeats on her roof.

Whoever the prankster was, he was good. Deciding that it was best to ignore the noise, Deidre settled back down into her covers and closed her eyes.

A half hour passed, and still, the sound of hoofbeats could be heard, clacking away on the roof over her bedroom. Tossing and turning, she knew that she wouldn't get any rest until she dealt with the idiot who refused to give up the prank.

It was probably Tommy Lawson or Billy Murphy. Both boys had crushes on her, but she didn't like either of them. They were typical eighth-grade boys, immature and pimple faced. She was so far beyond boys like that; she liked high school guys. Even so, they could still get her in trouble if they woke her parents up with their prank. Those boys were gonna get an earful from Deidre when she got to them.

In her robe and slippers, Deidre found herself at the front door, peeking through the peephole. Unable to see anyone, she flipped on the light switch, opened the door and stepped out onto the tiny porch at the front of her house. With one hand on the porch's iron railing, she placed the other over her eyes, trying to make out any figures who might be lurking on the lawn or behind the bushes by the living room windows. There was nothing to see, but still the beating of hooves could be heard on the roof of her house. Never stopping to ask herself why the sound hadn't woken anyone else up, Deidre didn't bother to question her actions.

She was a big girl, and big girls didn't believe in ghosts and spooks, so she walked into the driveway and turned to the front of the house. Looking to the roof, Deidra was shocked by what she saw.

Some kind of huge rooster or bird was on the roof, strutting around up there as if it were mad. It was dark in the wee hours of the morning and she couldn't make out more than the outline of the animal, but it was big, at least as big as her father. Roosters didn't get that big, so what was it?

No matter what it was, Deidra wasn't going to get any sleep until it left, so she picked up a rock from the front garden and threw it at the creature. Her aim was true, and the rock struck the side of whatever it was that was dancing on her roof. Now she had its attention, but did she really want it?

All that Deidre had wanted to do was scare the strange bird away, but now it was turning to acknowledge her. As it turned, the face of the animal became clear, and the young woman had to stifle a cry of disgust. The thing had the head of a collie dog and the long face of a horse. Its ears were small, like that of a monkey, and for the first time, she noticed its wings.

Turning to run, the girl was desperate to make it to the front door. Having gotten a good look at the beast, Deidre was scared. She had left the door ajar, and now more than ever, she wanted the comfort of her home. As she reached the bottom step, something hard and dull grabbed the girl by the left arm and clamped down tightly, hurting her. Deidre let out a startled yell, one that was mixed with pain, before she was jerked off of her feet and into the air. The sensation of leaving the ground was strange and frightening for the girl as she watched her front yard rush away from her feet. Hanging from one arm, which felt as if it was being pulled away from her body, she couldn't find the strength to look at her attacker.

Whatever kind of bird it was, it was strong, and she wanted it to let go of her. Using her right fist, the teenage girl punched the side of the strange animal, and that hurt her hand. The animal's torso was hard and covered in wiry hair.

When the animal dropped her on the roof of the house, she thought that her ordeal might be over. But any thoughts of her escaping died when she heard the heavy flapping of tiny wings as they set the creature on the roof. Scared shitless and unable to move, she watched in terror as the beast craned its head and turned its body her way. Like a kangaroo, the thing hopped on two skinny legs, legs that should never have been able to carry the weight of the beast. Awkward, its movements almost silly, Deidre normally wouldn't have found anything frightening about the creature. But on her roof, in the darkest hours of the morning, she found that she was terrified. Friendly animals didn't grab you by the arm and fly away with you.

The roof was steep, and getting to her feet, Deidre was sure she would tumble off of it. She couldn't run on the roof, so she stood her ground, hoping to frighten the beast off. Terrified by the monster she was face-to-face with, she found herself unable to scream as it got closer. Maybe she could fight it off.

When the beast hopped closer still, she knew she didn't stand a chance. Her arm hurt. There were teeth marks on it, but the creature hadn't drawn blood. She thought about jumping from the roof, but when she looked over the edge, it was a long way down, and she was too scared to leap. *Screwed, I'm completely screwed*, thought the young girl, who all of a sudden, didn't feel so grown up.

On the roof in the moonlight, Deidre could finally see the entire creature, and it was even more terrible than she had thought. Along with the collie's head and the horse face, the animal had small wings like a bat and a tail like a devil's. Its torso was like that of a greyhound, and it was covered in wiry hair. The front legs of the animal were like that of a dog, which ended in paws that were held in front of it as if it were praying. With the legs of a crane and hoofed feet, the thing was the strangest creature she had ever seen.

The eyes of the creature flashed beet red, and it hopped with purpose now. Malice shone clearly in its cruel eyes, and drool spilled from the edges of its equine mouth. The animal meant to harm her, she was certain of it.

Without warning, the creature began to dance in place on its two hooves as its bat-like wings flapped wildly. Shaking, with her hands clenched in fists and her lips quivering, she was terrified by the abrupt and strange behavior of the creature. Was it angry or happy, and was there any way that she could get away from it?

Standing on the roof, with tears rolling from her eyes, the girl was without hope. There was no doubt in her mind that the creature was angry; its red eyes seemed to bore that message into her mind.

When it stopped its frantic dance, it faced her. Craning its neck forward until she could feel its breath on her face, the creature let out an ear-splitting scream. Much like the bark of a dog, but far louder, the steely scream hurt her ears and made her close her eyes. When it was over, Deidre opened her eyes. She could see the lights on the houses across the street as they came on. *Maybe they would scare the thing away?*

All hope ended when the creature sprang on her, its horse-like teeth grabbing her by the leg before shaking her violently and then slamming her against the roof. The last thing that Deidre Cheek did before she died was scream at the top of her lungs. Her screams soon ended when the hooved feet of the monster pounded her furiously against the gritty shingles.

The scream of his daughter awoke Bruce Cheek from his sleep. He could have sworn that the scream had come from outside, but that was impossible, his daughter was in her room.

Jumping from his bed, the man threw open the door to his room and rushed down the hallway in search of his daughter. The door to her bedroom was closed, but she never locked it, and the handle turned easily. Opening the door, Bruce was shocked to see that his daughter wasn't there. Her covers had been thrown over to one side and her robe and slippers were gone. If she had gone outside, she was going to be in some kind of trouble when he found her.

All thoughts of punishment stopped when the creature let out its steely scream, which was followed by a scream from his daughter. *Oh God, oh please don't let anything be wrong with her*, her dad begged silently as he bounded down the steps to the front door, which he found ajar.

Fear overtook the man as he ran into the front yard. His head whipped from side to side in search of Deidre.

He could hear his wife inside the house as she called the name of their daughter, but there was no response. Adding his voice to that of his wife's, Bruce called out for his daughter. *Where was she*, he wondered, *and how come she wasn't answering.*

The lights of the houses across the street were on. The commotion and the screams had woken the occupants of the nearby homes. People had come out of their homes, squinting against the lights over their doorways, trying to see what was going on.

A loud thump on Bruce's roof caught his attention, and the man turned.

Dancing on the top of his house was the strangest creature he had ever seen.

The thing stood ten feet tall and looked like something from a science fiction movie. *What the hell is it? What is it doing on my roof, and where the hell is my daughter?* Those questions slipped to the back of his mind as he watched the crazy, unbelievable animal stomp up and down on a heap of rags on the roof of his house.

It wasn't long before Karen joined him in the yard, and together they watched the strange occurrence taking place on their roof. The roof was wet around the heap of rags, but Bruce couldn't make out the cause.

Stopping for a moment, the creature craned its neck forward and let out another of its strange screams. That was enough for some folks; they scrambled back into their houses, locking their doors behind them.

It must have been tired of stomping the pile of rags, because it began to dance on the roof, away from the clump of clothing, and for the first time, Bruce could hear the sound of hoofbeats.

While Bruce watched the animal in amazement, Karen focused on the pile of rags that the creature had lost interest in. As she scrutinized the rags, she noticed that they were pink and that a slipper was discarded to the side of them; it too was pink. Realization struck her, and fear came over her face. It wasn't a pile of rags up on the roof, it was Deidre's robe and slippers.

When it dawned on her that the clump under the clothing was her daughter, Karen let out a blood-curdling scream of her own, and then she fainted. The scream of the woman alerted the animal to the presence of the others, and it suddenly stopped its dance.

A smile seemed to come over the awful, equine visage of the animal before it beat its wings and flew away into the night, leaving the stunned man on the front lawn speechless.

Bending down to his wife, Bruce slapped her gently on the cheek.

"Come on, honey, wake up. It's gone now," Bruce said as he drew her back to her feet.

Waking up, reality settled on the groggy woman and she looked at the roof, mumbling, "Deidre."

It wasn't normal for Sheriff Andy Wright to get a call at four in the morning. *Something had better be really wrong.*

Climbing from his bed, he took the phone from his wife and said, "Yeah, this is Sheriff Wright." After listening to the person on the other end of the line, Andy said, "All right, hold the scene and call the detective. I'll be there in a few."

Hanging the phone back up on its base, he wondered to himself, *what is wrong with people?* Someone had broken into a house in the Crystal Springs subdivision and killed a girl. *What was the world coming to?*

His thoughts stayed with him as he got dressed and collected his car keys.

When he arrived at the scene, he wasn't surprised to see the neighborhood in an uproar. Every house he saw had someone, or two someones, standing on the porch, watching everything that went on at the olive-colored house on Thirty-Fifth Avenue.

Finding the deputy who had called him, Andy asked, "Bob, what the hell's going on here?"

Taking off his Stetson and scratching at his head, the deputy spoke. "So far we know that Deidre Cheek was murdered. Her body is still on the roof. I'm waiting for the medical examiner and a crime scene technician before anyone disturbs it."

"Anyone see who did this? There's lots of people around," stated the sheriff, who didn't look at all pleased.

"I'm way ahead of you, boss," Deputy Joiner said. "We've talked to several of the neighbors and the girl's parents, and they say that they saw the perpetrator."

Shaking his head and thinking that his men had done a good job, the sheriff said, "Great. What's the guy look like? Let's go and find him."

The look on the deputy's face said it all. "You see, that's the problem, sir. We got a great description, but you're not going to like it."

It took several attempts at giving the description before the sheriff realized that Bob Joiner wasn't pulling his leg. The scene of a murder was no place for such nonsense. Wright was about to tell him that, when he realized that the deputy was serious.

The night was a long one, and it turned into the next day. From the medical examiner to the crime scene technician who worked the scene, everyone was perplexed. Bloody hoof prints were collected from the roof, and some small, wiry, red hairs, but other than those, nothing of evidentiary value was found.

The news media had a field day with the interviews they did with neighbors, and the story began to sweep the nation: "Horse-faced demon kills girl in New Jersey as neighbors watch helplessly. Film at eleven."

The official cause of death was murder by blunt force trauma. There was no listing of a horse-faced demon in the report.

The case was also listed as still open.

Though the sheriff's office refused to identify the killer, the people of the tiny subdivision in Burlington knew who it was. The Jersey Devil was back again. After disappearing for nearly eighty years, the demon child of Samuel and Deborah Leeds was back. *May God watch over his faithful.*

3

November 3, 1984

A thin blanket of snow covered most of the northeast, along with the town of Burlington. The appearance of snow in the beginning of November promised a cold winter. From the millions of acres of the Pine Barrens on the west side of Burlington, to Bristol, Pennsylvania, where the Pine Barrens ended, snow covered everything. The sky was gray and menacing, almost daring the world below to give it a reason to punish them again.

Still, the snow was a welcome sight for some. For children, it meant a giant playground of white powder from which they might make snowballs or sleigh ride upon. School would remain open for the day, but upon getting home, every child in Burlington would take advantage of the winter's first offering.

For adults, it wasn't as bad as it seemed. Sure they would have a longer commute into the office, but the view on their way to that office would be spectacular. There was nothing like the view of snow-covered limbs on the trees, trees which had lost their leaves and had been brought to prominence again by the glistening white powder that covered them.

There was little use for snowplows when the blanket of frozen precipitation was only a half-inch high. The people of New Jersey were used to far worse. It would take more than a light dusting of snow to keep them from work or school.

Upon exiting his home that morning, Sheriff Andy Wright was surprised by what he saw in his front yard. The snow had been expected; the local weatherman had been right for the first time in years. But it wasn't the snow that bothered Andy; it was the tracks in his yard, and seemingly every other yard in the neighborhood.

Crouching down to get a better look at the tracks, Andy noticed that they were cloven, like the tracks of a deer. There was no rhyme or reason to them, they simply were. It was as if a herd of deer had come stampeding through the neighborhood the night before, leaving behind the proof that they were there.

Being a hunter, Andy noticed something odd about the tracks. There were no droppings accompanying them. So many deer would have left the signature pellets that always littered the ground, showing where they had been. *Why hadn't these?*

Shrugging off the strange occurrence, Andy climbed into his white Ford Crown Victoria police cruiser and headed for work. He'd forgotten his cup of coffee, but a stop at the 7-Eleven could solve that. He wasn't particularly fond of the coffee there, but it beat what they made in the office. Mud tasted better than what they passed off for coffee at the sheriff's department.

"Good morning, sheriff," was the first greeting he heard after entering his office. Standing by his desk, with a steaming cup of java in her hands was his secretary, Lori Dillon.

Lori was still attractive for a forty-year-old mother of four, but Andy rarely gave it much thought. His wife was as beautiful as the day they had met, and she had given him a wonderful daughter. He didn't stray.

Leaning over the fine desk made of Jersey pine, Lori allowed the man a look down her low-cut blouse. *He never takes the bait, but each day was a new one, and you never know when he might,* thought the woman without a conscience. Lori had been divorced for six years, through no fault of her husband. She was the kind of girl who needed excitement, and after just three years of marriage, she had begun cheating on her spouse. The man had tried to look the other way, but eventually twelve years of embarrassment turned into shame, and he had to leave. The love of his children could no longer keep the man at home. Lori didn't miss him; the money he sent every month for the children kept her living a lifestyle that she'd become accustomed to.

Realizing that she may have remained leaning over the desk for a moment too long, Lori retreated, straightening the bottom of her blouse as if it were no more than a nuisance.

Andy hated that part of the day, but he put up with it. As well as being a tremendous flirt, Lori Dillon was the best secretary he had ever had. She seemed to know what he was thinking and what he needed even before he did. He tolerated things from Lori that he would never tolerate from others.

The file that he wanted was on his desk, and he had to choose between it and the newspaper in his hand. The case file won out.

Andy Wright was a good sheriff. He believed in public service. Andy opened the case file, wishing he had a stiff drink in his hands as he flipped through the pages in the manila folder.

The photos of the Cheek girl were enough to give Charles Manson nightmares. Although they disturbed him, he knew that he would have to study them if he was going to find any clues about the man who had killed the little girl. Six eyewitnesses claimed that it was the Jersey Devil….. *Ridiculous!* It was Halloween after all; maybe some nut job had worn a costume while perpetrating the crime. That was the only explanation that made any sense, because the Jersey Devil didn't exist. Like Bigfoot and the Loch Ness Monster, it was a myth, something that mothers told their children to keep them in line.

Having been a cop for twenty-three years, Andy had seen a lot of terrible things, but the photos of the dead little girl might be the worst yet.

Hair and bloody hoof prints had been recovered from the scene. It was likely that the hair had come from the costume, but how in the hell could the bad guy walk on such thin legs and stand ten feet tall? Stilts? That would explain a lot. The guy was wearing stilts.

Andy's reasoning sucked, but he refused to believe that a devil had come to Burlington to kill the little girl. For an hour, he went over the material in the folder and when he was done, Andy Wright was no closer to solving the case. It was going to be a long day.

November 3, 1984, 7:39 p.m.

Driving up to Leeds Point, Harvey Kramer and Stacy Warner were anxious. The twenty-year-old man had been dating the seventeen-year-old girl for three months; they were keeping it a secret from Stacy's mother. What had started out as flirting had turned into dating for the couple. There was nothing seedy about what they were going to the point for. Harvey and Stacy were in love. Making out was all that they had in mind, but still, they had to keep the fact that they were dating from Stacy's mom.

Mrs. Warner didn't care much for Harvey, and for no reason at all, she had forbidden Stacy to see him. The two in the car were Catholics, and they had met at a church retreat. Even so, Mrs. Warner didn't like boys with long hair and unshaven faces. "A gentleman should have a proper haircut and be mindful of how he looked," she always said.

As Harvey and Stacy drove over the bridge that led to the top of the hill, the pair took in all of the sights. The Pine Barren Forest covered most of the ridge, which overlooked the town of Burlington. With no streetlights and little chance of an interruption from the police, Leeds Point was the perfect place for their secret love to blossom. No more than thirty cars a day used the road and the bridge, which led from the forest into the town below. A wide shoulder on the side of the road that gave them a breathtaking view of the city below them was the perfect place to park.

Without a care in the world, the pair embraced and their hearts caught fire.

Stacy felt good in Harvey's arms, better than anyone before her, and he knew it was right. Harvey knew that Stacy was a good girl, and he didn't mind. She was a breath of fresh air to the man who had only dated "hot chicks" previously.

If only they could tell Mrs. Warner that they were dating. He hated hiding things from the woman and knew that God wouldn't approve of the subterfuge.

At first, he thought he was hearing things and he ignored the rustling of the trees around them. It snowed the night before and Mother Nature might have had more of it in store for Burlington.

When Stacy pulled away from him to ask, "What was that?" Harvey knew that something was in the woods around them.

"I don't know," he said. "Maybe it's a bear or an owl."

"You're probably right," the girl said as she moved her lips close to his again.

Their lips had barely met when they heard a barking coming from somewhere above them; it was a bark that seemed to come out of nowhere and yet from everywhere at once. It wasn't the bark of a dog. It was somehow different; something steely, almost like it was coming from an amplifier.

Looking through the steamed up windows of the red Toyota Celica, she couldn't see anything in the darkness. The clouds covered the moon and the stars. The night was as pitch as coal.

"What on God's green earth is that?" she asked, knowing full well that Harvey didn't have an answer.

Stacy was right, Harvey didn't have an answer for it, but he was going to find out. "Wait here," said the young man as he reached for the door handle.

Grabbing Harvey by the shoulder, Stacy pulled him back toward her saying, "No way. You're not leaving me alone in here. Besides, you don't even know what it is. Suppose it's a bear, then what?"

The macho portion of Harvey's brain got the better of him. He wasn't going to sit and wait for something to happen, he wanted to know what was causing the noise, and he wanted to know now.

Reaching for the door handle again, he was startled when the next steely bark seemed to come from right over the car. In fact, the man was so startled that he snatched his hand back, striking Stacy in the eye with his elbow as she leaned over him.

"Ouch! That hurt. What are you doing?" The blow from Harvey's elbow caused her eyes to water, and she grew angry.

"I don't know what I'm doing. I thought I was going to go out there, but not now I'm not."

He was frightened. The color that had left his face said so. Reaching for the car keys in the pocket of his blue jeans, he brought them out with a trembling hand. As he tried to separate the ignition key from the others, he was spooked when something big rubbed against his side of the car; his trembling hands fumbled the keys. The keys bounced off of the seat and fell to the floorboard under his feet.

No sooner had the keys struck the floor jingling, than the barking began again. This time it was louder, closer, forcing the scared young girl in the front seat to slide down onto the floorboard. *The scream from the animal is terrifying, almost unholy,* thought the girl as she grabbed the crucifix that hung around her neck and began praying.

The sound of hooves prancing around the outside of the car was nerve-racking and Harvey was in no better shape than Stacy. He kept his head above the steering wheel, too frightened to take his eyes off his surroundings. For just a second, he thought he caught a glimpse of long, skinny legs as they moved past the driver's window. The legs of the animal were like nothing he'd ever seen before and he let out a small squeal of fright.

His breathing grew harder as his hands felt around on the floorboard, but no matter where they searched, he couldn't find his keys. Trembling on the floor of the car next to him was Stacy. The poor girl had heard his squeal and the tears had begun to flow from her eyes.

"Shit, shit, shit. Where are they?" Harvey mumbled to himself as his hands searched for the elusive keys.

Looking over at Stacy, Harvey could see that she was scared out of her mind. The girl was scrunched down in between the front passenger seat and the dashboard of the car. She looked positively pitiful. He could barely see her face, but her sobs were evident; she was terrified.

The girl wasn't the only one who was terrified; Harvey was barely able to keep it together as the horrible, barking scream continued to trumpet out into the night. Not only was the barking scary, it was maddening. It was as if merely hearing it could freeze his heart in place.

While his eyes searched for the thing that he thought had disappeared into woods, a new noise cut through the silence of the night. It was the sound of rushing wind. It was as if a giant bird was flying around the car; the force of its wings was sending great wafts of air crashing against the vehicle.

If Harvey's heart had been racing before, it was absolutely beating out of control now. Adding to the sound of the wind was the loudest bark yet, a bark that sounded as if it was coming from right next to him. He shied farther away from the car door. His hands were searching frantically. His mind was racing. If only he could find the keys, he could get them out of there.

Adding to his fright was the sound of Stacy's voice as she begged God not to let the Devil get her. The idea of a devil or monster had never entered his mind, but now he couldn't get it to go away.

The more he struggled to find the keys, the more his labored breathing fogged up the windows to the car. Soon he couldn't see a thing on the outside. Trapped in a whirlwind of beating wings and a barking sound so terrifying that it made his skin crawl, he nearly wet his pants.

When Harvey Kramer's right hand wrapped around the keys to the car, he blew out a sigh of relief.

But his relief was short-lived as something heavy landed on the roof of his car, causing it to sag. Dropping the keys back to the floor, Harvey winced as the metal above his head groaned and protested against the weight of the creature that stood upon it.

A yelp from Stacy was the only thing that reminded him of her presence. He was frightened in a way that he'd never been frightened before, and his fear caused a chill to run up and down his spine.

Whatever it was that was on the roof was moving around, almost dancing. He could hear what sounded like hooves beating on the top of the car, and the sound caused the tears at the edges of his eyes to fall down like large raindrops.

With his windows fogged up, he couldn't see anything.

"What the hell are you?" Harvey screamed at the top of his voice. His scream only served to further frighten the girl next to him.

As if in answer to his question, a face pressed against the window of his door, and the breath of the beast fogged up the window even further. The only things he could make out were the red, beady eyes of the animal. Everything else was obscured by the fog on the window.

With a flap of its leathery wings, the creature flew back onto the top of the car. Scared stiff, all Harvey could do was listen to the dancing beast on top of his car and pray that it would go away.

The tires of his car gave a slight bounce when the creature jumped off of the car and landed on the ground next to the passenger's side of the vehicle. Without warning, it began its assault on the car again, landing back on the roof with vigor and threatening to cave it in fully.

Harvey and Stacy screamed in unison.

For a moment, Harvey wondered if God was punishing the pair for hiding their love from Stacy's mother. How had he gotten them into such a mess? All he had wanted was some alone time with Stacy; it was innocent.

He was mumbling to himself, his mind almost lost to the terror that surrounded him.

Harvey tried his best to squeeze down onto the floor of the car like Stacy had. He knew it was impossible. Though he wasn't fat, Harvey wasn't exactly a small guy, and no matter how hard he struggled, he couldn't get his body below the wheel.

Abandoning the thought of hiding, Harvey's tortured mind sought any alternative to dying in his car. In his delirium, he thought he might have a chance if he could get out of the car and run away.

The wailing of the animal was nonstop as it continued to bring the roof down into the vehicle.

Damn. He was frightened, and there was no place to go. Every time he started to open the door, something frightened him, and he stopped. If Harvey didn't get free of the car, he was going to be crushed.

Deciding that he had to take a chance, Harvey grabbed the door handle and pushed the door open. As his head and left arm cleared the doorjamb, the creature came down hard again on the roof. This time the metal could no longer hold the weight of the beast, and the roof collapsed. The frame of the vehicle bent and the windshield blew out, showering everything around Harvey with broken glass.

He howled in pain as the doorframe crushed down on him. His scream was almost as inhuman as the barking of the creature. Sharp metal from the frame cut into his right shoulder, pinning him, which left his head and arm trapped outside the Toyota. The pain was bad. Unable to think, Harvey could already feel his warm blood running down his side from where the metal had sliced into his flesh. Stuck with no way out, he began to cry. No matter how hard he struggled against the ever-pressing doorframe, he couldn't free himself.

On the passenger's floorboard, Stacy screamed. The horror of it all was more than her fragile mind could take. The scream was a single, long, drawn-out melody of fright that split the night like an axe. Shivering and in shock, the poor little girl from Burlington knew that she was going to die. She could hear the screams of her boyfriend. Had he already been taken? Was she next?

The waiting was beyond torture for the girl, who cried out for her mommy to come and save her.

Wrapping her arms around herself as tightly as they would go, Stacy made herself as small as possible. Every time the creature landed upon the car, the roof came closer to her. Crying, her tears and makeup mixed, running down her face.

The terrible monster on the roof of the car kept barking, and the metal roof continued to groan as it was forced down into the vehicle, but there was nothing she could do. The sound of Harvey gasping in pain, as the roof cut further into his body, broke her heart. There was nothing she could do for him; she couldn't even help herself.

When the metal was forced even further into his body, Harvey Kramer gave a muffled cry of pain. What he didn't realize was that his head and arm had been cut off. As he died, he felt no more pain. When his head hit the ground, he could see the end of his severed arm.

He should have been horrified, but he wasn't. Instead, he felt a strange feeling of euphoria come over him. The euphoria was caused by a lack of oxygen to the brain, but it was a welcome emotion for the man, who had felt nothing but fear and pain for the last ten minutes of his life.

For another twenty minutes, the devil pounced on top of the car until it was sure that the girl inside had been crushed as well. By the time the beast left to find more mischief in the dark, the car looked as if a huge boulder had landed on it and then rolled off, leaving a mass of bent and twisted metal behind. As the devil flew off into the night, a frightened little girl sobbed. Trapped in a tomb of metal, she wondered if anyone would ever find her.

November 4, 1984

Looking over the crime scene, Sheriff Andy Wright was puzzled. He knew that the damage on the right side of the car was from when Stacy Warner had been cut out. The firemen had said that it was a miracle that she had survived. None of them had ever seen a car so completely flattened outside of a junk yard. How she had managed to make herself small enough to escape serious injury was beyond their imaginations. In fact, other than minor cuts, some bruising and a black eye, Stacy Warner was all right. At least, her body was all right.

When she had been pulled from the car, her eyes had been wide open, and she couldn't blink. She said not a word. It was as if she were in a coma. The girl had been rushed to the hospital, and her mother was notified.

Andy's deputies had been searching for her all night because her mother had reported her missing. If Deputy John Shelly hadn't thought to look for her on Leeds Point, they might still have been searching. *Miracles happen every day,* he told himself, *but this one was close.*

Moving over to the blanket that covered the body of Harvey Kramer, the sheriff rubbed a hand over his face and blew out a breath of air. How was he going to tell the Kramers that their son had been cut in two and that he didn't have a suspect yet?

The truth was that he had a suspect, only he refused to believe that it could be true. All around the car were cloven hoof tracks. The roof of the car was covered in dirt, and wiry red hair had been found on the car and the ground around it. *Okay, it wasn't the devil, so what was it? Could a man crush a car like that?* No, Andy didn't think it was possible. *A bear? Yeah, maybe a bear. Bears weighed enough and were strong enough to do that to a car, weren't they?* The first thing he was going to do when he got back to the office was call a forest ranger. A forest ranger would know if a bear had done this.

Circling the car for any evidence that might have been missed, the sheriff couldn't get over the shear carnage of the scene. It was as if someone had taken a giant sledgehammer and smashed the car in on itself.

It was times like these that Andy Wright wished he still smoked. *What he wouldn't give for a cigarette right now.*

Making his way to the rear of the car, Andy was stunned and annoyed at the same time because of what he saw there. Leaning down next to the rear left tire was a man Andy didn't recognize, *probably a reporter.*

"Ahem," the sheriff grunted to make the man aware of his presence.

When the man looked up, Andy noticed that he didn't look like any reporter he had ever seen before. He had dark, wavy, black hair, and a tiny crucifix hung down from his left ear by a short gold chain. The man reminded the sheriff of a movie star or a rock musician.

Rising to his feet, the man, who stood a modest five feet nine inches and looked to be around thirty years old, offered the sheriff his hand.

"Hello there, you must be Sheriff Andy Wright. I'm Raef Lorenz. I'm here on behalf of the Church of Rome."

The Church of Rome? What were they doing here? Confused and not knowing what to say to the man, Andy asked, "Are you a priest?"

"Not anymore," the man answered with a disarming smile. "The church sent me to check on your problem."

How the hell did the Catholic Church know about his problem, and why would they send someone to help?

"This is a police matter, nothing that involves the church. I can assure you of that."

Raef gave a knowing smile. Nobody wanted interference while trying to solve a crime, especially not from a former priest. It just didn't sit well with most people. He was used to the looks he got and the questions that had to be on the mind of the sheriff, questions that the man would never ask. It was the same in every place he went; he couldn't avoid it. He looked more like a rock star than a priest, and that was just what he was going for. His new life was satisfying. It allowed him to serve both God and himself.

Dressed in black denim jeans and a maroon button-down shirt, Raef wore no coat. It was only fifty-seven degrees that day, but still, he wore no coat. For as long as he could remember, he had rarely needed one. Sure, when the weather got bitter, Raef wore a coat like everyone else, but it would need to get much worse than this before he would pull one over his shoulders.

Deciding that the sheriff was about to shut him out, the former priest said, "Sheriff, I'm not here to step on your toes. I only came because I was asked to by the church. It's sort of what I do." Seeing that the sheriff was listening, Raef went forward with his statement. "I'm only looking to help. None of what I discover or deduce here will go to any newspaper. The only person I report to is the archbishop at the Vatican and you. That is, if you allow me to help."

Still not sure about the man in front of him, Andy let go of his hand. His tight grip and warm smile seemed sincere enough, but Andy was no novice law enforcement officer. It would take more than charm to get him to agree to anything.

"Look here, Mr. Lorenz, I'm still not sure what to make of your offer or of how you can be of any help to my investigation. Would you mind joining me for a cup of coffee at the diner in town? I'd like to know more about you and what you do before I say yes to anything."

"I understand, sheriff. Point me in the right direction, and I'll meet you there," said the man without a coat.

Before he entered the diner, Raef made a phone call. The number was one he knew by heart. Raef was one of the few people in the world who could call it directly.

When the line on the other end was picked up, Raef said, "Pardon my interruption, your excellence. Is this a good time?"

The man on the other end of the phone was Archbishop Thomas Wells. He was delighted to hear from the man in America. He thought very highly of him. What Raef Lorenz did for the church was the work of the divine, and the archbishop had told him so many times over.

"Yes, Raef, it's a perfect time. What is it that you have found?"

"Well your excellence, so far, I have three eyewitnesses who claim to have seen it. They all tell the exact same story, describing it the same as in our text.

"I regret to inform you that a young man became the latest victim of the creature last night, but a girl survived. She is nearly comatose, and I haven't been able to interview her yet. I don't know that I'll ever get the opportunity either. She's in a very bad way.

"I have seen cloven foot prints with my own eyes, and I collected a hair sample that I believe belongs to the creature."

"Excellent work, Raef," the archbishop said, his approval apparent in his voice. "I knew I had chosen wisely when I asked you to go to America."

Seeing the sheriff's patrol car coming down the road, Raef excused himself from the conversation and entered the diner.

Hungry Jacks was a typical American diner. It smelled like a mixture of french fry grease and tobacco. The booths were narrow—a clear indication that the proprietor wanted to squeeze as many tables into the building as he could. The tablecloths were made of cheap plastic and were in dire need of replacement. The checkerboard pattern of red and white did nothing to add any charm to the place.

Moving a green ashtray made of glass to the windowsill, Raef waited for the sheriff. Raef hated smoking and everything to do with it. His parents had been smokers when he was growing up, and everything about the terrible, disgusting habit had put him off. Cigarette smoke was the reason that Raef hated eating out. There was nowhere that he could go and get a meal without smelling the distasteful odor of stale cigarette smoke. Some places offered non-smoking sections, but who were they kidding? Even in the non-smoking section he could smell the aroma of the cancer sticks that people poisoned themselves with.

Peering through the window, Raef could see the sheriff as the man talked into the microphone on his cruiser's radio. The conversation was heated; Raef could see that from where he sat. Something like that was never a good thing right before you were going to ask a man to allow you in on his investigation.

A shadow to his left told Raef that someone was there. Standing next to the table was a pretty woman of about twenty-six. With jet-black hair and brown eyes, she stood straight and had an air of confidence about her that was rare in waitresses.

What is she doing working in a place like this?

It was another mystery, one that would have to be solved later, because the sheriff was walking through the door.

Before he took his seat in the booth, Sheriff Wright kissed the girl on the cheek and said, "Morning, darling."

Yet another mystery for Raef to solve. *Could this be the sheriff's wife?*

The question was quickly answered when the waitress said, "Oh, good morning, daddy. Is he with you?"

"For now, he is honey. This is Mr. Raef Lorenz. He used to be a priest."

What a shocker, thought Raef as he heard the sheriff proclaim him off-limits. No one dated a used-to-be priest. Still, Raef was unaffected by the sheriff's statement. It came with the job.

Reaching out to shake the woman's hand, Raef said, "Hi. You can call me Raef. It's a pleasure to meet you, miss?"

"You can call me Kerri. It's nice to meet someone new for a change."

Her slight accent was cute and she seemed to have an upbeat view of the world around her. When she bit down on the pen she was holding, it stirred something in the former priest.

Doing his best not to alert the sheriff to his discomfort, Raef lowered his eyes.

After they were done with their greetings and the food had been ordered, Sheriff Wright got right down to business. "Mr. Lorenz, what was it that you said you did for the church again?"

Yet another smile came to Raef's lips as he answered the sheriff. "I didn't," Raef said. "But, if you can keep an open mind, I'd be glad to explain it to you."

Adjusting the Stetson hat on his head, the sheriff grimaced, feigning boredom. "You won't find a mind more open than mine, Mr. Lorenz. I'm still here, so if you're going to explain yourself, now would be the time."

Sitting forward, Raef knew that it was time to lay out some of his cards.

"What I do for the church is complicated; it's unusual. The church hires me to chase down the supernatural, wherever it might be reported."

A sly grin came over the face of the sheriff.

"So you're a ghost hunter, is that it?"

"Sometimes," Raef said, as he brushed back his wavy hair. "Other times, it's far worse." Doubt—no, downright disbelief—was on the face of the sheriff.

"I understand what you must be thinking right now," Raef said. "You think that I'm nuts. I can assure you that I'm not, sheriff. I have been all over the world, investigating reports of ghosts and demonic possession and most of the time, what I find is explainable. But, on the rare occasion, I find something that leads me to believe that something supernatural is taking place, and when I do, I try to discover the cause of it."

"Can you tell me if Elvis is still alive?" smirked the sheriff. He had heard enough.

He got up from his seat, his meal not yet having reached the table. The sheriff wished Raef a good day before leaving the diner.

Shit, thought Raef, *the man didn't even give me a chance.*

Not that it mattered. Raef would still investigate the appearance of the Jersey Devil, only now it would be more difficult.

Having the inside scoop on what the police knew was always helpful in any case. Without the help of the sheriff, it would just take him longer to sort things out.

His next stop would be the hospital and the teenager who was most likely still there. If he could get her to tell him what she had seen, he could record it as having come from an eyewitness. His place was investigating the appearance of the supernatural. The church decided what to do about it.

Sometimes it was hard not to get involved. Like the time in Kenya when a young teenage mother had been sure that her unborn baby was possessed. She reported hearing voices at night, devil voices that spoke to the child, telling it to be patient, it's time would come. At first, Raef had thought that it was just a bunch of baloney, but things had happened that had changed his mind for him. On the belly of the woman were scratches that looked like writing, but they were in a language that was unknown to Raef or anyone in the African village.

By sheer luck, a professor of linguistics from Harvard happened to be there at the same time as Raef. The writing had intrigued the man, and he had copied the letters down. The man was a genius of script, and before long, he had solved the puzzle. As it turned out, they were reading the writing upside down. The writing was in Greek, a language that the afflicted woman could not possibly have known. Translating it was simple for the educated man. It read, "I'm going to kill you, mommy."

Pictures were taken, and Raef had decided to stay in the primitive hut that the woman lived in. His tape recorder had picked up the strangest sounds at night, sounds that had come out of thin air. Stumped, the man had sent the recordings to the Vatican, where scholars would try and decipher any meaning in them.

The day after the Vatican received the recordings, he was told to leave Africa. His mission was over. No one ever told him why, and the archbishop assured him that, sometimes, it was best not to know.

If the child in the woman wasn't possessed, he would have been shocked. There was no other answer for it.

Just when he was about to get up and leave, his food arrived.

Kerri looked pretty. Even the ugly uniform she wore couldn't hide her curves. She promised Raef that her father had already paid for the meal and said she would consider it an insult if he didn't eat his food.

He didn't want to insult the woman, so he remained and ate his food, before it grew cold.

Every once in a while, he caught the woman staring at him, and he smiled. She was cute, but her dad had already marked her as off-limits. Besides, he was there on behalf of the church. He didn't have time for romance.

Romance, now that's a joke. When was the last time anything romantic happened to me? It wasn't the reason that he had left the church, but he did struggle with thoughts of the flesh.

There were a number of women whom he thought were worth his time, but it never seemed to work out. Though they protested when he blamed it on his job, he was never able to get close to them. It wasn't their fault.

He was so removed from normal people, thanks to his profession, that no one else could understand. Sometimes he felt alone in a world that was filled with evil. There was plenty of evil in the world, but there was plenty of good too. He had seen his share of both, but what he did for the Roman Catholic Church often left him alongside evil.

Looking over his shoulder as he left the diner, Raef watched the beautiful woman as she took another order. There was something about her, but he doubted he'd ever get to explore it.

4

November 4, 1984, 3:57 p.m.

Camden Memorial was busy. It seemed as if everyone in the state of New Jersey was injured or ill.

Making his way to the reception desk, Raef was met by a frowning old lady wearing a nurse's uniform and horn-rimmed glasses. The hospital was overrun with patients, and she was clearly not in the mood for Raef.

The closer he got to the information desk, the more the woman tried not to notice his approach. *If this was typical of American hospitals*, he wondered, *how did anyone ever get better?*

"Hello," he said to the snarling beast of a health care professional. When she ignored him, he was more forceful. "Excuse me, do you happen to work here, by chance? I thought that the lovely outfit you wore might indicate that you did." The woman was not impressed by his attempt at wit, but it did get a response from her.

"Uh, duh," came the insult from the woman. "May I help you with something?" she asked in the most unattractive drawl he'd ever heard.

This one is a charmer, he thought as he answered her. "Yes, ma'am, I'm looking for Stacy Warner. Can you tell me where she is?"

"You and about thirty other reporters," squawked the woman as she continued to type at her computer. The only time she took her hands off the keys was to push her glasses back onto her nose, otherwise she acted like he wasn't there.

He was about to give up when he noticed the crucifix hanging around her neck. If he played his cards right, he might get some help yet.

"Sorry to have bothered you," he said as he began to walk away. Turning back suddenly, he asked, "Is there a chapel in the hospital, someplace a priest can offer a prayer for someone?"

After allowing his Irish accent to come out fully, Raef wasn't surprised by her response.

For the first time since he had entered the hospital, the bitter old nurse behind the desk looked at him.

"Did you say you were a priest?" the woman asked.

Lying wasn't something he did easily, but there were times when it was necessary.

"Why yes, ma'am, I am," responded Raef. "I'm on holiday in the States, and when I heard about the little girl, I was moved. I wouldn't say that the Lord sent me here, but something drew me. I just wanted to be of service. I don't usually dress like this, please excuse me."

The woman was a devout Catholic and if a priest wanted to visit the girl and offer her prayers, the nurse wasn't going to deny a man of God.

"I'm so sorry, Father. The girl is in T-4. They haven't moved her yet."

Thanking the nurse and offering her a blessing, Raef headed for the trauma unit. T-4 was a trauma room, which was usually used for the badly injured or the critically sick. The girl must have been worse off than he thought.

When he reached the door to the room, Raef knocked. The woman who answered looked as though she hadn't slept for days. She wore no makeup and had been crying. Her red eyes could use some Visine, and he wished he'd thought of it before coming to the room. She was easy to read. A single mother, Stacy was all she had in the world.

Wanting to balance his need to see the girl with compassion for her mother, Raef introduced himself. Surprised when the woman greeted him with kindness, he was allowed into the room.

New Jersey was filled with Catholics. Its large population of Italians and Irish made it so. Finding out that the Warners were Catholics made it easier for the woman to accept Raef's assistance, and it was probably the only reason he'd been allowed into the room at all. He didn't care about someone's religion; he saw people for who they were. Though he still considered himself Catholic, Raef was open-minded.

The interview with the woman went well, she even asked him to say a prayer over her daughter. She didn't care if he wasn't a priest anymore. Ms. Warner found him to be a breath of fresh air from the stiff lipped chaplains who the hospital had sent in to see Stacy.

Kneeling down next to the girl, Raef made the sign of the cross over his chest and began. He said the prayer out loud; he was not embarrassed that he believed in Jesus. The prayer wasn't overly long, but it was heartfelt, and it brought some peace to Ms. Warner. When he was done, he began to rise from his knees.

Offering Ms. Warner a half smile that said, *I tried my best, there was little more I could do*, he began walking away from the girl's bedside. He was sure that the shock showed on his face when a hand reached out and grabbed him by the wrist; the hand belonged to Stacy Warner.

The grip was strong, and he almost pulled away.

When the initial shock wore off, Raef got back on his knees and sat silently, the grip on his wrist not wavering in the least. The eyes of the girl remained open, and he could see twitching in the right one. Was it possible that he had reached her? If so, he knew that it was God who had guided him there.

His compassion for the girl overrode his desire to interview her. Reaching out with his right hand, Raef smoothed back the hair that covered Stacy's forehead. The gesture was genuine; he cared about her well-being.

Running his fingers through the girl's hair, Raef whispered to her.

"Hey there, Stacy. I'm Raef. I used to be a priest, and your mother asked if I might pray over you."

The twitching in her eye got stronger, and he continued to whisper. "You are such a strong girl. Your mother loves you very much. She's not mad at you. She's just glad that you're safe. I've never met you before, but I can tell you this: God loves you."

The mention of God made her grip his wrist even tighter. It was a good sign that maybe he really was reaching her.

Pressing her hand to his lips, Raef kissed the girl on the back of her hand and began whispering again. "I don't think I've ever met someone as resourceful as you. You made it. Whatever happened on that ridge, you survived it."

The mention of the ridge made her mouth tighten up. She screamed. The scream was the first sign of awareness that anyone had seen in the girl, and Ms. Warner began to cry.

"It's all right, little one. Come back to us. We love you."

"Mommy!" hollered the girl as her eyes blinked back tears and she reached out toward Ms. Warner. Both of the Warner women cried as they held each other and gave each other reassurances of the love they shared. The show of love between mother and daughter nearly brought a tear to Raef's eye. He was deeply moved.

As he was about to leave the pair to themselves, Ms. Warner turned to him with tears in her eyes and said, "Thank you. Thank you so very much."

The words were music to his ears, and he knew that it was not by his words alone that the girl had returned to her mother. A higher power had heard his prayer and answered it. He wasn't surprised.

A feeling of elation and a smile on his face was all that Raef left the hospital with, and it was enough. He would bother the Warners no more. They deserved to be left alone after what they had been through.

Walking through the parking lot to his car, Raef was surprised to see a familiar face. Even without the waitress uniform, he knew it was her.

"Hello there, again," the woman said when she saw him. It was an obvious indication that she had sought out his conversation.

He was pleased to see Kerri, especially now that she was wearing a pair of jeans and a tight-knit sweater. He was seeing a whole new side of the woman and he wasn't disappointed. Maybe his luck was changing for the better.

"Hi there. What brings you here?"

"It's that little Warner girl. My heart goes out to her and her mother. I feel badly about Harvey Kramer, too, but there's not much I can do for him now."

Her concern was sincere. There was more to her than met the eye. After relaying the story of what happened in the trauma unit, minus any intervention from himself, Raef asked Kerri out for a cup of coffee.

When she was hesitant, he said, "How dangerous can it be? I used to be a priest."

The coffee in the Java Jungle was good; only in Paris had he tasted better.

Raef watched the woman with intensity as she told him about herself. She was a graduate of Brown University, but somehow life as a scholar wasn't fulfilling for the woman. She was smart, and she knew that she didn't want to be a waitress forever. For the time being, being a waitress allowed her time for self-evaluation. Unable to decide what it was that interested her, Kerri was taking her time. She didn't want to be someone who rushed into life. Thanks to her father and mother, she knew she could be anything she wanted to be.

The more Raef listened to her, the more she became attractive to him. She wasn't just another pretty girl. She was an intelligent woman, and that, above all else, drew him to her. She was particularly interested in history, but she couldn't decide which period she wanted to study. She loved them all.

As he talked to her he realized just how well-versed, she was about history, both US and European. He allowed her to talk about herself as much as possible. He found her fascinating and could listen to her speak all day. It was obvious that she was a free spirit, one who accepted things as they came her way.

A free spirit himself, Raef couldn't take his eyes off of her. After an hour or so of conversation about herself, Kerri blushed and apologized for the long version of her life.

"No reason to apologize. I enjoy listening about you," Raef said with a wink of his eye. "You could go on all night if you wanted to."

She blushed even brighter and gave a sheepish smile before asking, "How about you? How does an ex-priest find himself in New Jersey, and what business could you possibly have with my father?"

Looking at his watch, he asked the woman, "Do you have the time? Mine is a long story as well."

It was nearly 6:30 p.m., but she said she had nowhere else to be.

"How about I buy you dinner and you tell me your story?" she asked. "I bet it's worth the price of the chow."

The invitation was intriguing, even though Raef had work to do. Still, what could a little dinner hurt? He could work late if he had to. To decline her invitation to go to dinner might hurt her feelings, and that was the last thing he wanted to do. "Who am I to refuse an invitation to dine with such a beautiful woman? I graciously accept, but only if you'll let me pay. The Church of Rome is very generous with road expenses."

They took separate cars and met at a place called Kangaroo Katie's. The place was jam-packed with people waiting to be seated. She had to know that it would be busy at that hour of the day, which led him to believe that she wanted to spend more time with him.

Kangaroo Katie's was well lit and spacious. The bar rested two steps above the dining area and stools surrounded it. Kerri spotted a couple getting up from the bar, and she grabbed his hand, nearly jerking him from his feet as she led him to the newly vacated seats.

"You gotta be quick or else you're gonna miss out," said the smiling woman as she sat down on her stool.

She wasn't kidding. As they reached the stools, Raef could see several people trying to beat them there. Only the keen eye and quick feet of Kerri had earned them a place to sit while they waited for a table to open up.

Bellying up to the bar, Kerri ordered an apple martini, and Raef asked for a Guinness. The head on his beer was nearly perfect. Unfortunately, it was served to him cold. *There is nothing better than a warm Guinness, but when in Rome …* he thought as he sipped from the glass.

While at the bar, he studied the men and women who frequented the restaurant. The clientele was mostly made up of middle-class yuppies, the shirt-and-tie crowd. The women there seemed to have come straight from work. Their short skirts and tight dresses were slightly wrinkled. A few families were in the dining area, but for the most part, Kangaroo Katie's was filled with young suburbanites trying to relax after a long day of work. It reminded him of the pubs in Ireland, only there were less darts being played, and the people were too well dressed.

Kerri broke the silence, asking, "You're name is Raef. Are you French?"

Nearly choking on his beer, the man replied, "No, sorry, but I'm not. Actually, I'm Irish."

Shifting in her bar stool and taking a sip from her glass, Kerri said, "Irish? Your English is perfect. Why don't you have an accent?"

Shifting back to his thick Irish drawl, Raef said, "Is this whet ye'r wantin' to hair, lassie?"

Laughing at him, Kerri slapped him gently on the shoulder. "That's nice, but I think I prefer the American one better."

"Have it your way," Raef said with a sigh. "Women. You can never speak enough languages for them."

He followed his statement up with a laugh, and she joined him. Her smile was bright, and the snaggletooth on the right side of her mouth was sexy.

A snaggletooth was what he called a tooth that overlapped others. It was common in girls from the United Kingdom, and he had always found it attractive. He also found her laugh infectious. She was an unexpected bright spot on his trip. *The Lord works in mysterious ways.*

Draining the last of his beer, Raef said, "All right then, I shall start."

"I was born in a city called Drogheda. I wouldn't expect you to know where that is, but it's not important to my story. Ever since I was young, I was drawn to the church, meaning the Roman Catholic Church. By the time I was sixteen, I knew that I was going to be a priest. I can't say that God ever spoke to me personally, but somehow I knew that I'd been called to his service. My parents were tickled to death. There was nothing more honorable for an Irish Catholic lad to do than become a priest."

After rolling his eyes into the back of his head as he said the words, Raef could see that Kerri could sympathize with him. Parents often projected their desires on their children. How many children had become something they never should have been because of a parent's ushering?

"I was a quick study in the seminary. Having competent knowledge of the Bible before I entered helped. After the seminary, I was sent to Oxford, where I studied early western civilizations. My specialty was religions of the world.

"When I was ordained, I was sent to Rome. The archbishop there had taken an interest in me and my knowledge of the world. Before I knew it, I was traveling to Africa, Spain, Australia, and so many other countries that I lost count of them. I was sent to study and uncover religious artifacts that might be of interest to the church.

"I was no Indiana Jones. I had no interest in trekking through jungles or the catacombs of the dead. What I was interested in was religions. Wherever I discovered a new one, or a sect of one that wasn't well-known, I took notes about it, reporting my findings to the church. I guess I wasn't cut out for the work they placed me in, because I rarely discovered anything new. Because of that I wound up as a parish priest in Virginia; nothing could have bored me more."

Raising her hand slightly, as if she were in school, Kerri said, "Sound's like Indiana Jones stuff to me. That had to be incredible, traveling to all those foreign places and meeting so many interesting people. Tell me, Raef, are the pyramids as mind-blowing as I expect they would be?"

"It wasn't long before Catholicism in America began to turn me off. I was raised in the old church, not the new one that was ever-changing in the States. In America, I was becoming disillusioned with the church. Instead of accepting what was, Americans always wanted the church to change into what they wanted, and it did. Before I knew it, there were ribbon-waving ceremonies and electric guitars playing rifts behind the hymnals. I lasted for three years before I had had enough. This wasn't what I had been called to do, and I began to doubt my calling as a priest.

"Oh, and to answer your earlier question. Yes, it was something that could make you doubt your significance in this world."

He could see in her eyes that she was sympathizing with him and it made him feel better. Raef wasn't at all embarrassed about his past, but it was nice when someone could understand the pain that was involved in finding out that what you had planned to do for the rest of your life, what you had planned to be, was less than satisfying and that you were slowly dying inside.

"Word of my disdain reached Archbishop Wells in Rome. He had always liked me, and somehow my failings as a priest didn't surprise him. On March 6, 1979, I was called back to Rome, where my fate as a priest was decided. I didn't argue when I was granted papal dispensation to leave the priesthood. I accepted.

"Archbishop Wells pulled me aside after the meeting and said he had a proposition for me, a job. The job was to go where the church sent me and investigate reports of the supernatural. This included hauntings, the speaking of tongues, the image of the Virgin Mary appearing, and sometimes demonic possession. The last of which is why I'm here in Burlington."

Raef expected her demeanor to change, but it didn't. She was lost in his story, and he liked it, so he moved on.

"What I do for the Church of Rome is simple. I go where they send me and investigate. I take and record interviews. I also collect evidence to either support or disprove what is being reported. I never get involved in whatever action the church takes next. I'm no longer a priest, I have no authority over the powers of evil in this world; at least that's what the church tells me. So far, I haven't had any problems with that. I would like to know what the final outcomes of my investigations are, but no one ever offers me any information, so I leave it alone. That's the way the church likes it.

"As for why I'm here, that's simple. I'm following up on reports that the Jersey Devil has returned to Burlington."

The words struck her like a ton of bricks, and for several seconds she was speechless. *The man is handsome and interesting, and now this? Perfect*, she thought, she loved the occult. For as long as she could remember, she had been searching out and reading about Big Foot or Champ the sea serpent, which had been seen in Lake Champlain. She wasn't sure that she actually believed they existed. In fact, she was leaning toward them not existing. But, seeing the passion of the man in front of her for discovering the unnatural, it was enough to make her change her mind, almost.

She was the daughter of a sheriff, and had been raised Lutheran. Though she wasn't a practicing Lutheran, she still believed in God.

Church didn't hold any interest for her; it never had. Kerri would much rather have gone hiking or played touch football out in the street than go to church when she was a kid.

Now that she knew what Raef did for a living, she had a ton of questions for him. There was no way to keep them in.

"What makes the church put any credence behind this latest sighting of the Jersey Devil?" Kerri asked, her face serious.

At least she isn't calling me crazy yet, thought Raef as he began to answer her. As they ordered another round of drinks, her name was called over the paging system, and they were led to a table.

After they had placed their orders, Raef said, "To answer your question, they don't. It was I who brought it to their attention and suggested investigating the possibility that a devil has been released on earth again. Things on the paranormal end of church investigations have been slow, so the archbishop agreed."

It wasn't the whole truth, but it wasn't a lie either. The church didn't make it common knowledge that it actually investigated matters like the Jersey Devil. As far as it was officially concerned, demonic possession and ghosts didn't exist; but that wasn't exactly the truth either.

As the pair ate their meal, Raef answered several questions for the woman. He could see that her mind rejected some of his answers; but it wasn't unexpected. Finding out that the supernatural was real couldn't be easy for nonbelievers.

Before she could ask another question, Raef asked, "Do you believe in God?"

The question threw her off. She hadn't been expecting it.

Wiping the corners of her mouth with her napkin she said, "Yes, of course I believe in God."

Taking her hands and staring into her eyes, Raef asked again. "No, don't give me the generic answer; I want your true feelings. Do you believe in God?"

His touch and the way he asked the question were unsettling. It didn't offend her. There was no judgment in his eyes. This time her answer was firm, with no matter-of-fact tone to it. "Yes, I believe in God. What's that got to do with any of this?"

"I'm sorry, but without knowing, I couldn't tell if I should continue or not." Letting go of her hands, Raef gave her a smile and continued. "If you believe in God then you have to believe in the Devil, correct?"

When she nodded yes, he continued.

"Let me assure you that he exists and that temptation and evil are a part of this world as sure as heaven above us. I have seen and uncovered things that most men and women aren't ready to hear about. It would frighten them too much for them to accept that it exists."

He could see from the look in her eyes that she was frightened. But she also seemed eager to hear about his latest investigation.

"In 1735, a man and a woman named Samuel and Deborah Leeds brought something into the world that was never meant to be." As he explained about the birth and death of the infant, he could see her mind racing with the possibilities. When he was done recounting the tale for her, she looked blown away.

Shifting uncomfortably in her chair, Kerri said, "I thought that it was just an old wives' tale, a story to make children behave."

"That often happens with a story so old, but this one has merit. Leeds Point, where the Kramer boy was murdered, is named for the family that once lived there."

"Really, how can you be certain of that?" asked Kerri, gulping down the remainder of her martini.

"The Catholic Church has an extensive library. People would be astounded by what you can learn there."

Looking at his watch, Raef realized how late it was.

"As much as I would like to continue the conversation," he said, "I have to go. Would you like to accompany me tomorrow? I'm going to some of the places in the story to try to prove that they exist."

"I'll have to blow off work, but I'll be there," she said. "Tell me when and where."

After telling her where to meet him, and what time they would leave, they parted ways. Both of them wore smiles as they separated for the evening. Raef decided that work could wait until the morning. It would be more pleasant with Kerri by his side.

5

November 5, 1984, 3:16 a.m.

Steam poured from the nostrils of the devil as it hopped and skipped on its long, crane-like legs through the pasture on the Dugans' farm. The farm was on the far west side of Burlington where pine trees had been removed for the paper industry in years gone by.

Norton and Penny Dugan were both the children of farmers. Farming was in their blood and they didn't want to let go of it.

The soil in the area wasn't worth a damn and it was a struggle to get anything to grow there, but that never fazed the Dugans, who had bought the property to run a dairy farm. Their herd of 120 dairy cows was considered big. Housing the herd and growing the feed that fed it on thirty acres of land was a chore, a chore that six sons, ages nine to seventeen, helped to handle. The boys rose early, chasing the cows and taking from them the creamy milk that would be pasteurized and then sold at market. None of the pasteurization was done on the farm. The milk was sold as a raw product.

Though they were well liked, the Dugans stayed to themselves, the boys having enough work on the farm after school to keep them out of trouble.

As it pranced over the pasture, the devil made sure to fix its eyes on every cow that it found. The cows made mooing noises and rushed off at the sight of the creature, unable to meet the gaze of the beast.

The only animal that wasn't frightened of the creature was the Dugans' family dog. The eighty-pound German shepherd came racing across the field when it saw the creature, but the devil wasn't frightened.

Waiting for the dog, its heart rate increasing, the devil bore into the animal with its beady, red eyes.

As the dog got closer it slowed, beginning to whine, its tail tucked between its legs.

The devil closed in on the dog, never taking its eyes off of the faithful canine.

Whining changed to whimpering, and it wasn't long before the dog started to have seizures. The stare of the devil was not only intense, it was also lethal, and lingering on the eyes of the beast for too long caused the dog's heart to stop beating.

When the dog rolled over dead, the devil let out a bark of triumph. The steely vocal outburst of the creature was loud and the lights on the house came on.

"What in the hell was that?" Penny Dugan asked. She had been jolted out of her sleep by the loud barking of the devil.

"Don't know," her husband said, his eyes wide open and his heart beating so hard that he could almost hear it. "Get the kids, Penny. I'm for grabbing my shotgun."

Before his wife was through the doorway to their room, he added, "And no one goes outside, not for nothing."

Penny did as her husband ordered, and soon, all of the Dugans were huddled together in the upstairs bathroom of their farmhouse, each person scared out his or her mind.

Berating himself for forgetting to dial 911, Norton Dugan knew that he would have to go back into the bedroom and make the call.

A loud thump on the roof of the house made him change his mind, he wasn't going anywhere. As the Dugans remained huddled, reciting prayers, something danced on the roof of the house. What sounded like hooves tapped out a dirge of horror.

Rumor of the Jersey Devil had been floating around town for days, and Norman Dugan had no doubt what it was that was dancing on his roof. He wasn't the most religious man in the world, but Norman could feel the evil that was on his roof; he would swear he could. It was fifteen-year-old Jefferson who spoke, breaking the silence in the room.

"Dad, you have a shotgun. Why don't we go out there and kill whatever it is?"

Mussing up the boy's hair and pointing at the ceiling, Norman said, "Because that isn't natural. It's the Devil that's on our roof."

Nothing more had to be said. The Dugan family remained in the house, hoping against all hope that the devil would pass them by.

For hours, the devil danced on the roof without pause, causing Penny's teeth to chatter and Morgan to faint. The creature's unholy barking and relentless prancing on the roof left all of the Dugans without breath; each of them was afraid to say a word, which might alert the devil that they were there.

The devil was angry and almost willing to break the covenant that prevented it from entering the home of the Dugans.

It wasn't long after Saint Michael, the archangel, had defeated Lucifer and his host of devils that the covenant had been drawn up. If summoned to the earth, any devil could remain so long as it didn't enter a domicile without the invitation of the owner. The covenant also said that night was to be the time of the Devil and his minions. During the day, they would be held powerless by the sun. Once summoned and the world was dark, any devil could do harm as it pleased.

Unfortunately for the Devil and his minions, holy men would be a bane to them, restricting their actions and forcing them back into the fiery realm of hell. Things had changed in the modern world, and holy men, even men of strong faith were few and far between. This time, the Jersey Devil would have no equal.

Though the devil wanted badly to break the covenant and seek its fun, it knew that to do so would bring punishment. The Father of Lies was not one to anger. His anger often led to thousands of years of torture and even the Jersey Devil wanted to avoid that suffering. So, for now, the devil would have to be happy with the mischief it had caused that night. The death of the dog would bring pain and suffering to the family; it would have to be enough.

Throughout the night, the devil roamed the Pine Barrens and the cities around them to no avail. People were frightened and remained in their homes. No one was coming out until the sun rose and when that happened, the time of the devil was over.

November 5, 1984, 9:30 a.m.

A light blue Mercury Marquise pulled into the front parking lot of the Holiday Inn and stopped alongside the curb. Waiting anxiously for the handsome man to exit the hotel, Kerri couldn't wait another minute for their adventure to begin.

There was no long wait. Raef was through the front doors, and jogging to her car as it pulled in. Plopping himself in the front passenger seat, he asked, "Are you ready? I promise you, you are going to learn more about the supernatural today than you ever imagined. Prepare yourself."

She gave him a smile that said, "Bring it on," and pulled away from the curb.

The pair crossed through Burlington until they hit a road called the Burlington Overpass, which led up into the hills, and soon they were crossing over a bridge.

"Stop the car," Raef said when they were in the middle of its span. Pulling over as close to the edge of the bridge as she could, Kerri did what the man had asked her.

"If you're going to ask me to make out, at least wait until we get up on the point," the woman said with the sly smile on her face.

"Once again, you misjudge me," Raef said as he climbed out of the Mercury. "Come on, I'm not going to push you over the bridge. It's the first piece of evidence in the road to solving the mystery."

He didn't have to say another word. While making out with the man wasn't a bad idea, solving a mystery was an even better one, for the moment. Approaching the side of the bridge, she stood next to Raef and waited for him to explain.

"Do you remember the story I told you last night about the birth of the Leeds' baby?" When she nodded yes, he continued. "Well, this is the rickety bridge from which the deformed child was cast into the river." Seeing that she was still with him, he said, "Right here, in this very place is where Samuel Leeds tossed his child into oblivion."

Brushing her windblown hair out of her face, Kerri asked, "How can you be sure of that? This bridge is new."

"The old one was torn down ten years ago and replaced by this marvel of modern science. The torn-down bridge was the one that replaced the rickety old bridge in my story. I did some research at the library in Camden before coming here. At least three bridges have been built here. After making so many repairs on lesser structures, the City of Burlington decided to build this wonderful expanse of metal and concrete. From what I've read, this bridge has been the scene of a lot of bad accidents, and several suicides as well."

Kerri had heard about the accidents and the suicides. The man was thorough; she should have expected that from him.

"All right, I'm convinced. What's next?"

"Next we get to the top of the ridge and park the car there. Are you up for some hiking?"

Pulling her coat tightly around her, Kerri said, "I was born to hike. Hope you can keep up."

Watching the man get into the car, Kerri realized for the first time that he wasn't wearing a jacket. It had to be fifty degrees outside; *was he nuts*? Still, he did look good in his royal blue sweater. It fit him well, showing off a muscular body that she couldn't take her eyes off of.

Parking at the same spot where Harvey Kramer and Stacy Warner had been attacked, the pair got out of the car again. For no reason that she could think of, the place creeped Kerri out, and she couldn't wait to get out of the car and begin their search.

For an hour and a half, they searched the weeds and brush along the ridge, which overlooked Burlington. Kerri was about to suggest looking elsewhere when she tripped over a piece of lumber. As she fell to her knees, Kerri was looking down at a long, thin board that was about eight feet in length. The elements had stripped it of paint and termites had nearly finished the job of making it one with the land again.

"Over here," she called to Raef, who was busy looking for clues about twenty yards away from her. "I found something."

When he finally fought through the weeds that separated them, Raef kneeled down and said, "I do believe that you did find something, something important."

The man began to brush weeds back from over the top of something, something that over time, had partially sunken into the soil on the ridge. As he brushed and dug, Raef tossed sections of lumber and a still connected crossbeam from a house at her.

Dodging the section, she said, "That's not funny, mister, keep your wood to yourself." No sooner had she said it, than she realized what she had said. "What I mean is that you need to be more careful."

His mind laughed as he continued to dig up pieces of an old house. The wood was old, so old that most of it fell apart in his hands as he tried to uncover it or pull it from the earth. Within a half hour, Raef had uncovered the crossbeam of a roof, two steps, a light fixture, and a sink. Tired, he sat down and announced, "There's no doubt about it. This is the place."

He was probably right, but what kind of companion would she be if she didn't make him prove it, she wondered. "This proves nothing, Raef. Maybe someone used this site as a dumping ground. It wouldn't be unheard of."

He couldn't deny that she was right, because she was.

Getting to his knees, Raef began to dig deeper into the soil. Weeds, rocks, and pieces of wood came flying out from where he knelt. This time Kerri was smart enough to stand in front of where he worked. When Raef struck something solid that wouldn't budge, he grew agitated by it. He needed to find some proof, something that would validate his belief that this was where the Leeds' house had once stood.

After finding a piece of wood that might withstand his digging, Raef shoved it under the item and pried the thing from the ground.

When it came free, he wasn't sure what to make of it. It was made of metal, and when he began to scrub the dirt away from it he could tell that it was an old whisky flask. Both sides of it were rusted, and dirt was encrusted around that rust. Using a rock, Raef began to scrub the dirt and rust away from the flask.

Kerri watched with interest. She didn't believe that the flask would bring them any proof that this was what they were looking for, but why not let the man try? Raef's elbow grease paid off and soon he was smiling. His smile made Kerri give out a fake sigh of disgust as she said, "Let me guess, you found something."

Turning the flask toward the woman, Raef's smile turned into an ear-to-ear grin. At first, Kerri couldn't make out what the writing on the flask said. Leaning in closer, Kerri could make out the writing and a smile found her face too. The writing on the flask read, "S. Leeds." They had found their proof.

Feeling good about themselves, Kerri and Raef made their way back to the car.

Seemingly from out of nowhere a rotten log crashed down over the back of Raef's head, and he went down hard.

Turning, Kerri was confronted by the man holding the other end of that broken log in his hands. The man was tall, at least six feet three, and his arms were covered in tattoos. On his forehead was the tattoo of a pentagram, a six-pointed star. His face was ashen and his eyes were red.

When he raised the remaining portion of the log over his head, Kerri cringed, bringing her arms over her own head for protection. Knowing that she was going to be cracked over the head with the log, Kerri thought, *shit, where did this guy come from?*

The attack never came, and she was surprised to hear the man with the log grunt in pain. When she looked down, she saw that Raef had rolled over onto his back, and apparently from the way the madman was holding his crotch, Raef had kicked him in the balls.

Turning onto his side and getting to his feet, Raef was still groggy. A blow to the head from a log, even a rotten one, could put a hurting on someone.

The man with the tattoos no longer held the log, but he seemed to have recovered from his injury. Charging, the stranger looked as though he meant to tackle the former priest.

Ready for the attack, Raef stepped to the side as the tattooed man changed his mind and threw a left hook at Raef's chin. Stepping away from the stranger's punch, Raef grabbed the man's wrist as it whizzed through empty air, twisting the man's wrist so that his arm was turned at an unnatural angle. With his left leg, Raef sent a martial arts–style kick into the man's ribs.

Kerri heard the man's ribs snap and she cringed. The kick from Raef must have been a strong one and Raef didn't seem to be done with the man yet.

Still holding the man's wrist, Raef grabbed it with his right hand as well, and pulling the wrist out wider still, he forced the man's body to flip over. Once he had the madman on the ground, Raef twisted that same arm behind the man's back, locking it in place so the man couldn't move for fear that his arm would be broken.

"Get to the car," Raef barked, his voice showing the strain of his encounter with the man. "Get your dad and tell him to get his butt up here."

Racing back to the car, when Kerri turned the key to start the engine, nothing happened. She had forgotten to lock the car when they left it, and now she noticed that the hood was ajar. Someone had been fooling around with her car.

At about the same time, she noticed the black Harley Davidson motorcycle that was parked against a tree. The man had obviously followed them and done something to disable her car, but why?

Cursing out loud, the woman ran back to where Raef still held the man pinned to the ground. She was out of breath when she got there. Finding her breath again, Kerri said, "Raef, he's disabled my car. It won't start."

"Oh boy," said Raef, who had just saved her from getting her skull cracked open. "We need to get out of here, now."

Using his right hand like a knife, Raef struck the stranger on the side of his neck and the man was out cold. Raef wasted no time getting to his feet and grabbing Kerri's hand. She didn't resist, and her legs fell into rhythm with his as he started running farther into the Pine

Barrens, which had reclaimed the ridge where the Leeds' house had once stood.

"Why are we running?" Kerri asked, her feet continuing to fall one after the other in front of her.

Raef didn't look at her when he said, "Because we're not alone."

She had never thought that there might be others who had come with the stranger. Of course, neither of them had seen the stranger until he had struck Raef over the back of the head.

Fear gripped Kerri, and she kept running. It was then, when she found it coming in handy, that she was grateful for her running class at the gym. She had hated it every day that she had gone, but if she got through this, she would never complain again.

It wasn't long before they heard the sound of rustling tree limbs and brush being trampled. Kerri's fear reached a whole new level, and soon she was outdistancing Raef.

Seeing that Kerri would run on without him, Raef slowed his pace and looked for a place from which he could ambush someone. The trees were tall but not very wide; there was no place he could hide. The option disappeared quickly as a man appeared. He ran around a large bush, waving a knife in front of him.

Never bring bare hands to a knife fight, thought Raef as he watched the man bear down on him. This one was covered in tattoos just like the first guy had been. He was shorter and stockier, but somehow, he looked as if he wasn't there, like he was in some sort of a trance.

Feigning a duck to his right, Raef went down on one knee as the stranger sliced at his face with the knife. The stranger missed the face of the former priest by just inches. Raef got a good look at the knife. It looked sharp. The attack put the stranger off balance and Raef used it to his advantage. Grabbing the man's ankle, Raef twisted, sending his off-balance attacker sprawling to the ground. Getting to his feet, Raef had no time to press his advantage as another man closed in on him, this one carrying a tire iron.

Ripping his sweater off, Raef twisted it tightly and waited for the new man's attack. This biker was taller than the one with the knife, but he had the same glazed look in his eyes, a look that said his actions weren't his own. Raef couldn't worry about that for now, the man wanted to hurt him, badly.

As the biker bore down on Raef, ready to clobber him with the tire iron, Raef snapped the sweater in his hands like a towel at the beach, striking the madman in the eye with its end. Crying out in pain, the biker dropped the tire iron and put his hands to his face. Temporarily blind, it was going to be a while before the biker was back in the fight.

There was no time to relax. Raef wasn't out of the woods yet. Raef could hear the stranger with the knife getting to his feet. If he didn't deal with the blinded biker then, he might find himself fighting both of them at once. Not proud of what he was about to do, Raef punched the blinded man in the throat. It was a killing blow, something that Raef had promised himself he would never do.

When it came down to you or them, there was really no other choice … at least that's what his father had always told him. His father was a wealth of knowledge and life lessons that the former priest paid close attention to. His dad said such things as though they were easy decisions to make, but every decision had its consequences. Having never been involved in a life-and-death fight before, Raef was shocked at how quickly the decision to kill had come to him.

The sound of the man's trachea crushing in on itself made Raef sick, but it couldn't be avoided. He and Kerri were still in trouble. Only God knew how many bad guys were chasing them, he couldn't chance the man surviving and getting to Kerri.

The injured man fell, clutching his throat. With his trachea crushed, death was only minutes away. He wouldn't be bothering Raef again.

A stinging pain brought Raef out of his thoughts and he turned to see that his right arm had been cut deeply on his bicep. The cut had gone through flesh and even muscle. It hurt like a bitch, but he couldn't let it deter him. Anger clouded the mind of the former priest, anger that he didn't know he had in him.

When the man with the knife lunged for him again, Raef spun, sending a back swing kick into the side of the stranger's head. Raef's heel struck the stranger on the right temple and he went down like a sack of potatoes.

There was no time to see if the man was alive, Raef didn't even have time to retrieve his sweater. Others might be coming. Racing at top speed, Raef could feel the blood running down his arm. He had nothing to use to stem the flow, so he just kept running.

He could have been wrong, but Raef thought he heard the sound of feet rushing through the forest behind him. He never looked back.

Hoping that Kerri was all right, he had no chance but to let her run away, while he faced the threat. Most of all, he wanted to make sure she wasn't harmed. She was special; he didn't know how he knew it, but he did.

It wasn't long before Raef came to the edge of a river. Looking across the water, he saw Kerri standing on the other side. She was soaking wet. She waved to him, motioning for him to swim across the water.

If she can do it, I can do it, he thought, so he dived into the water. The icy temperature of the water gripped his chest tightly and he began to hyperventilate as his head broke the surface. Thanks to the adrenalin in him, his body didn't go into shock, but still, his lungs refused to take in air. By focusing on his breathing, Raef was able to get it under control and he made the swim to the other side.

By the time he got there his lips were blue. So were Kerri's. Now they were soaking wet and freezing with no car. *Could things get any worse?*

Taking Kerri by the hand, Raef began to run again, but the shivering woman forced him to stop.

Pointing to his arm, she asked, "What happened to you?"

"I got a little cut. It's no big deal. Let's keep running. We need to get out of here."

Raef was shocked when Kerri took her coat off and ripped the shirt off of her back. Standing in the Pine Barrens in just her bra and her blue jeans, the woman wrapped her shirt around his cut, stemming the flow of blood.

When she put her coat back on, the cold, wet garment sent a chill through her body, but it was better than being naked.

"All right, now we can run," Kerri shouted as she took off into the forest again.

Freezing cold and injured, Raef would never forget the quick glance he had stolen at Kerri's nearly naked torso. Though he should have been focused on other things, his mind latched on to that sight. He was a man, after all.

Shaking his head, Raef followed Kerri.

They ran for another half hour before they found a road. As they walked down the road, it wasn't long before a car pulled over and offered them a ride back into town. They were dropped off at the sheriff's office, and the deputies brought them in, summoning medical attention for Raef.

Things had just gotten interesting. They had to be on to something.

Before she left the sheriff's office later that day, Kerri learned that something strange had happened in the wee hours of the morning. The Dugans had reported that something had killed their dog and stomped on their roof all night long. They had spent the night terrified in the hall bathroom of their home. Not only had their dog been killed, but for some strange reason, none of their cows were able to produce milk. The Dugans' cows were famous for their generous output. It just wasn't normal.

Her father had already deemed her house unsafe, so he had a female deputy go there in her stead to retrieve her clothes. Until the sheriff figured out who had attacked them, she would be staying at his house. She loved her dad, but somebody had to tell him that she wasn't a little girl anymore. It wasn't going to be her, but somebody had to tell him.

Once she had dry clothes on, Kerri had a deputy drive her to the hospital to check in on Raef.

Receiving two staples and seventeen stitches, he had been sewn back together again.

Finding Raef, she waited until they were alone to speak. "Who the hell was that on the ridge, and why were they chasing us?"

"If the church is interested in the return of the Jersey Devil, don't you think he is too?"

Waving her arms around, she asked, "What do you mean by he? You couldn't possibly be talking about the he that I think you're talking about, can you?"

Looking down into his lap, Raef let out a breath of air. When he looked back up at her, Kerri could see in his eyes that indeed he meant what she thought he meant.

"All right, now I'm confused," she said as she flopped into a chair and stared at the wall of the hospital room.

"I'm sorry. I never should have involved you in this. Those men who chased us; they were sent by him. It's probably best not to speak his name."

He could see the fear in her eyes. It was real. To her this had been just an adventure. She had never dreamed it would come with consequences.

"The forces of evil are everywhere. I wasn't kidding when I told you that. It seems that someone doesn't want us digging into why the devil has returned. There are no coincidences in this world. The Jersey Devil is here, and someone wants to keep it that way."

Once again the woman surprised him as she took his hand.

"Someone just tried to kill me," she said. " Now I'm really mad. Get your ass off of that table and let's find out more about this devil.

6

Darkness found the northeast early in November.

By the time Kerri and Raef left the hospital, twilight had already begun to fall over Burlington. No one wanted to be caught outside after dark, but Kerri had a stop that she wanted to make, a stop that she absolutely needed to make.

When the deputies had gone to Leeds Point and searched the ridge, they had discovered Kerri's Mercury sitting there with the hood ajar. A quick inspection of the vehicle had shown that the cables attaching the battery to the starter had been removed. It had been a simple matter to reconnect the cables, and the car was running again. She was glad to have her car back. She felt stranded without it.

Turning down Adelphi Road, Kerri stopped in the driveway of a cute, two-story house with maroon siding and beige shutters.

"Wait here. I won't be a minute," the petite woman said to Raef as she exited the vehicle.

Once inside the house, Kerri raced up the steps to her bedroom. Thanks to an inheritance from her grandfather, she had owned the house for three years. It was all she had in the world that she could call her own.

In the top drawer of the nightstand, she found what she was looking for. Placing the Berretta nine-millimeter handgun in her purse, she left the house. Her father had warned her that it wasn't safe to return to the house for the moment, and as usual, she had ignored him. If the men who had attacked her on the ridge knew where she lived they might wait there for her, it could be dangerous.

She had no intention of staying the night in the house. Kerri just wanted her gun. It made her feel more secure. Raef and her father might not approve of her carrying a gun, but what they didn't know wouldn't hurt them. She would be damned if she was going anywhere without being armed, at least until she was sure it was safe.

By the time she returned to the car, night had fallen.

If Raef was concerned, it didn't show in his demeanor. When she questioned him about it, the former priest said, "With God on my side, why should I be frightened," and he meant it.

She wished that she shared his confidence because she was still frightened. As they drove, Kerri turned and asked, "Where did you learn to fight like that? Are you some kind of secret agent?"

"I wish," the man replied. "It would be more exciting than the truth."

He never took his eyes off of the road. Raef scanned the roofs and treetops for any sign of the devil. He was wary of the dark, especially with the attack from earlier in the day.

"I took a few karate classes when I was a kid. I guess I remembered some of it."

It was the truth, but only the half of it. From the time he was six, Raef had studied tae kwon do. As a teen, he could have competed for an Ireland national title in his weight class, except his parents couldn't afford to send him.

He had never stopped his studies of the martial arts. Wherever he traveled, he studied the local techniques.

The church frowned upon his study of the martial arts, but he countered their arguments by saying it was great exercise. When he had told the church that the martial arts helped to bring him discipline, the church had backed off a little. Discipline was something that the Catholic Church could understand, and it reluctantly allowed him to continue his studies.

Because he realized that through his use of the martial arts, he had probably taken a man's life that day, Raef had a lot of soul-searching to do. Along with his soul-searching, there would be a lot of prayer. Although he had acted in self-defense, it still didn't sit right with him. He had taken a life, which was something that he'd vowed never to do. Of course that was when he was a priest, and he wasn't a priest now. Did that count? Could he revoke a vow just because he was no longer a priest?

He hoped so, because otherwise, his soul was in mortal danger.

The pair remained silent until they got to the home of the sheriff. Andy Wright gave Raef a hard stare when the man entered his house. He hadn't liked the looks of the man upon first meeting him. Long hair was for thieves and drug abusers. Which one was Mr. Lorenz? Thinking that he'd made it clear that his daughter was off limits, the sheriff asked the pair to have a seat in the family room.

The sofa was made of soft, brown leather, and Raef nearly melted into it when he sat down.

The rest of the room was as cozy as the comfortable couch. A mantle over the fireplace held the awards that the sheriff had acquired during his long career in law enforcement; there were many. On top of the console television was a statue of the Virgin Mary, and Raef was pleased to see the religious icon in the house. A mixture of family photos and paintings, none of which were in matching frames, covered the walls of the modest home.

Mrs. Wright was busy in the kitchen with dinner. Her humming was pleasant if not a little off-key.

When Raef's eyes found those of the sheriff, he knew it was time for an explanation. The man didn't look happy with him. The sheriff was overly protective of his daughter, but who could blame him? You don't take someone's daughter for a second date to somewhere where outlaw bikers try to kill her; it just doesn't set a good first impression.

Not surprisingly, the sheriff didn't care why the bikers had been there. He was only concerned with his daughter's safety. If the investigator from Rome wanted to get himself killed, he was welcome to do it. The sheriff did however wish that he would do it in a different town. Where should Raef start? Did the man even care to hear it?

It took nearly an hour for Raef to describe in detail the birth of the devil and some of what he had discovered since coming to Burlington.

The sheriff was impressed by Raef's investigative abilities, though he never said it.

As Raef finished telling the sheriff about the attack at Leeds Point, he left out the part about killing the tattoo covered man. Being arrested for murder wouldn't be good for his investigation.

Andy knew that Raef was holding back, but he couldn't force him to tell all that he knew.

Looking from Raef to Kerri, Andy said, "After you left for the hospital, I sent a couple of deputies to Leeds Point. They found Kerri's car, the battery had been detached from the starter. No bodies were found on the ridge or in the Pine Barrens. Whoever attacked you was gone by the time my deputies arrived."

Hearing that made Raef's eyebrows rise in surprise. He was sure, he'd killed the man, but stranger things had happened. If he hadn't killed the man, then he needn't worry over it any longer.

"There was no evidence of any kind to collect," continued the sheriff. "Other than Raef's sweater and some blood on the ground, a trail of which led farther into the woods, there was nothing to find. If my daughter hadn't been with you, I might not believe your story, Mr. Lorenz. Why are you really here, Mr. Lorenz, and why have you gotten my daughter involved?"

Kerri tried to speak, but her father cut her off with a hard stare. He wanted to hear it from Raef. The man had a lot of explaining to do.

As he sat on the couch, Raef had both of his hands in his lap. He stared down at the floor, but when the sheriff was done talking, he looked up. So, this is what it was like to have your girlfriend's father grill you before a date. Having never dated as a teenager, he'd never experienced the hard gaze of a suspicious father before. It was much worse than he'd imagined it would be, and he wasn't even dating the girl.

"It's like I told you before, I'm here to investigate the reappearance of the Jersey Devil. When I heard about its latest appearance, it piqued my curiosity. I petitioned the church to send me, and they readily agreed. The church delves into all sightings of the supernatural or demonic activity that comes to the attention of Rome. Most of it is quickly dismissed, but some has to be investigated.

"The last credible sighting of the devil happened in 1966, just north of Burlington. A farm was raided. Geese, ducks, cats, and two dogs were supposedly killed by the devil. One of the dogs was a large husky, capable of defending itself. The dog was torn to shreds by something that left behind a pair of cloven footprints. People in the area reported hearing strange screaming during the night. They barred their windows and locked their doors, frightened that some unholy monster had been unleashed on them.

"From my interviews with the people who saw the little girl get killed, and the hoof prints I've seen since I came here, I have deduced that the Jersey Devil is in fact back in the world of men. Couple those things with the attack on your daughter and me today, and I would say that I'm sure of it. The Jersey Devil has returned to Burlington, sheriff, but I still don't know how or why."

Interrupting, the sheriff said, "What do you mean when you say 'how'? According to local legend, this thing's been making occasional appearances since it was born. Do you mean to tell me that it comes and goes?"

"You're right," Raef said, "but not completely. You see … the Vatican has an extensive library, and its records show that the devil made an extended and rather auspicious visit to the area in January of 1909. From January 16 through the 23, it plagued the people of Burlington, adding the town of Bristol, Pennsylvania, to its haunting grounds. Records indicate that Monsignor E.W. Minster was sent, and he exorcised the devil from the town. At no time in recorded history has the devil ever killed a person, so why now?"

Unable to hold back her question any longer, Kerri asked, "Are you saying that someone has called the devil to come back to Burlington? How is that possible?"

"The forces of darkness often use pawns to unwittingly unleash devils into our world. Any person can be used as a gate, so long as he or she is willing. There is always someone who feels slighted by God or has a need that the creator cannot fulfill. These men and women often turn to Satan and dark magic as a means of attaining what they want. If Lucifer bothers to talk to them at all, it's only because he has a use for them. The Lord of Lies is just that, a liar. He will promise the world and never deliver. When people like Samuel Leeds become desperate enough, they tend to lose sight that their agreements with the Devil are one sided affairs."

Breaking back into the conversation, the sheriff said, "A gate, what do you mean by a gate?"

By now the sheriff was sweating under his Stetson. Keeping his hands in his pockets so that Kerri and Raef wouldn't notice that they were shaking, he tried to keep calm, but it wasn't something he was very good at.

Reaching into his thoughts, Raef looked for a way to describe a gate to the sheriff, in a way he might understand.

"A gate is something or someone in which the spiritual world can allow spiritual ideas and concepts to come into the natural world in order to shape it. In the New Testament, Matthew 16:18, it reads that the church is aggressive against the gates of hell, but even so, that doesn't mean that the agents of hell don't come through every now and then."

Deciding that he had to expand on his explanation, Raef added, "The strategies and schemes that are born in hell can therefore, gain access to the earth through people who are gates. It has been that way since Simon Peter was given the keys to heaven and earth."

Too nervous to sit any longer, Andy Wright began to pace the family room as his brain attempted to digest what Raef had said. Stopping behind his recliner, Andy asked, "But why would the devil continue to plague Burlington? There is no one left here who was involved in the baby's desecration."

"I understand your confusion," Raef said as he got to his feet. "But you're not dealing with the Leeds' baby. You never were. The very second that the baby in Deborah Leeds' womb was offered to Satan, it was no longer human. That which was born into the world that night was a devil."

"I don't get it," Kerri said. "If the Leeds asked for their child to be the Antichrist, why was it possessed and deformed? Why weren't their unholy prayers answered?"

While the trio was talking, Andy had turned to the dry bar and poured three short glasses of scotch.

Raef had never been so thankful for a glass of whiskey in his life. Taking the glass from the sheriff, Raef answered Kerri's question.

"It is written in the New Testament that the Antichrist will be born of a jackal. This is in direct contrast to the blessed birth of Christ himself. It is Satan's desire that the Antichrist be a perverse opposite of Christ, a way of infuriating God. Because it is scripture, it must be so. There is no other way to bring the birth of the evil one into the world. What I'm saying is that, because the Leeds' baby was made in the traditional sense, it didn't fit the criteria necessary to be the Antichrist.

"Simply asking the Prince of Darkness for such a thing must surely have angered him. I don't think that Satan ever meant to keep his promises to Samuel Leeds. What would he gain from giving anything to Samuel Leeds? Most likely Satan obtained his half of the bargain first. With Leeds' usefulness gone, Satan would most assuredly have turned his back on the man. He obviously made all kinds of promises to the Leeds, never meaning to fulfill any of them."

Now he was really animated, his arms going this way and that as he gave his sermon to anyone willing to listen to him. It felt great to teach a lesson about God and the Devil. Raef had forgotten just how empowering it could be.

"The church believes that Satan saw the Leeds' baby as beneath him and sent another of his foul minion to possess the child and destroy it. By changing the physical nature of the Leeds' baby, the devil that answered the call of the Leeds turned the child into its own likeness. What was born in that house on the ridge that night was a devil, not a child. If it mirrored a demon, it was because it was a demon. It was no baby that Samuel and Deborah Leeds released upon the world that night."

"Jesus," Kerri said as she downed her glass and pulled her sweater tighter around her neck. All of a sudden, she couldn't seem to get warm.

Her father's glass was empty as well. Father and daughter stood there in the low light of the family room, their faces as white as ghosts.

When Mrs. Wright called the group into the kitchen for dinner, none of them felt like eating.

November 4, 1984, 11:26 p.m.

Coming home late on the Amtrak train, Sandy Moeller had nothing on her mind other than a good night's rest. The advertisement executive had been in Baltimore for nearly a week. Though the Hyatt Hotel she'd stayed in was nice by hotel standards, she longed for the familiarity of her own mattress.

The train station was dark and empty. It lay on the eastern edge of town, a block from the recreation center and City Hall. As the train came to a stop, Sandy noticed for the first time that it was raining. *Great, and me without an umbrella*, the woman thought as she watched the large drops of moisture splash against the metal waiting platform that ran the length of the depot.

Running from the train to the overhang on the outside of the depot, Sandy was soaked from head to toe. Her luggage soon joined her, thanks to the porter, and the train disappeared into the darkness of the night.

There were few lights on around the depot. Two spotlights adorned the rear corners of the building, and one was hung over the glass front doors. Dark and dreary, Sandy waited for her no-good, alcoholic husband to pick her up. If he had forgotten to pick her up, it would be for the last time.

She only tolerated the man because he made a good sitter for her three cats while she was away on business. They hadn't had a real marriage in years, and the one-night stands that she entered into while away on business were all that she needed from life.

As she lit her cigarette, Sandy noticed a shadow hanging over her. The cold rain kept her from investigating the cause of the shadow. It wasn't until she saw the shadow move that she grew worried. Her sixth sense was buzzing; something wasn't right. While she stared at it, the shadow moved along the edge of the overhang, changing shape or disappearing altogether depending on the intensity of the light.

Taking a deep drag from the cigarette, Sandy nearly choked on the smoke as a shrill cry of steely evil erupted from somewhere on the roof above her. For a second, she stood frozen, not wanting to alert whatever was on the roof to her presence.

Moving farther down the rear side of the building, Sandy noticed the shadow reappear and follow her. No matter where she moved, the shadow followed, it was as if the thing was playing cat and mouse with her.

For the first time, she could hear it as it moved. A sound like that of hooves on a piece of cardboard greeted her ears, and then another inhuman scream split the night. The hair on her body began to stand on end, and she shrank back. With her back against the building, Sandy wondered what the hell was making the noise on the roof. Was it kids playing at frightening her or was it worse?

Shaking like a leaf, Sandy had never been more terrified in her life then she was at that moment. *Where was that damned husband of hers?*

"Go away!" yelled the woman, "I have a gun."

If that didn't make whoever was on the roof go away, what would, she asked herself.

Scared, Sandy slowly craned her neck out from under the hangover and looked to the roof above her. To her relief, the shadow was gone and the sound of hoof beats on the roof had ceased. Maybe it was some pervert who had decided to leave her alone. The promise of a gun was enough to frighten most predators off.

Waiting another twenty minutes under the overhang, Sandy remained quiet.

Before long, she realized that her husband wasn't coming. She would have to walk a block or so to find a cab. In the freezing rain, that wasn't much of a prospect. If she didn't catch pneumonia, Sandy was gonna kill that man of hers.

Cautiously, she stepped out from under the overhang and took a peek at the roof. Relieved that nothing was there, she moved out into the rain. After shuffling down a flight of steps, she found herself in an empty parking lot. There was a light on at the end of the parking lot. Squinting her eyes to focus on the object, she could tell by its shape that it was a phone booth. The pay phone at the end of the large lot promised her some help.

Leaving her luggage behind her, she made for the phone. The click-clack of her high heels against the pavement was the only noise she heard in the dark. That was until she heard the flapping of wings from behind her. Instinctively she ducked as something heavy crashed into her back and rolled away from her.

Knocked down to all fours, the woman scraped her palms and knees on the hard pavement, ruining her new stockings. She stayed on her hands and knees. Sandy was afraid to get up. She looked up and down, but she couldn't see anything in the darkness. The flapping was gone, and the sky was empty.

A tear formed in the corner of her eye, but she forced it back. Sandy was a strong woman. She would get through this in one piece. Whatever had struck her, it was gone now or so she hoped.

Getting to her feet, Sandy turned back toward the depot for one more look. There was nothing there, and she was relieved, but her relief lasted for only a split second. The sound of hooves clicking hard against the pavement behind her sent chills up her spine. She wasn't alone. Scared to turn around, she shivered in the cold rain. Whatever it was, it was between her and the pay phone. There would be no getting around it. Sandy was drenched, her cries coming in loud sobs. Her lips quivered as the rain washed over her hair and down her face.

As it ran down her face, Sandy's makeup made her look like the heroine from a Tim Burton movie.

Though her brain screamed at her to run, Sandy wanted to know what it was she was running from. A slow turn brought Sandy to where she could see the creature, and her jaw dropped. Not thirty feet from her was a pterodactyl. It was gigantic, much bigger than she had ever dreamed one would be. The thing had to be ten feet tall, and it was moving towards her.

Frightened far worse than she had ever dreamed she could be, Sandy was frozen in place; her legs refused the insistence of her brain to run.

As the creature drew closer, the woman realized that it was no pterodactyl. Its wings were small and bat-like. The creature reminded her of a deer that was standing on its two hind legs. The front legs of the beast were short and were held bent in front of the creature. It was crazy, but the thing actually looked like it was praying. But it was the head of the beast that made her cringe and frightened her most of all. The equine face with its beady, red eyes was pure malevolence. Those eyes stared at her with malice, entrancing her with their soft glow. They were bright embers, like those from the end of a lit cigarette. Her heart began to beat quickly, and she tore her gaze away from the creature.

Turning on a dime, Sandy ran for the safety of the depot, it was her only hope.

When she reached the side of the building again, Sandy watched in horror as the creature skipped and danced towards her. The beast was in no hurry. Its prey was trapped up against the building. She had nowhere to go. The hooves of the monster gave off an eerie clicking as the creature climbed the steps to the depot, announcing its arrival.

She found herself racing along the side of the building, searching desperately for a way out of danger. She no longer heard the sound of the footsteps, but she wasn't about to stop. Crying, she made for the front of the building. The depot was closed for the night. She had been on the last train and she was late. Maybe, if she could break the front glass doors, she might find a place to hide from the beast. When the glass broke, it might trigger the building's alarm and bring help to her. Would it be in time?

Turning the last corner, Sandy could see the light hanging over the doors. She was almost there.

The sound of clicking hooves as they struck the ground behind her made her lose her breath. That's when a vice clamped down on her right forearm and she was lifted from her feet. She knew that her arm was caught between the teeth of the beast. She could see one of its red eyes and feel the breath of the creature, its nostrils close to her arm.

With the ground rushing away from her, she screamed as she ascended into darkness. As they climbed steadily higher into the sky, Sandy could smell the odor of wet dog. That odor was one of the reasons she had cats. She hated the smell of wet dog.

Of all the things to be thinking about, she scolded herself as she looked in all directions for any indication of where she was. While she was in the folds of the darkness, the light over the glass doors of the depot was the only thing she could make out.

Her arm hurt badly, so badly that she thought she might faint from the pain. She prayed for the beast to release her before her arm was torn from her. As if in answer to her silent prayer, the creature did just that. She fell to the platform below. Twenty-five feet was a long way to fall, and when her feet hit the ground her ankles shattered. Her scream split the night, and pain, like miniature bolts of electricity, shot through her body. She lay on the platform for a moment, writhing back and forth as the pain washed through her body like a disease.

Even though she hurt worse than she had ever hurt before, the determined woman cried out in rage against her pain.

Sandy Moeller may have been in agony, but she wasn't ready to give up her life yet. Dragging her legs behind her, Sandy began to crawl towards the light and the glass doors that might bring her salvation. Every inch that she gained was wrought with crippling pain, but she kept going anyway. She cried out into the night. The pain was nearly unbearable, but she was close, if only she could find the strength to pull herself forward.

The door was in reach, just two feet away.

Screaming out in frustration and pain, Sandy fought against her desire to quit. She was crying and moaning. Her legs were numb with pain, but still she crawled. Reaching the doors on her stomach, Sandy stared into the glass, wondering how she was going to break it.

It was then that an equine face, one of pure evil, appeared in the reflection of the glass and she knew she was done.

With a squeal of delight, the devil grabbed Sandy around the waist with its horse-like teeth and lifted her into the air. It shook its head violently to and fro. The creature slammed Sandy face-first into the wooden wall and metal walkway. Taking out its rage on the woman, the devil shattered nearly every bone in Sandy Moeller's skull. Limp and barely conscious, Sandy let out a grunt as the vicious creature threw her ragged body through the glass doors, which shattered around her.

As she lay on the floor of the depot, glass shards all over her, Sandy died. A deep laceration on her throat from the broken window glass had sealed the deal. Her eyes were wide open as she lay there dead. A pool of dark blood grew around her.

Craning out its neck in triumph, the devil wailed into the raging downpour of water and wind. The sound didn't travel far, but for the moment, the devil was satiated. The muscles at the base of its wings began to tighten and the tiny wings, which appeared to be far too small to propel the creature into the night, beat hard. As the devil flew out into the darkness, it wailed again and again.

7

November 6, 1984, 4:10 a.m.

The sound of the rain as it struck the roof on the sheriff's house was pleasant to the man. Though he had been offered a place to stay for the night, Raef wasn't surprised to find himself in the basement on the couch. He didn't really mind. Most of the places he went in order to investigate reports of the supernatural were far worse. Sleeping on a couch sure beat sleeping on a termite mound in Niger.

In the rain forests of Borneo, Raef had been made to sleep high up in the canopy in a makeshift hammock. So deep into the forest, it hadn't been safe to sleep on or even near the ground. Leopards and scorpions didn't discriminate. An ex-priest was as good as a true one.

Watching shadows move along the ceiling, Raef wondered what had became of the man he had struck in the larynx. *Could he possibly have survived? No way*, Raef thought. He had heard the man's larynx crush against the back of his spine; the man had to be dead. *But if he was dead, where had the body gone? Was it possible that the others had removed it from the forest? Probably.*

He had been offering prayers to God and searching his soul for hours, and still he couldn't decide if what he'd done was right. Had his need to protect Kerri overridden his vow not to take life? Maybe, but Kerri was an innocent. She didn't deserve to have her head bashed in by some biker with a bad attitude.

The bikers were another mystery. They had obviously been sent to stop him and Kerri from discovering anything new, but why? What was there to gain from keeping them away from the secret? Pulling the covers up to his chest, Raef decided to sleep on it. If his tortured soul would allow him a few hours of rest, he would gladly accept it.

He had no idea how long he'd been out when he heard the sound of rushing feet coming down the stairs. They weren't the silent steps of a secret lover. They were the hurried steps of someone in need.

"Raef," Kerri's voice said. "Raef, are you awake? We need you upstairs."

Rolling off the couch, Raef tried to clear his eyes of the sleep in them.

"For God's sake, what time is it?"

When he didn't react very quickly, Kerri said. "It's nearly five in the morning".

"It's on the roof. I think dad's going out there to shoot it."

Her last words struck Raef like a bucket of cold water. He rushed past her, up the steps to the main floor of the house. The man who had been all but asleep a second before was wide-awake.

When he got to the front door, Raef planted himself in front of it. He was lucky he had hurried. The sheriff was coming down the hallway with a shotgun, his intentions clearly written on his face.

"Sheriff, please wait for a second and hear me out before you go out there."

The sheriff was in no mood for talking, the thing was on his roof and he wasn't happy about it.

"Get out of the way, Raef. This isn't the time."

Raef's concern was real. He had to keep the sheriff from going outside. It might be the difference between life and death. "Please, sheriff, give me just a minute. That's all I want."

By that time, Kerri and Mrs. Wright were in the hallway. The women in the family were frightened to death.

With her voice quivering, Kerri begged, "Daddy, please listen to Raef."

"All right, rock star," the sheriff spat in his direction. "You have one minute and then I'm going out there."

There was no time for bullshit. Whatever had to be said needed to be said then.

"That thing out there on your roof … You can't kill it with bullets, sheriff. It's not of this world."

A light came to Andy's eyes, he was actually listening.

"You might succeed in driving it off, you might not. If it stays and fights, you're going to lose. I wish I could say this in a different way, but if you go out there, you're going to die."

Upon hearing Raef's words, Mrs. Wright fainted, falling to the floor in the hallway. Kerri dropped to one knee, slapping her gently on the cheek.

When he saw his wife faint, Andy's desire to go outside faded. He went to the side of his wife and daughter.

Mrs. Wright was starting to come to and the sheriff promised her that he wouldn't go outside. Getting to her feet, Kerri moved to Raef and gave him a kiss on the cheek.

"Thank you," she said, tears streaking down her face.

Stunned by the show of emotion, Raef stood stiff as a board. He didn't know what he should do next.

Deciding that the family should be left alone, he went back to the basement. He wasn't likely to get any sleep, but at least he wouldn't be attending a funeral in a few days.

November 6, 1984, 9:05 a.m.

As Raef walked out the front door of the Wright's house, a bitter wind struck him in the face. It was the kind of wind that went right through him; there was no avoiding it. Overnight, the temperature had gone down significantly, making it a cruel twenty-six degrees outside. Now he needed a coat. He would have to make a stop at his hotel room for it.

While they had eaten breakfast, the sheriff had received a phone call that sounded serious. He hadn't said a word to Kerri or Raef before he pulled on his coat and Stetson hat. With a fresh cup of coffee, he had left for work. It was going to be a long day.

Kerri had offered to drive Raef to his hotel and he had agreed.

Once in the car, she turned on the radio to find, "Heavens on Fire," by the rock band Kiss playing on the stereo. Blushing, she went to turn the dial, when Raef's hand reached out and grabbed her hands. The touch was gentle and it sent shivers down her spine.

"Really, it's all right. I like rock music," he said as he drummed on the dashboard and sang badly.

He knew the words. How in the blazes did he know the words?

"Can you tell me more about the devil? Is there a way to destroy it or exorcise it?" Kerri asked.

"This is where it gets tricky," the man said as he started into a long speech.

"First of all, I'm no exorcist. Only a priest can perform the rite of exorcism. The next thing is, I don't solve the matters that I investigate, the church does. I only do the footwork. Someone else comes in and cleans up. I'm not done investigating yet. I have to discover how the devil was brought back into the world, which will give the church a good reference point to start from."

Watching as her mind processed everything. He wondered why he was telling her. Hadn't he already involved her enough?

When she motioned with her hand for him to continue, he couldn't stop himself.

"I'm kind of a nerd when it comes to the supernatural, so stop me if I bore you. One thing that is paramount if the devil is to be stopped is to find out its real name. You might be shocked to hear this, but every devil has a name. Most of them will try to confuse and divert you away from it, but it's there; you just have to find it. Once you have the name of a devil, you might be successful at forcing it from the realm of men.

"I have talked to many a priest about the subject, and they all concur that finding its true name is the key. If it was summoned here, it can be banished here. I'm sure of it. I'm going to need some help from Rome, and if I'm really lucky, we might get that help.

"Why am I saying we? I mean me."

Turning to him, Kerri smiled and said, "Oh no, you don't. You mean us. I'm coming with you. Until this is over, I'm not going to sit idle. You can bet on that. With or without you, I'm going to keep on digging."

The determination on her face was real. She meant every word of it. God, but she was beautiful when she was determined, and Raef found it hard to look away from her. Finding her had been both good and bad. On the one hand, he liked her. She was easy to be with. On the other hand, he didn't want to endanger her. It had already happened once.

On the approach to his hotel, Raef noticed that something was wrong. It took him a while to figure it out, but then it struck him. The neon sign on the front of the hotel said, "No Vacancy."

What was going on? The hotel couldn't be full. The fair wasn't in town, and as far as he knew there were no conventions taking place close by.

"Is there any way that we can see the hotel from the rear," he asked Kerri.

"I think so," answered the woman. "What's wrong?"

"Just get me to the back of the hotel. I'll fill you in afterwards."

She couldn't figure out what Raef was up to, so she followed blindly. He must have known something, because when they reached the back of the hotel, he grinned.

Behind the hotel were at least fifteen motorcycles. So, they had taken control of the hotel, waiting for the man to come home.

The sheriff had a lot on his mind right now and Raef didn't want to add anything else. Besides, if the bikers were busy waiting for him to come back to his hotel room, the distraction would allow Raef to search the town, virtually unmolested. He hated to leave the employees of the hotel under the control of some outlaw motorcycle gang, but it couldn't be helped for now.

After quickly relaying his discovery to Kerri, she was more than glad to get away from the hotel.

"Doesn't get more evil or sinister than that," Raef said as they drove away.

"The next thing you know, they'll go to the cemetery and topple gravestones for kicks," Kerri added to his assessment of the bikers.

The second the words came out of her mouth, the light bulb in Raef's head turned on.

If he hadn't known for sure before, he did now. The cemetery, it had to be there. Where else would someone spark a desecration? "That's it, you solved the mystery," he said while slapping her gently on the shoulder.

Stopping at a red light, Kerri looked at Raef and said, "Huh, I solved what?"

"The old Whitmore Cemetery. Get us there, now."

Neither of them noticed the man behind the dumpster in the rear of the hotel. No sooner had they pulled away from the hotel, than the man ran inside and informed the rest of the gang.

There would be no escape this time.

The name of the biker gang was the Diablos. It was more than just a name; it was a way of life, a way of life that involved devil worship.

They knew what the ex-priest was capable of. This time they would be ready for him. Not one motorcycle was left at the hotel. It was all or nothing; the priest and the girl had to die.

The master had contacted them through the gang member they referred to as Jitterbug. Jitterbug was a psychic. He could receive the thoughts of the master. When the master had called to Jitterbug and given the bikers their orders, they had been honored. His words didn't come very often, but down to a one, the bikers would die to fulfill his wishes. One of them already had.

Parking on Thirty-Seventh Avenue, Kerri told Raef that she knew a way into the cemetery that would allow them to enter unnoticed. There were many busybodies in Burlington, and she didn't want them spying on her and Raef. Her reputation might not survive such an incident.

The patch of woods that separated the cemetery from the Crystal Springs subdivision wasn't any wider than seventy-five feet, and it wasn't long before they found the way that Conrad Beyer had used to enter the cemetery. They were in.

Though it was old and in disrepair, the cemetery was big. Weeds and brush were taking control of the land, and if something wasn't done soon, that process would become irreversible. The headstones were old; some of them dated back three hundred years. There was a time when the Whitmore Cemetery had serviced all of the greater Camden area. Once revered as a holy place, the cemetery had become a jungle of weeds and moldy, old headstones.

Raef thought that he had a sense for holy places, and this wasn't one of them. He felt sad as he looked at the broken headstones and weed-covered markers, thinking that the dead deserved better. Sure, their souls were gone, but when a family member came to the cemetery, it usually gave the family member comfort. But not this place, not now; it was deserted. If it hadn't been deserted by God, it had certainly been deserted by his flock. What a shame.

Being a scholar and understanding the power of such places, Raef wept inside.

Kerri could see that he was unusually quiet, and she chocked it up to him searching for a clue. If there was a clue there, it was doing its best to stay hidden.

It was Kerri who saw it first, the dark spot on the ground seemed out of place. Whistling to Raef, she motioned for him to follow her, and she was off.

Raef could see what she was running toward and he took off after her. For some reason he felt a sense of urgency, a need to rush, but he couldn't understand why.

As the pair neared the spot, Raef could already understand some of what had transpired. The mass of gold and burned-out gems on the ground was significant to him, and him alone. Desecration, it always pained him to see it. Whatever the metal had been a part of, it had been something that had been deemed worthy of sacrifice to the evil one. There was also a book on the ground. It was a small leather-bound diary of some sort. After grabbing the book and turning it over, Raef gasped and dropped it as if it had burned his hand.

His actions were strange to Kerri, who asked, "What was that all about?"

"Sorry," Raef said as he removed a handkerchief from his back pocket.

Resembling a rag, more than it did a handkerchief, the piece of cloth looked old. The rag was eggshell white in color and was adorned by roses and crucifixes that had been stitched into it by hand. It was a sacred cloth, one that would protect him against the evil that was the manuscript he wished to pick up. Most people would never believe that an object in of itself could be evil. They were wrong. The book on the ground was *Groban's Tome of Demons and Devils*. It was one of the most unholy books ever written, few would dare possess it, and even fewer would dare to read from it.

Glancing at the name on the headstone, Raef couldn't believe what he was seeing. This explained the return of the devil, but how could they stop such a powerful manifestation of the creature?

The thought would have to wait, because as he wrapped the book in the holy cloth, the sound of gunfire erupted around him and Kerri. Stuffing the book into his back pocket, the man grabbed Kerri's hand and yelled, "Run, but stay low."

Reacting to the sound of guns being fired, she squeezed Raef's hand tighter. What bothered her even more was that a bullet ricocheted off of a headstone, barely missing her face.

"Keep close to me this time. We're in big trouble," Raef called out as he ducked behind another headstone.

There was no place to hide, except for behind headstones. Few trees grew in the cemetery. None of them would offer any real protection against an armed adversary.

"Damn it all, Raef, what have you gotten me into this time," the woman cried out as she followed him.

Kerri was right. What had he gotten them into? How did the bikers find them, he hadn't seen any lookout. *Stupid fool*, he chided himself. *The lookout had been there. You just missed him.*

It was too early to panic. It wouldn't do them any good anyhow. What he needed was a way out, a way into the woods beyond the cemetery, but how? When he looked at the woman next to him, he knew he had his answer. Kerri had grown up in the neighborhood. She would know all of the hidden trails, wouldn't she?

Still looking for a way out of the cemetery, Raef shouted, "You grew up here, can you get us out?"

This was her turf. If anyone could find a way out, it would be Kerri. But as the bullets crashed into the ground around them, she began to wonder if she could do it.

Scanning the cemetery wildly, Kerri noted two or three places that she thought might work. No sooner had she begun to lead Raef in the directions of those escape routes, then they became closed off by armed gunmen. She noticed that the gunmen were bikers, and they were all full of tattoos, just like the ones on the ridge.

Frig and crap, she thought as she grabbed Raef by the hand and ran for the only place left to her. It had been years since she had used it, *would it still be there*?

Raef yelped as a bullet smashed into the headstone on his right, shattering the old piece of masonry. That one was close. They had to get out of there now.

Coming to some high grass at the far side of the cemetery, Kerri dove to the ground, taking Raef with her.

"Crawl," she ordered the man, and he wasn't about to argue.

If they remained upright, they were going to be cut down by the gunmen. Their only chance was to stay low and let the weeds and tall brush hide them.

The part of the cemetery they were in was in far worse condition than any other. No one had mowed the grass here for years, and the three-feet-tall plant life showed it. What he wouldn't have given for some real cover at that moment, but there was none to be had. He could hear the sounds the gunmen made as they ran through the brush. There were too many of them. In seconds they would be discovered, and then it would be over.

The hand that grabbed him and pulled him into a dark cave nearly gave him a fright.

Raef's feet splashed into water that cascaded in over his shoes, and his toes became soaked. The icy cold water of a creek sent a chill down his spine, and he began to shiver almost immediately. *Damn, this is cold,* Raef thought as his feet complained. With no coat and wet feet, he would freeze to death before the bikers could shoot him.

Taking his hand in hers, Kerri began to drag him through a tunnel of some sort. It smelled bad and it was slippery, but at least they were moving away from the gunmen.

"Where are we?" Raef whispered.

The response that came back to him sent a chill up his spine.

"We're in the drainage system. Shush."

They had entered the end of the drainage system for the Crystal Springs subdivision. This was where the storm water runoff entered the creek leading to the Shandy's Farm. The tunnel was round and nearly four feet tall. They could easily travel through it if they bent low.

Sloshing through the three-inch high water in the drainpipe, the ex-priest began to look for rats. He knew they were going to show up at any time now. Raef hated rats: he always had. Indiana Jones hated snakes and Raef Lorenz hated rats. They were his kryptonite.

"How did you know about this?" Raef asked Kerri as she continued to drag him along.

"My friends and I used to play down here as kids. This drainage system will lead us under the neighborhood. If I can remember which way to go, we might yet get away."

"Lead on, my sewage queen," Raef joked as they ran, hunched over, through the drainage system.

It was time to pay attention. The last thing that Raef wanted to do was to slip and fall into the slimy water. Though he was sure they were going to run into rats, he decided it was better than bullets. It wasn't long before they could hear the water splashing behind them and rough voices cursing at each other. The bikers had found the drainage tunnel and they were giving chase.

I bet that rats don't faze the bikers one bit, thought Raef as he continued to be pulled along by Kerri.

Hundreds of feet into the drainage system the pair encountered the first dilemma. The tunnel turned into a four-way intersection. One path led forward and two were on either side of them.

"Turn right. Go five steps and turn around," Kerri ordered.

While Raef did as he was told, Kerri did the same thing in the tunnel directly in front of them. Meeting back in the middle, she grabbed his hand and looked at his confused face.

"Come on," she ordered before taking his hand, pulling him down the tunnel on the left.

"What was all that about?" Raef asked.

"Well, when I was a kid, my friends and I used to play tag down here. I learned to make false footsteps in the silky grunge that serves as the floor of this place. It throws people off your trail."

"Beautiful and smart, what a bargain you are," Raef said.

Did I just say that out loud, he asked himself. *Damn, I really have to be more careful.*

She heard the words, and they shocked her. The minute they got out of this, if they got out of this, she was going to blush.

The bikers weren't stupid. Only seven of them had entered the drainage system in pursuit of the pair. Crowbar was the leader of the gang, and he was no dummy. He too had grown up in a neighborhood like this, and he knew exactly how the drainage system worked. Instead of playing games in the drainage system under his town, he had used it to traffic drugs. No one understood a drainage system like Crowbar. He would have the pair yet.

"This way," whispered Kerri.

She knew where they were going, even if she couldn't see it. For what seemed like hours, they crouched down, running through the tunnels under the subdivision. They turned here and there, but for the most part, they went straight. Kerri wanted to get to the far side of the neighborhood. If they could get to Thirty-Fourth Avenue, she was pretty sure she could get them to safety.

When they finally saw sunshine, Raef wanted to cheer. He had hated every second they spent in the tunnels. He was ready for some fresh air. A shadow that only partially blocked out the sunlight, alerted him to danger, and he grabbed Kerri, stopping her in her tracks. Making noise as they splashed through the water couldn't be helped. It was something that couldn't be avoided.

Not wanting to alert the man at the end of the drainage tunnel that they were wise to him, Raef marched in place, splashing as he did so.

When Kerri gave him a strange look, he leaned closer to her. She could feel his breath on her cheek and ear, and that sent another kind of shiver down her spine.

"There is someone waiting for us at the end of the tunnel."

"Are you sure?" she asked him. She hadn't seen anything.

Looking above him, Raef saw a sewer grate. It wasn't the kind you could see into, it was the round, thick, metal kind, the kind that kids dropped on their toes. He knew that some of the grates could be opened.

Saying a prayer to Jesus, Raef pushed cautiously on the grate. He didn't want it to make any noise to alert the biker that they were there. He wanted it to be a secret.

Kerri marched in place as Raef struggled with the grate.

When he heard the grate shifting against its frame, he smiled. This was exactly what they needed, but would it work? As the grate lifted, Raef straightened a little, peering into the bright sunlight of the day.

Of all days for it to be bright and sunny, why did it have to be today?

Squinting against the brightness, it took Raef a minute to be able to see any distance. When his eyes adjusted, he wasn't surprised. Waiting by the end of the drainage tunnel were two bikers. They didn't look happy. The bikers were only sixty feet away from him. It was too close. They would have to try something else.

Replacing the grate, Raef turned to Kerri and explained the situation.

She didn't look stunned. She just smiled and said, "I have an idea."

The idea was a good one, which wasn't surprising to Raef. Allowing her to get near to the end of the drainage tunnel, Raef lifted the grate and began to crawl out as if he didn't know that the bikers were there.

The second they saw him, they were on their feet, running at him. He let go of the grate and it slammed back into place as he dropped back into the grungy water. He sprinted through the drainage tunnel the best he could. Sprinting wasn't easy when you were bent over like an old man.

When he got to the end of the tunnel, Kerri was already waiting for him. Crawling out through the storm drain opening, the two squeezed their way to freedom, and they were off.

The bikers were sixty feet away from them in the opposite direction, but they were giving chase again. Racing west, Kerri used one hand and vaulted over a four-feet-tall chain-link fence. Following closely, Raef was again amazed by the woman. The pair raced to the end of the yard and jumped the rear portion of the fence in the same manner.

Rushing through the Pine Barrens that surrounded the neighborhood, the pair raced for freedom. Kerri took the lead, with Raef close behind her. He could hardly keep up, and he wondered what she must have looked like as a kid, running through these woods.

They were home free, Kerri was sure of it. All they had to do was run for about half a mile and they would be on the old dairy road that led into Camden. From there, they could flag down a ride and be gone.

Kerri was too far ahead to see the giant of a man that stepped out from behind a pine tree that Raef approached. Raef tried to avoid the man, but they went down in a heap on the ground. The struggle came to an end quickly. When he felt the cold steel of the snub-nosed revolver touch his side, Raef froze. No kick or karate chop was going to defeat a lead bullet. It was over. He had been caught. *At least Kerri had gotten away*, Raef thought from his prone position on the hard ground. Maybe she would contact the church and tell them what he'd found.

Forcing Raef's arm behind his back, the biker began to march him from the woods. There was a trail up ahead, one that Raef hadn't noticed until now. The black motorcycle parked on the trail looked out of place; it shouldn't have been there.

Laughing from behind him, the biker said, "You're good, but I'm better. The master has obviously chosen wiser than the creator of fags and queers."

Raef knew it was a taunt that was meant to get a reaction out of him. Though he knew that was the case, he still wanted to punch the man in the face.

Hearing the footfalls of the other bikers who had chased him and Kerri into the woods, Raef bent his head in defeat.

"Go and get the bitch," yelled the biker who had control of his arm. "She ran toward the old dairy road. She can't be far."

The pair of bikers raced off, and soon their footfalls could no longer be heard.

"You do know what they're going to do to her before they kill her, don't ya?" the biker asked.

The biker's breath smelled like stale tobacco, and spittle struck the back of Raef's head as he laughed. Hating the smell of tobacco, it was just another burden Raef would have to bear until he was killed.

The words of the filthy biker struck Raef hard, but no matter how he tried, the former priest couldn't come up with a snappy retort.

Raef never got the chance to answer him. The sound of a gunshot rang out from behind Raef, and he wondered where he'd been hit. There was no pain, and all of a sudden he realized that the pressure on his arm was gone.

Spinning around, Raef was shocked. Standing behind him, smoking gun in hand, was Kerri. The biker lay dead on the ground; his head split open and his brains spilling out on the pine needles and tufts of moss.

Lowering the gun, Kerri answered the biker's open question, "Those two idiots are going to end up the same as you. That's what they're going to do."

Raef didn't even realize he was doing it, but he grabbed Kerri around the waist and kissed her. There was no resistance from the woman; she kissed him back.

It was good to be alive.

Picking their way carefully out of the forest, the pair managed to hitch a ride into town.

The sheriff was in a mood, ordering his deputies to arrest any bikers they found.

"If they resist, shoot them. I don't care. I'll deal with it later."

There would be no investigation into his daughter. The biker in the woods was a victim of inner gang violence as far as the sheriff was concerned.

Only three of the bikers escaped the pursuit of the police, Jitterbug was among them. There would be hell to pay for failing, but at least they were still alive and free. The master would contact Jitterbug again; he was sure of it. Whatever the master asked of them, the members of the Diablos would see to it. It was what they lived for.

8

November 6, 1984, 1:09 p.m.

Things were hectic at the sheriff's department. Sneaking into an unused office, Raef and Kerri began discussing what they had found in the cemetery.

"What was that book you found next to the black spot on the ground?" the excited woman asked.

Even though she had just escaped a near-death experience, she still had a burning desire to know what was in the cemetery. Her education in history had made her naturally inquisitive. It was something that she couldn't turn off.

"The book is called *Groban's Tome of Demons and Devils*, and it's old, at least three hundred years old."

Removing the book and placing it on the desk in the unused office, Raef was loath to uncover it.

Kerri could see his reluctance, but she couldn't understand it. Reading his face, she soon understood what was going on … *He was scared, but why*? Seeing that Raef was locked in some sort of internal battle, Kerri changed the subject.

"What do you think caused that black spot in the earth over the gravesite?"

Raef was glad for the change of subject, but it was still a difficult question to answer.

"I think that was a person, or what was left of a person, anyhow."

"Are you serious?" Kerri asked.

"Yup," answered the man. "When it comes to Satan, it's not unusual for him to repay his servants in such a manner. Someone had to have read from the tome in front of me to bring the devil back into the world. I think he paid a heavy price for his service."

Finding it hard to grasp what she was being told, Kerri remained quiet. She had many questions, but none of them seemed important enough to ask.

"I found pieces of burnt cloth and some scorched pieces of bone at the gravesite. I think whoever called forth the Jersey Devil, he or she was required to give more of a sacrifice than he or she had bargained for. Did you happen to notice the name on the headstone at the gravesite?"

"No, I didn't. I was too busy running from the men who were trying to kill me. Why? What did you find?"

"The name on the headstone was Samuel Leeds."

The color washed away from Kerri's face. She was blown away.

Taking her hand in his, Raef gave her a minute to take it all in; it was a lot to handle.

"I think we know why this manifestation of the Jersey Devil is so much more powerful than the ones from the past. If the ritual to bring it back into the world was done at that gravesite and the proper sacrifice was offered … it's not good news."

Turning away from Raef and then back to face him, Kerri asked, "What makes it so much different than any of the other times the devil was called to Burlington?"

He could see that she needed to know. Being the curious person that he was, Raef would have wanted to know too.

"Evil can linger in places," he began with a sad expression on his face.

"If Samuel Leeds was as evil as the stories about him lead me to believe he was, that could prove to be a powerful contributor to the strength of the devil as it came through the gate into this world."

"I don't get it," Kerri replied. "How is it that evil can emanate from something after it's removed from the world? If there's nothing left there anymore, what does it hang on to?"

Pulling her coat around her for warmth, Kerri was beginning to get cold again. She was inside a building with the heat on, and just like the night before, she couldn't seem to get warm.

"Do you remember what I told you about good and evil? That evil exists and it can remain in places where its essence had once been strong."

She nodded her head no. She didn't understand.

"Have you ever gone into a church or a holy place and had a feeling of peace and warmth come over you?" Raef asked.

Kerri nodded yes, and he continued.

"That's because the essence of goodness is there. It permeates the place, leaving some of itself behind. It can happen in a cemetery, a house, or a field. It can even linger upon a person or his or her grave. Though the body is dead and the soul gone, goodness or evil can continue to exist there."

"Damn it's cold in here. Doesn't this place have any heat?" Kerri asked as her teeth chattered.

"Come on, let's go for a drive and maybe some lunch," Raef said. "I think we need a mental break."

November 6, 1984. 7:00 p.m.

In his hotel room at the Holiday Inn, Raef placed the book on the desk in his room. From a pack, which he had kept hidden under his bed, he removed a candle and a crucifix made of pure silver. A Bible and a ring given to him by Archbishop Wells joined the first two items on the desk.

The ring was said to have been a holy relic, which dated back to the crusades. Raef had done some research on the ring, though, and the closest it came to resembling any ring that dated back to the crusades, was a ring worn by Pope Innocent III.

Though not an exact match, the ring worn by the pope was said to have been one of five that had been crafted in France and given to kings and members of the Catholic Church. All of the rings were said to have been blessed by God, though the ritual wasn't specifically documented. Priceless, the ring was something he treasured.

During the crusades, the Catholic Church had searched all of Europe for holy relics. From the sacred Lance of Longinus, which had pierced the flesh of Jesus Christ, to a wooden cross said to have belonged to Joan of Arcadia, they had taken whatever they found wherever they found it and locked it away in their vaults.

Kissing all of the religious items in turn, Raef lit the candle and sank to his knees. For how long he prayed, he couldn't say, but his knees were stiff.

He wanted to open *Groban's Tome of Demons and Devils* and see what significance it had played in the return of the devil. Fearing demonic possession himself, Raef wanted God's blessing and protection as he searched the tome of absolute evil for answers.

When it came to prayer, the ex-priest was serious. When he had left the service of the church, he had remained a faithful servant of God and Jesus Christ. They were as much a part of his life now as they had been before he was granted his separation from the priesthood.

Something happened to Raef in that hotel room that night as he prayed, something that had never happened to him before. The most intense feeling of peace washed over him and he had a sense of love in his heart, a love that was inspiring. It made him feel protected from evil. His body felt light, and his mind went blank as if it was opening up for the very first time in his life.

When the feeling ended he was left breathless, the skin on his body was tingling. Had he just had an ecclesiastic moment or an epiphany? He was overwhelmed by his feelings, so he took a moment to compose himself again.

Upon opening his eyes and looking at the book of evil, which remained bound by the holy cloth, Raef no longer feared the tome. Crossing himself and giving praise to Jesus, Raef took a seat in the chair next to the desk and unwrapped the book.

On the inside cover of the book was written the name Samuel Leeds. For some reason, Raef wasn't surprised. The date written next to his name was 1733, two years before the devil had been born into the world. There was no publishing date written in the tome; it wasn't that kind of book.

Though it was called *Groban's Tome of Demons and Devils*, the book was a tool to create a gate for the agents of evil to come back into the world of men. The book had been hand-inked by an evil monk who had inscribed the ink with malevolence, even as he had used that quill to write the teachings and incantations in the artifact of lies. Inked with a quill, the book had to be ancient. The pages were yellowing with age, but time had done little to corrupt the otherwise well-preserved diary.

The book had seen harsh weather in just the past few days, but there was no sign that it had ever been removed from a shelf. Other than the notes that someone, presumably Leeds, had written on the edges and in the margins of the book, it was as if it had hardly been read. The notes had been written with a quill as well, and some of them were done in an odd, brown ink, which might have been blood.

Every chapter in the book started with a letter from the alphabet which had been artfully penned in beautiful script. The first letter was several times larger than any other letter of the alphabet in that chapter. It had to have a secret meaning behind it.

Written around the edges of the script were partial sentences and words. The phrase "Trust in the Mammon," was a recurring anthem throughout the tome. Written on the back cover was the phrase "Torture the eyes; they are the wells to the soul."

The phrases in the book made Raef's blood run cold. They were as diabolical as any thoughts he had ever dared think about.

"Crush the weak, and thy gains will be great," was another terrible phrase found in the book. Did it have any special meaning?

Time lost all meaning for Raef, and when the phone rang, he was shocked to see that the clock read, 11:16 p.m. Picking up the receiver, he answered, "Hey." He didn't know who might be calling him at this time of night. He only knew that he didn't want to identify himself right then. The voice on the other end of the line was familiar, if not a little unexpected.

"Raef, it's Archbishop Wells. Do you have any more news to report?"

It took Raef an hour to tell the archbishop all that had happened over the past two days.

The archbishop was disturbed by the news that the devil had gathered minions to protect the manifestation of evil in New Jersey. It wasn't unheard of, but he wanted to know what Raef had discovered that would bring such a fantastic show of power from the unholy one.

The tome was of significant importance, the archbishop was sure of that. When he learned that Raef had read into the text, he was extremely concerned. Such evil works had led more than one man of God astray. Raef assured him that he had prayed and taken precautions against such a happening, but still the archbishop worried. Instructing Raef that a courier would be there within the hour to pick up the tome, Archbishop Wells ended the call.

He only had an hour to unlock the secrets of the tome. It wasn't much time, but it was all that Raef had.

Prying open the book of evil for a second time, he noticed that the writings on the edges of the book seemed to have changed. New phrases such as, "Hate thy neighbor, take what he owns," and "Mammon is wise, she leads the way," were now written there. Was the tome itself leading him astray, or was there something to the changing text? Who was this Mammon, and why was she important? Maybe the archbishop was right, he shouldn't be reading the book. But he had to. It was the only means by which he might discover a way to banish the devil.

He studied the tome until the knock on his door came. Tired, even his soul was weary from reading the text.

Raef got up and answered the door.

"Who is it?" the tired man asked.

"I'm here for the package," a voice on the other side of the door said.

Many of the people who the church used to do their business were abrupt, and Raef was used to it by then.

As he opened the door, a fist enclosed in a set of brass knuckles punched him square in the jaw. Offering no resistance to the blow, Raef let his head turn with the momentum from the punch. It was the only thing that kept his teeth from being knocked down into his throat.

While his head was turning, he noticed a gleam of light that came from the blade of a knife in the other hand of the man who was rushing through the door of his hotel room. The man or woman, Raef wasn't sure which it was, was dressed in a black robe. A cowl of satin covered the person's face.

How could he have been so dumb? He should have asked more questions.

Reversing his momentum, Raef threw his torso back the opposite way, narrowly avoiding the blade of the wicked knife that his assailant wielded. The blade on the knife had been polished to a high shine. The metal was red, but Raef had no doubt that it was still keen. Eight inches long, the curved weapon reminded Raef of a mini scimitar. The handle was black, and the bottom of its pommel was carved into the face of a demon.

Raef had been caught off guard, and if his assailant knew how to use the knife, he was probably going to feel the blade. Fortunately for Raef, his attacker had lunged at him and was just as off-balance as he was.

Years of martial arts training took over, and Raef went into action. A spinning leg sweep kept him low and away from the knife, but his attacker deftly jumped over the attack and sliced down with the blade. A line of searing pain was drawn from the top of Raef's shoulder to the back of his left bicep, and he let out a cry of agony. Not only was the knife sharp, it seemed to burn his flesh as well.

Blood flowed from his arm. The flow was far worse than it should have been. *What the hell kind of weapon is he using?* thought Raef as he backed away from his attacker.

The hooded assailant wasted no time pressing his attack against the ex-priest. With his left arm all but useless, Raef was in desperate need of help. Kerri wasn't there to shoot the man and Raef didn't own a gun. The attacker came in with a martial arts front kick. Raef dodged it by turning to the side, only to be met by the knife, which was being slashed in a line of death at the same height as his face.

Using his right arm, Raef blocked his foe's attack by placing his arm against the attacker's elbow, stopping the momentum of the knife. Looping his arm inside that of the attacker's, he had to be careful, because he didn't want to be cut again. Driving his fist under his opponent's underarm, Raef locked his foe's arm against his own side, hoping to keep the blade away from him.

In a blur of motion, Raef brought his left knee up into the right kidney of the attacker. Hearing a satisfying groan of pain, he repeated the strike twice more. Releasing the man, Raef then spun, sending a back side kick into his assailant's ribs. It was the most powerful martial arts kick there was, and it sent his foe backpedaling against the far wall of the room.

As the two men became separated, Raef realized he was getting dizzy. The cut must have been worse than he had thought. He was losing a lot of blood. Even so, it was still early for him to be getting dizzy. Then it struck him like a freight train: *Poison. The son of a bitch had poisoned him.*

There was no time to lose. If Raef didn't end the fight soon, it wouldn't matter, because the poison would finish him for the man.

A sense of urgency came over Raef, and he charged the man. The attacker waved the knife in front of him, almost daring Raef to bring himself into range of the deadly weapon. Dropping his hips, Raef gave his attacker the impression that he was going to attack his legs. Changing his tactics as he jumped into the air, the ex-priest extended his right leg, his right heel leading the way. The attacker was able to change his arm motion as well, slicing down hard against Raef's calf with the wicked blade, but his attack failed to stop the momentum of the former priest. As he cried out in pain, Raef's heel caught the man in the throat, pinning the man's head against the wall behind him. The crack, which resounded loudly throughout the room, was sickening. It had a sound of finality to it.

Stunned, the paralyzed attacker sank to the floor slowly. His eyes widened in disbelief of what had happened to him. Raef, on the other hand, hit the floor hard and began writhing in pain. The poison had reached his gut, and it was tearing him apart from the inside. His throat was tightening, and his vision was blurred, but he was still facing his injured foe, conscious enough that he didn't want to take his eyes off the deadly man.

Even though he was paralyzed, the man could still speak. Most of what he said came out as gibberish to Raef, but it was clear that he was begging someone. Crying, his fear was obvious. Whoever he was frightened of, that fear was real. No matter how he begged or promised the unseen entity, it was apparent that the entity was displeased with the assassin.

Raef could feel the presence of the unclean spirit that was in the room with the two men, and it was beyond oppressive. Its evil covered everything like a blanket, causing the former priest to grind his teeth in defiance of the evil he was witness to that night.

Crying at the top of his lungs, the injured assassin continued to plead with the vile spirit.

Without warning, the man burst into flames, and Raef could smell the stench of his skin and hair as it was burned away from his body. The man screamed in abject terror as the entity in the room tortured his body with flames. Though he was dying, Raef was still affected by the sudden inferno. While the man burned, Raef swore he heard laughter, malevolent laughter, as his attacker was turned into ashes right in front of him.

Closing his eyes, Raef couldn't believe what he'd witnessed. The poison then took over and he passed out cold.

9

Groggy eyed and confused, Raef Lorenz woke up in a strange place. Tubes were sticking out of his arms, supplying him with the enzymes necessary to break down the poison in his body. It all seemed surreal to him. The only familiar thing in the room was the smile on the face of the petite woman who leaned over him.

Too tired to say hello, he offered Kerri half of a smile. Not even his face seemed to work, but at least he was alive.

The sheriff's daughter could see the confusion on his face. Raef clearly hadn't expected to live through his ordeal.

"Someone found you in your hotel room and brought you here. The man didn't leave a name. He only told the nurse that your precious things would be in Rome, and you could collect them when you got there. No one seems to know what to make of the stranger or his odd reference, but he did bring you here. My dad has a lot of questions to ask you when you're feeling better.

"From your injuries, I know that you were in a fight, but with whom? Something cut deeply into your muscle. Do you know what it was? On both your shoulder and your leg you were badly cut. Do you remember that?"

When Raef nodded yes, she sighed.

"Can't you go anywhere without a fight or getting into trouble?"

Apparently not, he thought to himself, his throat still not wanting to speak the words. He'd been through a lot, and all he really wanted to do was sleep.

"Oh no you don't, mister. You're not falling asleep on me now," Kerri shouted as she held his hand and squeezed tightly. She wanted answers, and she wasn't about to let Raef duck them by feigning sleep.

Shaking Raef lightly, Kerri forced him to open his eyes and look at her. She could see from the dead look in his eyes that it was no use. The medicine was knocking him out again. Her questions would have to wait.

There wasn't a whole lot she could do without Raef. Investigating the Jersey Devil had once seemed exciting to her, but now it was frightening. Strange things were happening in Burlington. It was just a matter of time until someone else was killed.

Her father had posted two armed deputies at Raef's room. He wasn't convinced that the man was safe. A general state of emergency had been issued throughout the city, and there was a six o'clock curfew. It was going to be strictly enforced.

She remembered driving to the hospital. The city had resembled a ghost town. Not a single child was playing in the streets and anyone who didn't have to be outside of his or her home, wasn't. It was eerie. She could almost feel the evil that was descending on the town. Something was about to break wide open. She hoped the town would survive it.

November 7, 1984, 9:22 p.m.

A long day at work was nothing new for Caroline Kelly. Twelve-hour shifts at the hospital were hard on her. The only good thing about them was that they allowed her more days at home with her children. The registered nurse liked what she did for a living, but it was hard being the single mother of three children under the age of seven.

Watching the children had been much easier when Bob had been around.

Her husband had left her ten months before for his boss. Caroline had always thought of Bob as effeminate, but gay? No way. Boy, had she been wrong.

Folding the day's laundry, Caroline heard the strangest sounds coming from her shed in the backyard. It sounded like rocks pounding against the roof of the small aluminum storage unit. *Who would do such a thing?*

Going to the back window of her kitchen, Caroline pulled away the curtains and watched as a strange bird hopped up and down on the shed. *What in God's name is that?* Caroline asked herself, staring at the most bizarre creature she had ever laid eyes on. Thinking that maybe some bird from a tropical location or a zoo had become lost, she found it hard to take her eyes off of it. *Was it bouncing up and down or was it prancing?* It was dark outside. She couldn't make out the features of the bird, but it was huge, the biggest bird she had ever seen.

Turning from the window, Caroline went to a drawer under the kitchen counter where she kept odds and ends. Grabbing a camera, she approached the rear door and unlocked it. The light over the small concrete slab that substituted for a rear porch was burned out. She had forgotten to replace the bulb again. Damn Bob and his need to be free.

Opening the door and stepping out into the backyard, she discovered she had missed her chance to get a picture of the bird. It was gone. She brushed the hair out of her eyes. Then she backed her way into the house, hoping to catch another glimpse of the mixed up creature. Cursing her luck, Caroline looked down in disdain at the camera that was going unused. Her neighbors would have freaked out had she been able to get a shot of the bird or whatever it was.

As she closed the door between the kitchen and the backyard, she heard noises coming from the roof of her home. Maybe she hadn't missed it after all. The noise was different from inside the house. Was it a reindeer or a bird that was on her roof? The steps of the bird sounded like those of a hoofed animal. Whatever was up there, it was prancing around as if it were anxious. Santa Claus wasn't due in town for a few months yet, so it couldn't be a reindeer.

She had a couple of choices. She could stay inside and listen to it, or she could go out and try to get a few shots of it. No one was going to believe her if she didn't get a picture, so she stepped outside.

When the cold November air met her face, she shivered. Winter was coming early.

Maybe it's the Jersey Devil, Caroline thought. Why that thought, of all the thoughts she could have had, had come to her, she didn't know. She had lived in Jersey for all of her life, and everyone in Jersey had heard tales of the Jersey Devil. In none of the tales was a person ever harmed, just livestock and pets, so what could it hurt?

Peering through the glass on her front door, Caroline couldn't see a thing. There was nothing but untarnished snow in her front yard. The coast was clear. Daring to open the door, she was pleased to see that none of her neighbors had taken notice yet. She wanted to be the first and only one to get shots of the incredible animal. Her front porch light was already on, so she moved farther into her front yard to have a look on the roof.

What she saw there amazed her. She couldn't take her eyes off of it.

Standing on its hind feet, the anomaly of nature turned to face her. It had a weird shape to its head, sort of like the head of a German shepherd or a collie. The face was something else entirely, resembling a horse with red, beady eyes that burned right through Caroline. The creature's tiny, bat-like wings rose high over its shoulders. They were impossibly small for such a creature to use them in flight. The wings opened and closed hypnotically. The rhythm of the wings' movement made something in side of her stir, but she couldn't say what it was. The tail of the creature was like that of a devil. Forked at the end, the long, hairless limb seemed out of place. The front legs of the beast were as unusual as the rest of it. The legs reminded her of the legs on a dog. Like a sinner who was praying for absolution, the creature kept them bent in front of its chest. If it was not praying, the animal might just as well have been begging for a treat. Its back legs, the ones that it stood on, were long and thin like the legs of a stork or a flamingo. They seemed awkward and far too flimsy to bear the weight of the heavy beast. That heavy body was reminiscent of a dog as well. Thick wiry fur covered a wide chest, which remained partly hidden behind the bent forelimbs of the animal. For the most part, the creature appeared to be rust colored. Other than the wings and the legs, its body seemed to be covered in red hair.

Raising the camera to her face, Caroline snapped off a photo of the creature. Not satisfied, she took three more pictures while the beast danced, becoming agitated on her rooftop.

The whole of it was incredible until the creature craned its long neck out and gave the most unsettling scream that she had ever heard. It was steely, like the trumpeting of an elephant, but no elephant had ever frightened her so much. Maybe she had gone too far. Maybe the devil didn't want its picture taken.

With renewed vigor, the beast began to dance in place, flapping its wings wildly, trying to get her attention. A sucker for the out-of-the-ordinary, Caroline Kelly put down the camera and watched the wild display. As she watched, Caroline met the bright red eyes of the creature. They resembled nothing she had ever seen before, and she couldn't look away from them.

The wings began their rhythmic beating again, and the tail of the creature swished back and forth. The eyes pulled her in, and she became lost in them. She could sense the danger, but no matter how hard she tried, she was unable to tear her eyes away from those of the beast on her roof. At first, the woman felt faint. It was as if her heart would stop beating, but it didn't. Standing in the cold winter air without a jacket or a coat, she was oblivious to the goose bumps on her flesh and to her lips, which were turning blue. She was lost in a dream that she couldn't wake up from.

When the voice entered her thoughts, she couldn't understand it at first. It was cruel and full of hate, the voice that filled her head. Like a fine mist that eased its way under doors or around a corner, the will of the creature wrapped around her senses until she could begin to understand what it was telling her. The images it revealed to her and the thoughts it gave her made her want to throw up, but she didn't.

Bright spirals of red and black began to cloud her vision, and she felt dizzy again. Rocking back and forth, but continuing to stand, she heard the malign thoughts of the monster. At first, they were subtle, shallow things that merely disturbed her, but soon they became harsh and battering thoughts that bore into her brain, removing all of her ability to ignore them.

The voice became insistent, telling Caroline that she was a whore and that her husband had left her for another man because she was worthless. The voice used words like "bitch" and "slut." It even referred to her mouth as only being good for one thing. Never in her life had anyone talked to her in such a manner. Caroline was a good woman who had helped friend and stranger alike. To hear anyone or anything talk to her as if she were a worthless bag of garbage sent her into despair. The insults continued and soon there were tears rolling down her cheeks. They froze to her flesh in the frigid November air, though she had no conscious knowledge of them. For endless minutes, Caroline suffered the indignities of the creature's words, unable to do otherwise.

When the devil made its final suggestion, her face cringed, and she began to teeter backward, though she never fell. Even though the beast had control of her, she tried to resist its commands.

"Do it," came the insistence of the devil. "Do it for us," it screamed into her head, hurting her.

With all of her might, she fought against the thing, but it was cruel and insistent, telling her to do that which she could not. The power of the suggestion was real, and the force behind its mental commands was beyond her ability to resist.

"You are nothing but a bitch, an empty vessel," the voice screamed in her head. "Do it and free us."

She was a strong woman, but in the end, that wasn't enough. She couldn't deny the needs of the master. Its will would be done.

Turning toward the house, Caroline Kelly moved like a zombie. Time seemed to stand still for the woman, who was not conscious that she even moved at all. Climbing the steps to the second story of the house, the woman stared forward like a china doll. Her facial muscles didn't move, and she walked stiff legged as she shuffled down the hall toward the rooms of the children. Passing the first door, the one behind which five-year-old Daniel slept, she continued down the hall.

The master commanded it. Its will would be done, she told herself, though Caroline was hardly there.

Stopping at the door on the right, the woman turned the knob and entered the darkness. Reaching into the crib, she gathered little Kathy up in her arms, pulling her close.

"Mama," came the sweet voice of her two-year-old as she was awakened.

The child was scared, her heart beating faster as she was taken from her room. The smell of her mother's perfume comforted her. All was well. Her mother was cradling her.

Moving to the end of the upstairs hallway, Caroline entered the bathroom. *The master commands it. Its will will be done* continued to reverberate through her brain.

Kneeling down next to the tub, the woman turned on the cold water and then the hot. Muscle memory was taking over. She had always drawn a warm bath for the kids. Placing the stopper in the tub, Caroline Kelly just stared forward. She never looked at the child, the sweet innocent face of her baby smiling up at her.

When the water was high enough, she placed Kathy into the tub face-first. It was the act of a monster or of a woman compelled by a force she couldn't resist. For a time, the child struggled under the strong hands of her mother until her body went limp. Through it all, the woman who had just killed her youngest was oblivious to her actions. *The master commands it. His will be done.*

Twice more that night, Caroline would walk down that hall and each time she would bring another of her children into the bathroom. That night, she took the lives of all whom she cared about in the world.

In the morning, when she woke from her trance, she would be devastated. Caroline Kelly would call 911, but by the time the police and medical teams arrived at her house it would be too late.

Morning did come and Caroline did make that call. When the police arrived, they found her body hanging over the side of her tub face-down in the water. She was dead. Caroline Kelly had drowned herself.

As shocking as the death of the woman was, it was nothing compared to the other discovery the police made. Floating in the tub around the head of the woman were her children; their mother had drowned each of them.

November 8, 1984, 10:13 a.m.

When Raef woke this time, he was far less groggy than he had been the day before. The poison in his body had been counteracted. Hungry, the first thing the man did was scarf down the distasteful eggs that were brought to him. He had been awake for an hour, and still there was no sign of Kerri. Was she mad at him?

When the door to his room opened, he expected to see Kerri Wright's smiling face. Unfortunately for Raef, another face from the Wright family greeted him, that of the sheriff.

Here we go, thought Raef. *I'm in serious trouble now.*

Grabbing a chair and turning it backward, the sheriff sat down, placing his arms over the back of the chair.

"We have a lot to discuss, don't we?" the sheriff asked.

"Uh, sure, what would you like to know first?" Raef asked.

The sheriff asked several questions at once, never taking his eyes off of Raef's. When he was done, the ex-priest hoped that he could remember all of them, fearing that to not answer one would bring more suspicion upon him. Sheriff Andy Wright was a serious man, and his face told Raef that no subterfuge, no innocently edited version of the truth would be acceptable this time.

Sighing before he laid his hands over his knees, Raef began. "This is going to be difficult for you to believe, but then again, I suppose most of what I've told you so far has been."

Looking into the eyes of the sheriff, Raef knew he was fighting an uphill battle. *One more try, Raef. Just in case it's your lucky day.*

"Are you sure you want the truth?"

Watching as the sheriff nodded his ascent, Raef knew he wasn't going to be able to get out of telling the man his story.

"What your daughter and I discovered in the cemetery the other day was a book of evil. We were looking for clues in the cemetery and got far more than we bargained for. I know we didn't tell you about the book, but we were afraid you would confiscate it, so we hid it from you.

"The book in question is a tome of unfathomable evil. Unless you were a theologian or a scholar of the occult, there would be no way you could know what you were dealing with. You might not think much about the evil that can be found in written word, but the Church of Rome does, and so do I, especially after what happened to me last night.

"I was in my hotel room studying the book, trying to see if it could unlock any clues to the mystery of the Jersey Devil, it didn't.

"Deciding that it was of no use to me, I agreed to have the Vatican pick up the tome after they called me. You would not believe how fast the church is able to move when they want to, and word was given to me that a courier would be there to pick it up within the hour. I was expecting a courier, but that's not what I got. When the knock came to my door, I saw no reason to use caution. Opening the door, I was attacked by an assassin in a black robe. He was armed with a knife. The knife was an instrument of evil, a wickedly curved dagger with poison on it. The man and I fought, and I broke his neck.

"As the poison took effect on me, I could swear that the man was speaking to some unseen entity, begging it for his life. I don't know if it was the effect of the poison or if it was real, but the man burst into flames and was reduced to ashes in my room. That's all I remember, I swear. I used to be a priest. I don't lie."

"No, you don't lie. You only withhold the truth. Am I right?" the sheriff asked.

Sighing heavily, Raef said, "Yes, you're right. I'm not at liberty to discuss everything I know with you. My employer isn't ready for the world to know all of their business."

Reaching into the pocket of his jacket, Sheriff Wright removed three photographs and placed them in Raef's lap.

"How about these? Do any of the images in the photos look familiar to you?"

Picking up the pictures, Raef turned them over and his breath became caught in his chest.

"Oh my God," he exclaimed. "How did you get these? They're incredible."

Removing a toothpick from the front of his uniform shirt pocket and jamming it between his teeth, the sheriff let the question linger in the air for a moment. He could see that Raef was familiar with the animal in the photos. It showed on the face of the former priest.

"I got these from a camera that was left on the lawn of a woman who drowned her three children last night."

Shock and repulsion came over Raef's face.

"No, Lord please, no," he said as he stared at the pictures. "It's far worse than I thought," Raef said as though the sheriff wasn't even there.

Sweeping his long hair back over his head, the man turned pale. He was tortured by what he was seeing. As if he had done the foul deed himself, the former priest felt dirty, unclean. His brain raced, and his mind searched for an answer.

"I knew that it was powerful this time, but this is something new, something unknown to the church."

The pictures in the hands of Raef were of the Jersey Devil. The sheriff explained that they were the very pictures that Caroline Kelly had taken from her front yard the night before. When Caroline had called 911, the sheriff had been among the first to arrive at the house, it was only a street away from his home.

Running up the front yard, Andy noticed the camera and picked it up. He hadn't put much thought into why he picked it up, he just had. Anything that looked out of place at a crime scene was usually of value. Old habits died hard.

The photographs were clear, though they were dark. Raef could see the outline of the creature and its red eyes. They were unmistakable to him. He had seen a picture of the devil before, a real one, not some fake from out of the *National Enquirer*. Like he had told Kerri before, the Vatican had an almost endless supply of resources. The photos were similar, though the ones from the Vatican were clearer.

Clearing his throat, the sheriff looked at Raef, who saw sincerity in his eyes.

"I've shown you all of my cards, I need you to show me yours. Every life in this town may depend on it."

The sheriff was right. It was time to collaborate.

Meeting the gaze of the man in uniform, Raef couldn't help but tell him the truth. The man with the gun belt on was not a theologian, nor was he a practitioner of the occult. If he were going to understand what it was he was facing, Raef was going to have to be the one to make him understand.

"Look, sheriff, the church has been investigating the appearances of the Jersey Devil since it first came into this world. Shocking, huh? I bet you're wondering why you never heard anything about it. That's because the church believes that men aren't ready to face the reality that the Devil exists. Not just the Jersey Devil ... the actual Devil himself, the one called Lucifer."

Raef could see that Andy was uncomfortable with what he was saying. Well, it was time for him to get comfortable, because unless they did something to stop it, the devil was going to continue to kill. It was time to take the gloves off. If Sheriff Andy Wright wanted the truth, Raef was going to smack him in the face with it.

Turning the pictures over so that he wouldn't have to be reminded of the children who had been murdered, Raef turned his attention to the sheriff.

"Like I told you before, my specialty is the supernatural, the bizarre. Anything paranormal, and I want to know about it. So does the church. The forces of darkness, Lucifer, and his minions, it's all too real. Every day all around us are those who would harm us if they could. Not just physically but spiritually.

"I know you are a church-going man, sheriff, but you have no clue what roams the earth with you on a daily basis. To put it bluntly, sheriff, I've seen shit that would make you holler uncle."

If he didn't have the attention of the man before, he had it then.

"The story of the Jersey Devil is sort of a hobby of mine."

"You've got some strange hobbies," the sheriff interrupted. "Don't give me any of your holier-than-thou bullshit. Just tell me what we are dealing with and I promise you, I'll do my best to understand it."

Laughing almost to excess, Raef could hardly believe that the sheriff wanted his help at all. The man didn't believe in the devil; that was as clear to Raef as the mustache on the sheriff's face.

"I can't deny the truth, sheriff. My hobbies would seem strange to you, but they have their uses. For a long time, I've thought that there was something more to the Jersey Devil than just an odd creature that creates mischief and kills livestock. Whoever it was that brought forth the devil this time, the powers of darkness have been waiting a long time for him or her."

The sheriff looked lost, so Raef would have to backtrack. He had to understand, he just had to. He waited for the nurse who had entered his room to take some readings. Raef began the second she closed the door behind her.

"This isn't just a coincidence. This has been a long time in the planning for the minions of hell. Someone wants to unleash them upon our world, and if we don't stop it from happening, it's more than Burlington that's at stake.

"If not for yourself then for your daughter's sake, you have to believe me. I like Kerri a lot. She's a great girl. But if the cloak of evil descending on this town isn't cast away, she is going to suffer too."

10

By the time Raef was done explaining it to the sheriff, the man had lost all of the color in his face. Sheriff Andy Wright could deal with bad guys, and thieves. Devils and the forces of evil he couldn't handle.

Raef had dressed and was out of his bed before the conversation with the sheriff was over. Checking himself out of the hospital, he had a lot to do.

He wasn't surprised to find that the Holiday Inn no longer wanted him as a guest. He had expected as much. His suitcase and belongings had been packed and were waiting at the information counter for him.

Climbing into Kerri's car, Raef didn't know how to tell her that she was out of the investigation. She had made a brief appearance when the sheriff was grilling him and was told by her father to wait for Raef outside. Raef had promised the sheriff that Kerri would be placed in no further danger, and Raef always kept his promises.

On the car ride to Kerri's house, they talked about what they had discovered so far. Raef told Kerri about the writings in the tome of foul deeds. Though he couldn't find any meaning behind it then, he did now. She pressed him hard to explain, but he refused, having remembered that he wasn't supposed to involve Kerri any further. His having the knowledge was bad enough, knowing any more about it would put Kerri in danger. Raef had made a promise.

"Damn you, Raef Lorenz," the unhappy woman behind the wheel shouted. "You owe it to me to tell me. I've gone through a lot on this investigation of yours. I think that I'm entitled."

He couldn't deny her words, but he'd made a promise. Raef was shocked when the car came to a screeching halt next to the Pine Barrens on Huggins Road.

"Get out," the woman said, her lips were trembling with anger and her eyes faced forward.

"Excuse me?" Raef said. He was shocked by Kerri's behavior.

"I said get out, and I meant it," the woman shouted again. "If we're no longer working on the investigation together, then I've no reason to keep company with you any longer."

Opening the door, Raef looked back at her. His eyes were filled with deep hurt. He had thought she was different than that.

"I'm sorry to have been any trouble to you, Kerri. Thanks for the ride."

As she drove away, Raef looked around him. There were no houses and he hadn't seen a car in a while. It was going to be a long walk back into town.

The cold air on that November day made him jog for a bit. It also gave him a chance to think about what he had learned. It was hard to shake off the hurt he had felt when Kerri had booted him from her car, but he had no control over what she did. In fact, he had little control over anything at that particular moment. The devil, unfortunately he had to get back to the devil.

While in the bed at the hospital the night before, he had come to an epiphany of sorts. The name, Mammon, it was the name of the Jersey Devil itself, he was sure of it. He now understood what Samuel Leeds was doing. He had been talking with the devil named Mammon. Mammon was no she; there were no female devils, not true devils anyway.

Somehow Leeds had made a pact with this Mammon and had decided to change his mind at the last minute, when his wife asked that the child be born the Antichrist. Deciding to change the deal in its own way, Mammon had taken the open invitation of the Leeds and possessed the baby in Deborah's womb. To further bring despair to the Leeds and punish Samuel for his treachery, Mammon had taken his true form, twisting the flesh of the baby. But something went wrong and Mammon was born helpless. When Samuel Leeds threw the creature off of the bridge, its newly inhabited form had died and it had been cast back into hell.

Over the years, the devil had been called back into the world, taking the form of the Jersey Devil, its true, hellish form. Most of the archangels that had been cast out of heaven had taken on the shapes of beasts. It was said that Lucifer himself had ordered it. Though they could have remained angelic in nature, Lucifer and his downcast devils had wanted nothing to do with God or the forms he had given them.

What Raef really needed was to see the book of evil again. If he could look into it again, he might be able to discover how to rid the world of the creature. He knew that he would never see the book again. He would have to find a library, an old one, and see what it could tell him about Samuel Leeds. What kind of deal had he made with Mammon?

Raef finally managed to flag down a car and get a ride into Camden. With his suitcase in tow, Raef entered the old Camden City Library. He hoped to find something on microfiche that might lead him to an answer. Genealogy would be the place to find what he was looking for. Raef was led to a small cubicle on the third floor of the library, and upon his request, an employee brought him reels that had information regarding the life of Samuel Leeds.

It was slow going to process the information that he received. But when he came upon a deed of sale for a piece of land, he knew he was onto something. Samuel Leeds was broke. How in the hell could he afford to buy a piece of land?

It was the next-to-last reel of microfiche that gave him the answer. Unknown to most, Samuel Leeds had put his home up for sale. He had owned two hundred acres of Pine Barrens on that ridge. The sale of his property would be just enough to cover the cost of the property he had wanted in Bristol, Pennsylvania. With yet another mystery uncovered. Raef knew why the devil had visited Bristol on the rare occasion. Burying the information he had gathered deep inside of his brain, Raef left the Camden Library. He had a lot of investigating left to do and very little time to do it.

11

Reaching the third floor of the old Camden Library, Kerri wasn't surprised to see the dark-haired man in the cubicle with his back turned to her. The earring that dangled next to his neck was a dead giveaway. It was obvious that she and Raef had come to the same conclusion. History involving the Leeds family was the only way they were going to learn more about the devil.

Watching the man scroll through files of information, she knew that she was beginning to feel something for him that she couldn't avoid. She felt badly for the way she had treated him earlier. She had been angry, but she wondered if her anger was really toward him or somewhere else.

It was obvious that he didn't want her put in any more danger than she had already been in, but that wasn't his choice anymore. For the first time in her life, Kerri Wright felt as though she was doing something that had meaning to it and she wasn't ready to quit just yet.

It was a simple yet maddening matter to allow time to pass. By the time that Raef finally left the library, Kerri was nearly out of patience. Rarely had she seen someone so into what he was doing that the rest of the world became shut out. He had to have discovered something, yet had taken no notes. The man's mind was like a steel trap, and hers was much the same. Having an Ivy League education could do that to a person.

The librarian on the third floor was a kindly old man named Cooper. When Kerri told him that her fiancé had just left and that she was hoping to surprise him with even more knowledge about his ancestry, Cooper was excited to help her. Pulling the materials that Raef had just looked through was no problem.

Soon Kerri was lost to the world, studying the files of microfiche.

What she found was astounding. It was no wonder that Leeds was broke. The way the man had run his business was risky, and it had finally caught up with him. Add some bad investments with his money to the equation, and he was ruined. The land deal that he had struck in Bristol, Pennsylvania, in June of 1735 struck her as odd. It didn't take the intelligent woman long to figure out that it had some special meaning, but what? If she was going to learn any more, Kerri was going to have to go to Bristol. Bristol was where she would find her answers. She was sure of it.

The first step was to find a realtor who sold property in the area. Even if the property in Bristol wasn't for sale, she could tell the man that she wanted to make an offer for it and that he would be in line for the commission on the deal.

Robert Vale of Vale Realty was more than happy to assist Kerri in the process.

After talking to Kerri on the phone, he did a quick query on the property, and what he found made his pockets begin to vibrate. If the deal went through, Vale's pockets would soon be filled with money. The piece of property in Bristol was fifty acres of Pine Barrens forest. On the east side of the property was a freshwater spring. The place would be worth a fortune.

Kerri mentioned that she wanted to see the property before she made any kind of offer for it, and she didn't want the owner notified until she did. It was a little unusual, but things had been tight in the real estate market, and Vale needed the sale. Promising the woman that he would pick her up at eight the next morning, the pair concluded their business with one another.

All Kerri had to do was wait.

November 8, 1984, 4:52 p.m.

Burlington wasn't nearly so big that he couldn't find someone by just asking. The deputy at the 7-Eleven convenience store knew exactly whom Raef was talking about when Raef asked about the woman.

On the drive to the woman's house, Raef had some time to sort through his thoughts. The fact that the dagger and brass knuckles hadn't been in his room when the police had gone to the scene bothered him. He knew that the agent from the Church of Rome, the same agent who had brought him to the hospital, had taken them and they were probably already packed away in a vault somewhere at the Vatican. They were the only pieces of evidence that might proclaim Raef's innocence in the case. With the man's body all but burned to ashes, Raef would be hard-pressed to prove he had nothing to do with the disappearance of the man, whose remains should have been left on the floor of the room. Raef might have killed the man, but he hadn't set him on fire.

What Raef really needed was another look into that tome of evil. Of course, that too was sealed in the vaults in Rome. He would never see the inside of the book again. If Samuel Leeds had planned all along to deceive the devil, Leeds would need a way to ensure that the creature wouldn't harm him for his deceit. The only way to ensure such a thing was to have some knowledge that the devil needed or to find a way in which to send the creature back to hell. The second was the more probable of the two choices.

The entity that had come forth on that night, more than two hundred years before, was powerful. It was likely that the devil would have killed Leeds outright and taken its chances with losing the knowledge that the man had. Unfortunately, it had been born helpless. Putting practicality before desire was the one thing that devils were not known for. Death, torture, and mayhem were all that they desired in their existence. Everything else was secondary.

What was it that Samuel Leeds thought he knew or thought he could use against the devil to keep it from destroying him? The real answer to Raef's question lay in Bristol, Pennsylvania. But the woman he was seeking out might have knowledge that could unveil the mystery of that property. He had to go to her first.

Parking alongside the curb on Thirty-Sixth Avenue, Raef gave a shudder when he saw the house in which the woman lived. Walking past the rotten picket fence in the front yard, he climbed the three steps that led to the front door and rang the bell. Probably, like everything else on the old house, the doorbell didn't work either.

Raef could hear a dog barking from inside the house, but it didn't sound too big. Raef liked dogs. He had never met one that hadn't taken a liking to him.

When Beverly Ann Anderson answered the front door, his heart fell into his stomach. Though he fought against his initial thoughts, he couldn't forget them. Standing in front of him was a witch. She was every bit the description from the fairy tales he had read as a child. There was no denying it. The right side of her face was drooping, a sure sign of a past stroke. It made her look as though she were scowling. The wart on the end of her nose didn't help either.

Forcing himself to smile, Raef said, "Hello, Ms. Anderson. I'm sorry to bother you this late, but I need your help."

Right away, Raef could sense her withdrawing from the door and he tried another approach.

"I'm here on behalf of the Church of Rome. I'm not here to sell you anything or preach the good word to you. I'm looking for information about a man named Samuel Leeds. Can you help me?"

Recognition became apparent on her face. She obviously knew something. The little dog, which was barking his fool head off behind her, knew something too. He didn't like Raef.

"What is it that you want to know about Samuel Leeds, Mr.?"

"Lorenz, Raef Lorenz. I'm sorry to bother you, but your name came up in some research that I was doing, and I had hoped you might be able to help me. I'm not here to sell you anything. All I want is a few moments of your time and maybe more, if you are so inclined."

Seeing that she was wary of strangers, Raef decided to break the ice.

"I used to be a priest. Now I work for the church in another capacity. I hate to be blunt, but time is wasting and that which I hope to avert is growing closer by the day. Do you know much about your own relatives, Ms. Anderson? The relative that I'm particularly interested in is Samuel Leeds."

He could see the change in her demeanor. She had gone from cautious to frightened, which meant she knew something. There was no need to mince words with the old woman. She understood the reason behind his visit. He could see it in her eyes.

"I think that Samuel Leeds is responsible for unleashing the devil again, this time from the grave."

If she was frightened by the knowledge, it didn't show on her face. But then again, little else did either, because of her deformity. He could see that she was lost in thought. The barking dog behind her was naught but an afterthought to the woman, though it bothered Raef tremendously. When she came back from her daydream, she opened the door up further.

"Come in, Mr. Lorenz. Maybe I can help you." Looking down at the dog next to her she said, "You're going to have to excuse Charlie. He doesn't like people very much."

"That's no problem Ms. Anderson, and thank you for opening up your home to me."

The man was as well-mannered as he was handsome, and right away, Beverly took a liking to him. She had feared that the day would come when a stranger would knock on her door and ask about her past. Beverly Ann Anderson knew she couldn't avoid it any longer, for it was there. What she needed was kept in the basement, and at her age, she couldn't possibly carry the trunk full of ledgers and documents up the stairs.

"Mr. Lorenz, I'm afraid we're going to have to go into the cellar if you want to know anything further. The papers are old. They're likely to fall apart in our hands. I haven't looked through the chest in years, but I'm sure we can find something that will be of use to you."

There was no mistaking her words. The woman knew something about the Leeds family and what it had brought into the world. Was she really going to help him or was it possible that she would try some deceit of her own? The only way to find out was to follow her into the cellar.

The cellar of the house had a strong odor of mold and mildew. It was obvious to the former priest that it was rarely visited and possibly never used. The steps leading down into it creaked as he descended, but they held his weight. There was no need for hand rails, he could reach out and touch the wall on either side of the steps.

When they reached the bottom landing, Ms. Anderson flipped a light switch. Raef was surprised to see a light bulb in the center of the basements ceiling light up. *At least something works around here.*

The floor of the basement was unfinished concrete, and though stained with mold, it was strangely vacant. On the far side of the room rested the chest that the woman had spoken of. It was made of cedar, something that was good for keeping insects away.

"Can you lift it?" the old woman asked. "The light down here is poor, and it stinks. In the kitchen there are chairs, and I can make you a cup of tea while we peruse through the papers."

"That would be wonderful," exclaimed Raef with a little more intensity than he had planned. The empty basement, which only seemed to contain the chest, gave him the willies. *Who kept an empty basement?*

He hadn't noticed it when he had walked across the basement the first time, but upon his return trip, Raef could see that something had once been painted on or stained into the floor. Whatever it was, it had been large and circular. The attempt to remove it with bleach had been successful, but the cleaning agent had left behind a trail of its own.

The next thing he noticed was that there were sections of the walls that had two small holes in them that had not been filled in. The holes were reminiscent of what you might find behind a candle holder that had once been attached to the wall. Just what was this woman into? Maybe he would find his answers in the kitchen.

While Ms. Anderson brewed a pot of tea, Raef began to remove the parchments, documents, and diaries from the chest. As he laid them out on the table, Raef came to the realization that it would take a lot of reading to discover what he needed to know. Time was something he didn't have, so he turned to the only other person in the room.

"Excuse me, Ms. Anderson. You wouldn't happen to have gone through the papers in this chest, would you?"

"Yes, of course I have. Why do you ask?"

Setting down an odorous stack of papers, Raef looked at his hands, which were yellow with the mold from the papers.

"Because I believe you might be able to help me save a lot of time, time that is a precious commodity right now."

He had to press a little harder as the woman remained silent. He needed to know what she knew. It was imperative that she tell him.

"You know, Ms. Anderson, I noticed the washed-out circle on the floor of the basement and the places on the walls where candle holders or sconces were once affixed. I think you know a little more about the occult and what is in the box than you are leading me to believe you do."

He hated to have to go this route, but he had no choice. Unless he made her believe he knew a lot more than he did about her, it was going to be a long night. People with dark secrets and skeletons in their closets could be nearly impossible to deal with. He was hoping that her advancing years would make her more prone to want the burden off of her shoulders.

Turning from the stove with sadness evident in her eyes, Ms. Anderson broke down. "It's a long story. Are you sure you want to hear it?"

Giving her his most sympathetic expression, Raef shook his head. "You have no idea how sure I am, Ms. Anderson. It could mean the difference between life and death for some."

"All right," the woman said. "But please don't judge me until you have heard the entire story. Promise?"

Raef promised. He was a good listener and he was sure to be interested in all that the woman had to say. He was finally getting somewhere. Her story might answer his dead-end questions for him.

"I came into possession of that chest in 1964. At the time, I had no idea what Samuel and Deborah Leeds were up to. They were relatives on my mother's side of the family, and no one talked about them. I am a lonely old lady and the contents of the chest filled many of my days and nights." Her hands moved of their own accord as she spoke and her eyes took on a glazed look. "As I read through them, it became clear to me that Samuel Leeds and his wife were into devil worship. With a little research into the diaries and papers in that chest, I was able to determine that Samuel had been conversing with one devil in particular, a devil named Mammon."

Stopping there, Beverly looked up at Raef and saw the name recognition in his eyes. There was no need to go into exhaustive explanation about Mammon; the former priest already knew.

"Samuel and this devil had made a deal that would bring the devil into the world of men. There was more to the deal, but no matter how much I read, I was unable to decipher what that was. After reading and discovering what Samuel Leeds had done, I decided to rectify his mistake and clear my family name. Though I am not a Leeds, I am still connected to the name, which has become synonymous with evil. You see, it was Samuel Leeds who brought the Jersey Devil into this world. For as long as I can remember, people have reported seeing the Jersey Devil as it danced on rooftops or killed livestock. One fable even proclaimed that the stare of the devil could dry up the milk in a cow."

The hands of the old woman were shaking as she paused to sip at her tea.

Raef could see the comfort that the warm mug of liquid brought to her.

"Even after the death of Samuel and Deborah Leeds, one of their children, Abigail Leeds, took on the family business of dealing with devils and demons. She was apparently responsible for bringing the devil back into the world for the second time, but her incantation was weak, leaving the Jersey Devil without the majority of its hell-spawned powers. Because of the weak incantation and its lack of true power, the devil settled into a pattern of mischief. Unable to work its mischief in the hours of daylight, the devil was little more than a ghost or a poltergeist. Though it could frighten, its powers were good for little else.

"What the devil desired was to be brought into the world with its full power, so it forced Abigail to send it from the earth. The bargain was that with the help of the devil, Abigail would perform a more proper incantation in the future, bringing the devil back into the world with its full powers. Before that could happen, Abigail Leeds contracted the measles and died."

She offered Raef a thin smile for a moment before she went silent again. Ms. Anderson stared blankly into her cup of tea. Raef could see that what she would say next would be difficult for her. Deciding against interrupting her thoughts, the former priest remained patient until she began anew.

"As I told you before, I was determined to right the wrongs of my family. Deciding to learn about magic and the occult, I began to go to Wicca meetings, where I learned much more than I would have thought possible. The first thing they taught me was that there were good witches and bad witches, but that is all hogwash. I didn't learn that until it was too late.

"Deciding that I would become one of these 'good witches,' I turned my full attention to Wicca. I bought one of the 'White Bibles,' one that was said to hold charms of curing and protection from the bad spirits of the earth and elsewhere. My intentions were pure, but as I learned too late, that is what the powers of darkness rely on.

"I practiced drawing the symbols and circles of protection for a year until I believed I was ready to bring forth the Jersey Devil. What I had planned was to bring the devil forth and then bind it to hell. I was naïve, but that didn't stop me from trying. The White Bible had an incantation for just such a thing, but it warned that any imperfections in the circle or the symbols, which had to be drawn to keep the devil contained within, would result in the devil becoming free and possible harm coming to the spellcaster. As I told you, I practiced for a year. I thought I was ready. I wasn't."

It was the first time that a witch had ever confided in him and Raef relished it. Her story was fantastic. Nothing else compared. When she continued, Raef had to shake himself out of his reverie in order to keep up with the story.

"Never one to rely on my own judgment, I brought in people from my coven to inspect the circle. They assured me it was perfect. I never told them what I intended to do with it, though they had to know. They should have warned me."

She began the next sentence with her eyes closed and a grim look upon her face. As deformed as her face already was, her look of determination only added to her frightful appearance.

"So, on a stormy night in late March of 1966, I called forth the devil, using the incantation from the White Bible. I lit the sacred candles on the walls of the basement, which I had kept free of any obstructions. I placed candles at each corner of the pentagram that I had drawn inside of the circle. Using goat's blood, which was the only acceptable alternative to that of a human, I flung the blood into the circle with a bucket. I was reluctant to enter the circle for fear of becoming entrapped within it myself, so I tossed the blood from the bucket.

"Reading the spell from the bible, I could feel power coursing through my veins. It was actually working. I was bringing the Jersey Devil back into the world of men. Sweat poured from my forehead and chills ran down my spine. I was completely enthralled by what I was doing. I can't explain to you the ecstasy of the conjuration, but I can tell you it far exceeded any that a man had ever brought to me.

"The moment was sweet, and I didn't want it to end, but like all things it did. By the time I was done, I was out of breath and my throat was dry. I had been yelling at the top of my lungs.

"When the swirls of mist and brimstone began to take form in the circle, I was prepared. But that only lasted until the creature took shape within the circle and I looked upon the terrible equine visage of the devil for the first time. Using the name of the goddess of the woods, for that's whom I worshipped then, I called on her to bind the devil and forever return it to the flames of hell. It wasn't success that met my prayers to the goddess; it was the laughter of the devil, a horse-like whinny that made my skin crawl and my heart freeze in place."

The chest of the woman was rising and falling rapidly as she told the story, and Raef worried that she might collapse. Reaching out to touch her hand gently, he assured her that she was safe.

"My breath was torn from my body, and I fell to the floor, clutching my chest. I thought I was having a heart attack, but it was far worse, it was a stroke. As I lay on the floor thinking that I would die, the devil casually stepped over the outline of my containment circle and looked me in the eye. Letting forth the most horrible scream, it leapt for the window at the top of the basement wall. Glass shattered, and wood tore free from the frame as the devil's head and shoulders found their way free of the window. Using its dog-like front paws to dig into the ground outside the window and its cloven hooves to scrape against the wall for leverage, the devil managed to entirely free itself of the basement and was lost to the night.

"I had accidentally released the devil back into the world. It was my worst nightmare come true. I had finished what Samuel and Abigail Leeds had started. I lay on the floor of the basement, crying, as my heart fought to find a rhythm, and then I passed out."

She was shaking violently now, her mouth quivering on one side. Squeezing her hand, the former priest rubbed it with his thumb and forefinger. The woman was a gentle soul. She didn't deserve to go through what she had or to bear the weight of her ignorance for so long in lonely isolation. He could forgive her for her mistake, and somehow, deep in his heart, he knew that God could too.

"When I awoke, my face was as you see it now. The gaze of the creature left me forever crippled and deformed, much like it had left the Leeds' baby two hundred years before. My shame was total. I couldn't face the world, so I remained hidden in this house. To this day I still keep to myself, ashamed of what I have done."

The story made sense to Raef. Ms. Anderson wasn't the first to try something similar and have it meet with failure. Assuring her that God could forgive her for the act, he offered up a prayer for the soul of the woman. She seemed thrilled to have someone pray for her. She said she had thought herself condemned to hell for her actions.

Realizing that the woman was in need, Raef talked to her as he had once talked to his parishioners. It made him feel good to ease the woman's soul. She had suffered far too much for her mistake.

When she became calm again, he decided he couldn't avoid asking her questions about the Leeds family. He had no choice.

"I recently did some research about Samuel Leeds and came across the deed of sale to a piece of land in Bristol, Pennsylvania. Is there anything special about that piece of land?"

The face of the woman next to him became animated and she seemed to break free of her self-lamenting.

"Why yes. Yes there is," the woman exclaimed as she tore through the papers until she found a folder containing the deed.

After handing the deed to Raef, Ms. Anderson allowed him some time to peruse it.

"The only thing of interest on that land is a freshwater spring. It was worthless in the day, but apparently, Samuel was desperate to have it."

Looking up from the deed, Raef poured himself another cup of tea. Letting the warm liquid wash down his throat, he said, "Why would a man sell two hundred acres and a house in order to buy forty acres and a spring, the forty acres being far less valuable than the two hundred?"

He had asked it out loud, though he didn't expect Ms. Anderson to know the answer to his question. He had thought that by asking the question aloud, somehow the answer might come to him, but it didn't. Damn, he was so close. Maybe there was something in the diaries that would explain the purchase.

"I hope I'm not overstepping my bounds here, Ms. Anderson, but would it be possible for me to borrow the contents of the chest? I believe that there might be something of value in them, something that might lead me to discovering a way of banishing the creature again. The creature didn't come back in a weakened state this time. In fact, I believe that it's more powerful than ever."

As she placed her teacup down on the saucer, Raef could see that her hand was still shaking. The saucer rattled as the cup vibrated against it, and then she spoke.

"As far as I'm concerned, Mr. Lorenz, you can have the damn contents from the chest. All they ever brought to me was pain and suffering."

Getting up from the table, Ms. Anderson went to the window in the kitchen and drew the curtains aside. Darkness had taken hold of Burlington and she feared for the ex-priest who sat in her kitchen.

"It's getting late, Mr. Lorenz, and I fear to let you leave. Too many strange things are happening in Burlington right now for me to feel right about sending you out into that darkness. Would you like to spend the night in the guest room?"

He had never considered the hour or the fact that he was homeless. Though he was afraid of what the guest room might look like, it was better than sleeping in the car that he had rented.

"The offer is very considerate of you. How can I say no?"

Ms. Anderson excused herself from the room to make sure that all was prepared for the man.

For the first time, Raef realized that Charlie the dog was lying comfortably under the table, and his head was on Raef's foot. The dog looked almost peaceful, *the lucky mutt.*

Sorting through the diaries, Raef found one that looked promising. It was labeled, "business consorts of another kind." If dealing with the devil wasn't another kind of business consort, then Raef didn't know what was. Opening the diary, he knew right away that he was on the right track. It was going to take some time, possibly all night, but he meant to know what was in the diary.

He had barely gotten into the ledger when Ms. Anderson drew him away from the kitchen and up to the second-story bedroom where he would take his rest for the night. He couldn't believe his eyes when he walked through the simple wooden door. The room was immaculate. It looked as if it had just been cleaned, but of course it hadn't. The double bed had fresh linens on it, and the room smelled of pinecones. A desk sat in the far right corner, and a tiny table lamp upon it was lit. A crucifix hung over the bed, and several pieces of art, which the homeowner herself had painted, were hung on the wall. The alarm clock next to the bed was set at the right time. The room was perfect. *How in the world did a woman who never had guests keep a room so well maintained for the guests that she was never going to have?*

After thanking her again for her kindness, Raef sat at the desk and opened the diary again.

He was in the right area. All he had to do was to keep reading. It would come to him. Then he struck gold in the form of a quill-written entry that he knew would lead him to an answer. He read:

> The master himself has certainly shown favor upon me. The land in Bristol is exactly what I need to take control of my business with Mammon. So far, the devil has been in control of our agreement, but that is about to change. If only I can raise the capital to purchase the land, I might yet be free of its demands. Although it frightens me greatly to do so, I mean to use that which lies upon the property as a threat against the devil. Now that I know he fears it and why, I shall use it to gain the upper hand in our relationship.

Mammon is the way, but I shall be in control of the way. I fear that purchasing the land will cost me everything that I own, but it is the only way. Abby is my confidant, she alone knows of that which I will attempt. She is my daughter, my lover, and my keeper of secrets. It is through her that I have promised Mammon the birth of another child if the one in the womb of my wife becomes insufficient. Only she, the devil, and I know that she bears my child. My wife shall never know. Either way, Mammon shall be born into the world again and bring a host of his brethren with him.

I have his promise, but I fear the promises of such fiends. Creatures such as he are wily and treacherous. I must weigh my steps carefully in all that I do in his name. Although the reward that was promised to me is great, it remains unfulfilled. I have regained none of my wealth or station in the community and, for some reason, I don't believe I ever will. I must readdress my desires with Mammon so that I am not deceived.

Raef knew that Samuel Leeds had entered into an agreement with the devil, Mammon, but the fact that he himself had impregnated his daughter went beyond disgusting. No evil was beyond the man. He had even corrupted his daughter. The diary made no mention of her age, but she had to be young, probably no older than thirteen.

A scratching that came from outside of the bedroom door interrupted his thoughts. When Raef opened the door, Charlie stole into the room and jumped on the bed. Resting his head on the footboard of the bed, Charlie watched Raef with interest. It was a little unnerving, but Raef was glad for the company. Reading the diary was giving him the creeps, and Charlie was offering him comfort.

Raef was many pages into the book before he found his next set of clues. Though none of the entries were dated, Raef was able to get some sense of the time frame.

The spring … it is known as the Blue Hole, but I know its true name. It is the key to my salvation from

Mammon, and my only bargaining piece against him. I now know that he does not intend to make good on his promises. He is a liar, but should I be surprised? If I have learned anything while dealing with the fiend, it is that the truth is not within him. He cannot be trusted.

Abigail has miscarried, and I had to send her away, as is proper when such a thing is discovered. The midwife has agreed to keep the secret, but only if Abigail was sent away from whoever may have done such a foul thing to her. I do not believe she suspects me. If she did, she would be dead by now. Murder is no longer something I fear to do. I will do what I must.

Even though she is beyond the normal years for childbirth, Deborah and the unborn child are doing well. The birth of this child is perhaps my last hope. Even now, I seek a way out of my bargain with the devil, but I must proceed with care. If the devil were to guess at my intentions, he would surely have vengeance upon my soul in either this life or the next.

The implications were simple. Samuel Leeds was a thing of evil; no different than the devil himself. With Abigail miscarrying, his ace in the hole was lost.

The spring in Bristol was the key to uncovering the mystery. Maybe Raef would discover its importance somewhere deeper in the diary.

Getting up from the desk, his thoughts went to Kerri. *Is she all right, and is she still mad at me*? All he wanted to do was protect her from harm. He couldn't do that if he drew her in further. What scared him most was that she was out there alone. The woman had a strong will. Would she be dumb enough to search for answers without him? He didn't have to answer the question. It had been on his mind all day, and he knew that she would.

Looking at the dog on the bed, Raef asked Charlie, "Do you have these same problems with women?"

The dog pulled both paws down over its face and whined. They were two of a kind. Even the dog didn't understand the opposite sex.

Taking a seat on the bed, Raef began to pet the dog. Charlie seemed to like it. His eyes closed and soon Raef could hear his tiny snores. Charlie wasn't a bad dog. It was more likely that he was just lonely. He was a lot like his master.

Thinking of Beverly Ann Anderson brought a smile to Raef's face. The Lord had once again shown him not to judge a book by its cover. He wouldn't call her delightful, but she was far removed from the monster that her deformity made her out to be. If only someone would reach out to her and befriend her, it might mean the world to the recluse. This wasn't the movies. That wasn't likely to happen. But Raef could still pray for her. While prayer didn't always work, it couldn't hurt. Raef had no doubt that God was listening. The creator would answer the prayer in his own good time. That had always been that way.

Going back to the desk, Raef sighed. He was getting closer, but he was also tired, the answer had better come soon.

Returning to his reading, he read:

> The day is almost here, and I am ready. I shall turn the tables on the devil and offer the child to another. By the time Mammon realizes what is happening, it shall be too late for him. He shall be lost. If by chance he finds his way into the world, I know how to remove him from it. The spring in Bristol, which I now own, is the key to his undoing.

> In the Pine Barrens not twenty miles behind my house, I have kept the man. He is old and disgusting of face, but he has the gift of seeing. Keeping him warm and fed all these years, though my family suffered, has paid off. It was he who located the spring, the gateway to hell from which devils can be summoned or banished. Though its waters are crystal clear, the spring holds the power to bind demons and devils to this world or their own. It is neither holy nor evil; it just is.

In the tome I carry in my pocket, it is sometimes written that natural gateways to the heavens and hell exist. I now see that it is true. Because the writings in the book are ever-changing, it has taken me years to learn this secret, and it is only through luck that it appeared to me.

The master will undoubtedly reward me for my treachery, for it is his way. He favors the strong, those who through the use of lies and deceit, outwit their peers. No matter the result of Deborah's child-birthing, I shall bring forth devils into this world. I alone know the way.

Skipping through the pages, Raef found the next entry he was looking for.

The birth has come, and yet I am undone. My child was born a monster, a monster that I removed from the world when I tossed it into the river by the rickety old bridge. May it find peace in the cool waters and offend me no more. I am without money and home. Tomorrow the bank will come and force me from this house. There is no place for me and mine in Burlington. The children shall have to be sent away and my wife shall go to live with her sister in Camden. Where I shall reside, I cannot say. I do not know the answer to the question.

Not only have I angered Mammon, I have angered the master. He denies me. I know this because I can no longer read the words in the tome, the words that once came so easy to me.

I have wasted no time in covering my tracks. The seer is dead and shall haunt me no more with his promises of knowledge. Though I possess the spring and know its secret, without the tome I am unable to call forth from it what I desire.

When Abby returns I shall try again to father a child with her. She will be a year older and likely able to carry my progeny. In my will, I have left all that I own to her. It is not that she deserves anything from me; it is just that I desire her to carry on my work. She above all others will understand. The darkness is within her. She will reach for it as I have.

They were the last words of any clarity in the diary. Samuel must have been stricken with smallpox before his next entry. He was said to have died within three years of the birth of the devil. *Good riddance,* Raef thought as he closed the book and got into bed.

He now knew the secret of the spring, but what good would it do him if he couldn't put it to use. The tome was in Rome, and even if he possessed it, it wasn't likely to show him how to undo the devil.

Sleep came begrudgingly to him that night. The sound of hoofbeats on the roof shook him to his core being, yet he did not awaken. In his dreams, he could hear the Jersey Devil as it screamed in the night, yet still he did not wake.

Through it all, Charlie sat at the end of the bed and growled at the door to the room. Like an undersized bodyguard, the dog watched over the sleeping man. Monster or devil, if anything entered the room, it would have to get by the dog if it wanted the man.

The man in the bed twisted and turned, calling out names that even he wouldn't have recognized. In his dreams he clearly saw the New Testament as the pages of the book opened before him in a whirlwind of motion. The pages passed by his eyes too quickly for him to read them, yet somehow he understood every word. Visions of rosaries and crucifixes filled his brain as well as the visage of the Blessed Mother. He saw visions of Jesus bringing the dead back to life and Moses throwing the tablets containing the commandments down upon the sinners under Mount Sinai. His brain was enthralled by the visions of lovely winged beings at war with one another, some of them being cast from a lovely city in the clouds. Though he could not make out a face, he was sure that he was watching God cry as the creator witnessed the war between the winged beings. The tears of the creator fell with the force of a waterfall upon the planet below them, filling much of it up with liquid pain. All that the tears touched sprang to life, and green grass was born.

There was no fighting the dream or the way it tortured his mind. Raef would dream until the sun found him, and Charlie would watch over him until then.

12

November 9, 1984, 3:45 a.m.

If Raef's sleep was tumultuous, Beverly Ann Anderson's was downright torture. Without reason, her eyes flew wide open. It was there, somewhere outside her bedroom window. She heard nothing in the darkness of the night, but she knew that it was there. She could feel it.

When someone looks upon the true face of evil, it is something that she never forgets. It permeates her soul and leaves a mark upon her. Never in Beverly Ann's life had she been as frightened as she was on the night she had first seen the creature. And that night, she was just as frightened by it. Fear filled her from the tip of her toes to the top of her head, and she shivered under the covers. She shook so hard that the headboard of the bed began to rattle. The former priest was in the room just down the hall from her, but she was too frightened to go to him.

She could hear Charlie growling from somewhere down the hall. The dog was on edge too. It had to be the creature.

It took every ounce of courage Beverly Ann had to reach for the pill on the nightstand and pop it under her tongue. The tiny nitroglycerin tablet made her feel better. One stroke was enough in this lifetime. If she could outwait the creature, maybe it would go away.

For the first time in years, she crossed herself and prayed to God. She had felt as though God had abandoned her some years before, but really, she had abandoned God. Tears rolled down her eyes as she prayed. If only God could make the devil go away.

Without warning the wind kicked up, and tree branches began to scrape the sides of the house along with its windows. Charlie began to bark. So why wasn't the priest coming to help her? Fear turned into desperation. She had to get help, and the only help available to her was sleeping in the room down the hall. Had she invited the man to stay for his own good or hers? She didn't know and she didn't care. All that Beverly Ann Anderson knew was that she needed his help.

Getting out of the bed was a chore for the old woman. There was no time to put on her slippers or her robe; she had to get to Raef.

The second her feet hit the floor, she could hear the flapping of wings as they beat against the wind and the window to her bedroom. Her throat grew tight and she nearly fainted then. Unable to move her body because she was frozen with fear, Beverly Ann tried not to look to the window where the insistent flapping continued its assault. Everything that she feared was coming true. The devil had come for her. She had always known that it would.

Her feet were stuck to the floor, though nothing held them there. Tears welled up in her eyes and she nearly screamed, but her throat was tight and dry. The sound wouldn't come. Her mind begged her not to look toward the window, but she couldn't resist.

Fear could do strange things to a person, and Beverly Ann found her head turning toward the glass in the wooden frame. It was the only thing that kept the creature from her, but it was a false security against the devil. Her eyes met the angry red lights of fire that stood out in the equine face of the beast, and she gasped. Its tiny wings flapped wildly, holding it still in front of the window as its eyes continued to bore into her. Beverly Ann had felt those eyes on her before, and she knew what was to come next.

Somehow she found the strength to close her eyes, but it didn't matter. The eyes of the devil were like hot lasers and they burned through her lids. There was nowhere to hide from the creature's gaze.

Behind her eyelids she could feel her eyes burning. They were on fire. She was not imagining it.

The scream that wouldn't come finally did, but it brought the woman no relief. Flames shot from her eyes like the breath of a dragon in a fairytale, and they quickly spread to her nose and mouth. She was a human torch with fire erupting from every orifice on her skull. Her mouth remained open, and the fire danced inside, searing away her tongue and turning her teeth jet-black. Her gums became dark and soon her lips burned away from her mouth. Moving through her skull, the fire found her brain, and it laid waste to the organ. Eventually burning through the top of her skull, the inferno of malevolence burned off her hair and any skin that it could find to feed on.

It took no longer than three minutes for the fire to consume her body, for hellfire was beyond any heat that could be produced on the earth. When her body, consumed by the fire, finally crumpled to the floor, all that was left of the woman was a single ring, the one bearing a crucifix upon it. Other than the ring, there was no proof that Beverly Ann Anderson had ever existed.

Flying wildly outside of the window to Ms. Anderson's bedroom, the devil took delight in its revenge. It had once spared the life of the foolish mortal who had brought it forth, into the world of men, and tonight, the devil had rectified the mistake.

Allowing the holy man to find the Anderson woman and to seek answers from her was another mistake. But no matter how hard the devil tried to awaken and beguile the man, the priest didn't stir. The creature could sense the hand of the Heavenly Bastard in the man's inability to awaken; for that, they would both pay.

The barking dog in the room with the man also served to keep the creature at bay. It was no simple familiar that guarded the man. It was something else altogether, something holy that the devil dared not cross. The powers of the holy guardian were strong. There would be no victory tonight.

Letting out a steely scream of anger, the devil took flight into the darkness. It had other things to do. For now the man was out of its reach.

The power of the devil was growing stronger. With each life it took, it consumed yet another soul. Souls were the key to its power on earth and soon it would be nearly invincible.

When it felt safe in its growing power, the devil would begin to bring forth those that had sworn allegiance to it. The group was made up of mostly lesser demons and devils, but they could serve a purpose. Mammon hated the prick from heaven just as badly as Lucifer did, but where the Father of Lies was unwilling to thwart the creator directly, Mammon planned to do just that. What the devil in the guise of the beast wanted more than anything was another fight against the archangels. Such a fight would bring about devastation, if not the total destruction of the earth.

During the last battle between archangels and those whom God had cast from heaven, the oceans had boiled hot, and fiery mountains had come to life from flat ground. The wind had flayed the earth and brought other mountains crumbling down into the seas.

The likelihood that Mammon and his legions of devils would win was remote, almost nonexistent, but it would still serve his purpose. The destruction of what God loved most was all that the devil cared about. Mortals and the world they lived in were just a means to an end for the creature of evil.

St. Michael's Church in Bristol, Pennsylvania, was beautiful to behold. The high-reaching spires and the steeple made of copper were still pristine after twenty-seven years in the weather. The stained glass windows showed the Stations of the Cross, which portrayed Christ's journey through the streets of Jerusalem, his crucifixion, and his death.

The devil cared nothing for the beauty of the church as he flew over the top of it, urinating and defecating on the structure. It screamed its unholy scream and dug rows of deep furrows in the grass at the front of the structure. It couldn't enter the building. The power it needed to accomplish such a feat was still beyond the devil.

Making as much noise as possible, the devil began to grin as people came out of their homes and looked through their windows. Fear and terror were its tools on that night. The people of Bristol needed to understand what the people of Burlington had already come to know.

For hours, the devil flew above the church, releasing bile and other vile substances from its body.

A police cruiser from the town's police department was called to the scene. When the young cop got out of his car, he drew his gun and fired. Though he hit the creature numerous times, it had little effect. Screaming out in anger, the devil flew toward the young officer and the man fled to the safety of his cruiser.

When the weight of the devil landed on the roof of the patrol car, the lights upon it shattered, and the roof caved in. Before the policeman could duck down enough to escape injury, the caved-in roof struck him on the head, knocking him out cold.

With the devil's job completed, it flew from the police cruiser and left Bristol behind. The actions of the Jersey Devil had left behind fear and horror.

The cop would survive his ordeal, only to be ridiculed for the rest of his career by his coworkers. Though many witnesses reported seeing the Jersey Devil that night, few believed them. The Jersey Devil was a fairy tale. It didn't exist.

November 9, 1984, 6:29 a.m.

Waking up, Raef felt as if his body had been involved in a tug of war between two giants. He was sore in his legs and his arms. His neck had seen better days as well.

Standing at the bottom of the bed was Charlie. He looked anxious.

"Hey there, little fella," Raef said in a calming, playful voice. "How are you doing this morning? I feel awful, if you want to know."

Getting no response from the dog, Raef checked his hair in the mirror and headed down stairs. "Do you think your mommy will mind if I make some coffee?" Raef asked the dog.

Since the dog didn't say no, it must be all right, Raef thought.

Rooting through the cabinets over the range, Raef found an open can of Maxwell House. The coffee maker was as clean as a whistle, and within minutes, Raef was holding a steaming hot cup of Joe. The coffee was good, but he couldn't seem to work the kinks out of his body. Truth be told, it wasn't just his body that hurt; his head hurt too.

The coffee had done nothing for his headache, so once again he rifled through the cabinets and drawers of the kitchen, looking for aspirin. After finding and taking two of the tiny tablets, he settled back into his chair and resumed enjoying his cup of java. While Raef sipped at the coffee, Charlie remained restless, pawing at the former priest's feet and whining. The dog refused to be let out; it wanted to go back upstairs.

"What's on your mind, boy?" the man asked the dog. Charlie was a smart dog. If he wanted to go upstairs, there had to be a good reason for it.

Taking the steps two at a time, Raef began calling out for Ms. Anderson.

Getting no reply from the woman, he began to worry. Elderly people were renowned for an inability to sleep late. This wasn't good. Reaching the door to Ms. Anderson's room, Raef could smell the odor of something burned.

After turning the handle, Raef wished he had never opened the door.

Ms. Anderson was nowhere to be found in the room. The black spot that had been burned into the hardwood flooring told Raef all he needed to know. The devil or one of its agents, had found the woman and dealt with her.

There was no sign of any forced entry into the room. *So how was it done?* Raef asked himself. The words of Sheriff Andy Wright struck Raef at that moment. "There was no sign that anything was amiss, but the children were dead and so was she."

The sheriff had been talking about Caroline Kelly's house and the events that had led to the deaths of her and her children.

The devil was growing in power. There could be no doubting it now.

Turning from the awful scene in the bedroom, Raef decided it was time for him to go. Everywhere he went, people seemed to die. It wouldn't be long before the sheriff was forced to arrest him. He had no alibi. Gathering up the diary and the papers that he deemed to be relevant, the ex-priest bounded down the steps and out the door.

Slipping out of the door ahead of him was Charlie. The dog ran to Raef's car, waiting patiently by the driver's door. *Smart dog*, Raef thought as he opened the door and Charlie jumped in. Taking a seat on the passenger's side of the Pontiac Grand Am, the dog looked as though he belonged. Beverly Ann Anderson was gone; Charlie needed someone to look after him.

Raef's first stop was going to be Kerri's house. She lived nearby. If she yelled and hollered at him to go away, at least he would know that she was all right. When he pulled in front of the house, things didn't look good. Kerri's car wasn't there, so he thought maybe she had slept over at her parents' house again.

After driving by the house of the sheriff, Raef was disappointed to see that Kerri's car wasn't there either. He had no choice. He was going to have to go to the sheriff. Kerri might be in danger.

The sheriff was less than pleased by what Raef had to tell him when Raef stopped by the office. Concerned, Andy Wright picked up the phone and dialed his wife. He was just as unhappy as Raef was to learn that Kerri wasn't there. At least she had told the missus where she would be for the day.

"Looks like she hired a real estate agent," the sheriff said without smiling.

Looking upset, Raef asked, "Let me guess, he's taking her to look at a property in Bristol?"

"Now how in the hell did you know tha …?" The sheriff broke off his question and gave Raef a hard stare. "You promised me that you would keep her out of this, remember?"

"Yeah, I remember," said Raef, "but I don't think she cares about our concerns for her. Sheriff, I told her she couldn't be involved in the investigation any longer, and she kicked me out of her car. I don't mind telling you that it was a long walk back into Burlington."

Seeing that the sheriff wasn't concerned about how long his walk was, Raef finished his deduction of what must have happened. "Aw,

Christ, she must have followed me to the library. How could I have been so stupid?"

Straightening his Stetson, Andy Wright asked, "What are you talking about? Why was she in the library?"

"It's simple, sheriff. I went to the old library in Camden yesterday. I went to their genealogy section hoping to find some information on Samuel Leeds. I needed to know what he was up to. I was at a dead end in my investigation. I found some interesting things out about the man, like he was broke but still trying to buy a piece of property in Bristol. Kerri must have found out too and decided to check it out for herself."

"Is she in danger?" the sheriff asked, his voice caught in his throat.

"It wouldn't surprise me. There's a whole lot of that going on around here right now," the ex-priest replied. "Sheriff, we have to find her."

Clearing his throat, the sheriff said, "There is no we. Stay away from my daughter, Mr. Lorenz, or I'll lock you up in my jail with your biker buddies."

Having said all he needed to say, the sheriff left the office and got into his patrol car. He was determined to find his daughter. This time she was going to listen to him.

With lights flashing and siren roaring, Sheriff Andy Wright headed for Bristol. The radio in his car was off and he was of a single mind that day. He was going to find his daughter. If she had come to any harm, there would be hell to pay.

A flat tire was all that the realtor needed. He didn't have a spare. The short cut he had taken down the old dirt road might well have just cost him a sale. His client didn't look too happy sitting in the passenger seat of his car.

Damn, damn, damn … why now? thought the man as he gazed upon the tire with the nail in it. The road was almost never traveled on, and it was going to be a long walk to anything that resembled civilization. Opening up Kerri's door, he peeked in and said, "I'm not sure how to tell you this, but we're stuck."

When she found out that Vale had no spare tire, she nearly choked the man. She had to get to Bristol before Raef. It was her only chance to get back into the investigation. *Someone doesn't want me in Bristol*, she thought as she looked into the cloudy sky.

"You don't have to take his side on everything," yelled Kerri.

She didn't care if Vale thought she was nuts, it didn't matter to her.

Getting out of the disabled car, she began the long walk home.

Kerri didn't wait for Vale to follow her. They were going to have to walk about nine miles, if she guessed right, and that would take all day. By the time they found a ride back to Burlington, Raef would already have visited Bristol.

As the pair walked, Vale tried to strike up conversation. Even when faced with an uphill battle, he was doing his best to make the sale.

"You really should see the freshwater spring on the land, it's quite remarkable."

Turning toward the man, Kerri asked, "Did you say there was a spring on the property?"

"Why yes," said Vale, "You should see it. I hear it's absolutely beautiful. The water is crystal clear and remains a cool sixty-eight degrees year-round."

A freshwater spring on the property? What could it mean? Forgetting that Vale was with her, Kerri's mind was working on the new information that had just been given to her. She had been a history major, and her mind was like a steel trap. Trying her best to remember anything in history that had to do with a spring, she came up with one legend: the Fountain of Youth. It was a freshwater spring located in Saint Augustine, Florida. Ponce de Leon was said to have found a spring that could reduce the effects of aging on a person, maybe even grant youth to the elderly. The spring in Florida was full of water that was saturated with sulfur. Smelling like rotten eggs, its taste was even worse.

Kerri remembered the family vacation to Daytona Beach, Florida. Her dad had insisted on stopping when he saw signs for the Fountain of Youth. He was a weirdo for anything strange, saying that Kerri's mother could use it. There had been absolutely nothing interesting about the tourist trap. It was little more than a well where you paid five dollars to drink a Dixie-cup full of the disgusting water.

Even if it wasn't the original Fountain of Youth, its origin had to come from some factual part of history. Like Stonehenge and Loch

Ness, every myth started from some fact. Maybe the spring on the land in Bristol had some mystical power to it. It would explain why Samuel Leeds was so desperate to own it. *What could a natural spring possibly do that would give the owner protection from the fiends of hell?*

Upon reaching Bristol, the sheriff had no problem getting directions to the property. As far as he knew, it was the only property in all of Bristol, Pennsylvania, to have a freshwater spring on it. Pulling up to the ranch-style fence that marked off the property, Andy was surprised to see that there were no cars there. Had he missed Kerri, or was she in trouble again?

Tire tracks from motorcycles had not escaped his notice as he drove down the dirt road to the place. If any of the bikers had followed Kerri here, she was in trouble. Most of the outlaw band of men had been caught or run out of town. *Had they come here?* Everyone seemed to know where he needed to be except for him. Andy was beginning to feel like he was behind the eight ball. A long-time cop, Andy was used to being ahead of the game, but dealing with demons and devils left him feeling alone. He couldn't share it with his men and he had no intention of joining that religious kook, Raef Lorenz.

Exiting his cruiser, Andy grabbed his shotgun and loaded a shell into the chamber. There were plenty of trees for cover, and he used them as he slowly walked the perimeter of the fence. With his shotgun in a low, ready position, the sheriff began to look for signs of life. He hadn't seen any motorcycles yet, but there had been no tire tracks leading out of the property, only in to it.

Jitterbug had been mentally warned that he should expect visitors. When the sheriff's cruiser pulled up to the property, the only thing that confused him was that it was from Burlington. *Now why would a cop from Burlington come to Bristol?* Something was amiss, but he would handle it the same as any other intrusion upon the property.

The sheriff wouldn't be the first cop killed by the Diablos. Jitterbug had killed at least three lawmen from the Midwest himself. The nine-millimeter Luger in his hand had been responsible for the death of one cop. It was about to be responsible for another.

Along with Jitterbug were Atlas and Hasty. Atlas was a giant of a biker. He was heavy muscle, which was always good to have when you got into as much trouble as the Diablos did. The man called Hasty was always in a hurry. His quick decisions, with little thought behind them, often got him in trouble with the law. If he hadn't been one of Crowbar's favorites, Jitterbug would have killed him and left him for dead long before.

The other two men were in position. If they waited patiently, which he doubted that Hasty could do, there would soon be one less sheriff in New Jersey.

They were there. He could almost smell them. Dirt bags had a distinct odor to them; it was always the same. The reason that he couldn't see them was because they knew he was there. Unless they had taken Kerri, there was no way that they could have known he'd be coming for them.

His only concern was for his daughter. If Andy had to kill a hundred bikers to save her, he was going to do it.

An ex-military man, the sheriff put his training to use. Collecting twigs and pine needles, the sheriff stuck them to his hat and his uniform. He stripped all of the brass from his uniform's shirt, because he didn't want the glint of the sun on his hardware to give away his position. Rolling pinecones and throwing rocks, the sheriff used the noise they made to move from tree to tree. The brush in the Pine Barrens was dry and crunched loudly under his footsteps. If he was going to get near bikers without being seen, he was going to have to be lucky.

A noise to the left of him made him crouch down low and suck in his breath. Fearing to breathe lest he miss another sound, Andy didn't exhale.

Shit, thought Jitterbug, hearing the noise that one of his bikers had made. It was loud and clearly gave his position away to the sheriff. Hasty was an idiot, and it would serve him right if the sheriff blew him away in the forest. At least Jitterbug wouldn't have to worry about the man anymore.

Slight of build, Jitterbug could move silently from place to place if he was careful, and he was always careful. His men were armed, one with a knife and one with a machete. If the sheriff found them before they had a chance to surprise him, they were shit out of luck.

Again came the noise from one of his men, and he cringed. Damn Crowbar for leaving him with such an idiot. The man was likely to get them all killed. A flash of green caught the eye of the skinny man, and he grinned. Fixing his eyes on the place where he had heard the noise, the outlaw smiled. The sheriff was moving in a straight line for him; all he had to do was sit and wait. The dark green uniform of the sheriff had given him away. Using what the forest had provided for a disguise was good, but the sun had decided to peak out at the wrong time for the lawman.

The hair on the back of his neck began to stand on end, telling him that he was in trouble. Twisting to his left, Andy was met by a man wielding a machete. Fortunately for the sheriff, he was the quicker of the two, and when he pulled the trigger of the shotgun, the force of the slug as it buried itself in the chest of the giant biker blew the man from his feet.

His cover was blown; it was time to take chances. Leaping over the dying biker, the sheriff was shocked when the man, who had a giant hole in his chest, reached out and tripped him up, sending him falling into a headlong roll.

Andy came to his feet, his instincts taking over and prompting him to duck away as a knife came across his face. The blade cut flesh, but thanks to his internal warning system the cut wasn't deep. Blood ran down his right cheek, the flow separating at his chin where some of it reached the corner of his mouth and, some of it trickled down his neck. The knife was so sharp that he didn't feel the pain, but he knew it would come later; it always did.

Spinning to his right, Andy pulled the trigger again and heard the scream of the knife-wielding biker as his face was blown back through his skull. The sheriff preferred to use slugs in his shotgun. Buckshot was good for men who needed room for error, but he liked to use slugs. The inch-thick plug of metal destroyed anything it came into contact with. Flesh held no hope against it.

He felt the pain before another shot rang out, but where had it come from? He fell to his knees. The bullet had entered his lower back, missing his spine by inches. Pain like that of a thousand hot pokers being jabbed into his body found him, but he had no time to be in pain. Somewhere out there was a man with a gun, who wanted to take his life. A fighter since the day he was born, Sheriff Andy Wright wasn't about to stop then.

The sound of leaf litter crushing under the foot of his assailant told him that the man was closing in on him. He wanted to turn around, but the damage to his back wouldn't allow it. The bullet had gone deep, doing more damage than he had realized at first. Stuck on his knees, Andy used both hands to point the shotgun over his left shoulder, and he pulled the trigger. He heard a man yelp, but it wasn't a scream of pain. He had missed.

The sheriff hadn't missed by much, and the slug that tore past Jitterbug's head almost scraped his cheek. By his count, the sheriff had one shell left in the gun, and seeing the recoil of the weapon on the lawman's shoulder told Jitterbug that he meant to use it.

Diving out of the way as the gun went off a second time, the biker was pleased to know that the sheriff was out of ammo, and soon he would be sending the sheriff to see the master.

Getting to his feet in a hurry, Jitterbug rushed the sheriff, tackling the man to the ground. Andy's cry of shock and pain was music to the biker's ears as they fell onto the dry earth together. The Luger was still in his hands as the biker climbed onto the sheriff's back.

Placing the gun to the back of the sheriff's head, Jitterbug decided to gloat before he killed the man. Why not have a little fun at the sheriff's expense. He had the time.

Drawing a small silver knife from inside his boot, the biker shoved the blade into the hole where the bullet had entered the sheriff. He screamed in pain, pain that was unparalleled. Taking the knife from the wound, Jitterbug watched as blood poured from the hole.

"How did that feel, Mr. Sheriff?"

The biker was not only a coward who attacked from behind; he was also cruel. Again the biker stabbed him. This time, the blade of the knife entered his right buttock and the sheriff wailed in agony.

If he was going out, he was going out fighting. Though he couldn't defend himself physically, he still had his mouth.

"Does that make you feel like a big man?" the sheriff asked through gritted teeth. "I bet your boyfriend shoves his cock up your ass the same way when he bends you over," the sheriff said.

"For that you're gonna bleed, pig."

Bringing the knife around to the front of the sheriff's face, the biker placed it between Andy's lips and drew it back sideways, cutting a long line from the corner of the right side of the sheriff's mouth, all the way to his ear.

"You like that, little piggy? Do ya?" asked the biker, cheer evident in his voice. "I got some more for ya. What do you say? Do you want to play with me?"

Reaching around to the front of the sheriff's trousers, the biker unzipped Andy's fly, undid his belt, and tugged at his pants. The sheriff knew what was going to happen, but the knife going into the wound from the bullet had left him unable to move his arms or legs. He was helpless, and unless something happened soon, he was going to get raped before he died. Closing his eyes, Andy Wright began to pray.

The biker was tugging furiously, and Andy could feel the pants sliding down his thighs. If he could feel the pants against his legs, why couldn't he move them?

With his pants and underwear resting at his ankles, the sheriff began to cry. Something like this could only happen to him in his worst nightmare, and now it was coming true.

Hearing the zipper of the biker's blue jeans come down, the sheriff begged for death. He didn't want to be alive while he was defiled; it was just too much for him to handle.

Opening his eyes for a moment, the sheriff noticed something shiny on the ground next to his face. In his haste to rape the man, the biker had dropped his knife on the ground. Without the pressure of the biker on his back, the sheriff reached for the knife and his hand obeyed. Though his fingers were still numb, they wrapped around the bloody handle of the weapon, and he squeezed it tight.

Fear shattered his illusion of escape when the biker parted his butt cheeks and entered him. The assault was painful, the insult worse. It hurt so badly that Andy sucked in air, unable to scream or cry out against his brutal attacker.

Leaning over the shoulder of the sheriff, Jitterbug placed his lips next to the man's ear.

"How do you like it, sheriff? Is this what you had in mind the first time you saw me?"

When the knife pierced the side of his skull and entered his brain, the biker began to shake and quiver.

Releasing the knife, Andy was comforted, knowing that he had killed the man who had so brutally wrecked his mind and his ego. Bringing himself into just the right position for the sheriff to use the knife, the biker had never realized that he had murdered himself. Andy was still shocked that he had found the strength to kill the man. If the cocky bastard hadn't leaned in to taunt him, the sheriff would still be suffering at the man's hands.

As it was, the mind of the sheriff was shattered. Being raped in the woods was more than he could bear. Clawing at the ground, Andy Wright was able to twist far enough to reach the biker's gun.

He was going to die. Nothing could stop it now. The pain in his face and his back was unbearable, and the memory of what he'd just been through was something he could never live with.

Placing the gun to his head, Andy Wright begged for God, his daughter and his wife to forgive him. He found it hard to pull the trigger and end his life, so the sheriff thought about the bravery of far better men than he, men who had given their lives in defense of their country, men who had died defending others.

The whimper that escaped the mouth of the sheriff was the last noise he would ever make. Pulling the trigger, the sheriff knew no more.

13

She had never been thirstier in her life than when the black, Ford pickup stopped and offered her a ride. She had left Vale in the dust hours before. He could fend for himself. If the idiot hadn't driven a car without a spare, she would have seen the property in Bristol by now and been back at home relaxing on her couch.

The man driving the pickup was a decent sort. He was in his sixties and his gray beard reminded her of her grandfather. Simple conversation flowed between the two as they pulled into town and he dropped her off at her house. Thanking the stranger for his kindness, Kerri got out of the truck. Then she climbed the steps of her porch and entered her home.

Her home had been ransacked. It was anger that found the woman first. Anger turned to fear, so she retraced her steps, quietly exiting her home. *Damn those sons of bitches*, she thought as she got into her car and started it. Her father didn't need anything else to deal with, but she had to report it to someone. Sometimes it came in handy having the sheriff for a father.

Driving by the park on Azalea Way, Kerri spotted a familiar face. Raef was sitting at a picnic table under an awning, reading over the pages of a book. Stopped at the red light, Kerri could see that he had a whole stack of papers, which were kept from blowing away by another book that rested on top of the stack.

Curiosity got the better of her and she turned into the parking lot. She was sorry for the way she had treated the man yesterday, but he had had no right to bar her from the investigation. *Yeah, sure it was his investigation, but she had helped him with much of it.* Her feelings had been hurt, and she had allowed herself to use him as an outlet for her pain.

Shocked when a familiar voice called out over his shoulder, Raef was surprised to see Kerri smiling sheepishly at him.

"Still friends?" asked the woman as she took a seat next to him.

She was forward, not even waiting for his reply before she took her seat. *Charlie didn't seem to mind her*, Raef thought, so she must be all right. Lying under the bench, allowing the cool leaf litter on the ground to get tangled up in the fur on his belly, the dog seemed content.

"Sure, I guess. I thought it was you who was upset with me?"

The color rushed to her cheeks when she said, "I'm sorry. I was hurt when you decided to boot me from the investigation. I'm sure that you had a good reason for it, but I never let you explain."

He was happy that she was back. He had never meant to hurt her feelings.

"I was forced into making a promise to your dad to leave you out of the investigation. He threatened to throw me in jail, otherwise."

She chuckled as she said, "That sounds like my dad alright. I did some searching, and I think I found something of value for you."

"Did you get it after you followed me to the library in Camden?" Raef asked.

Again she blushed.

"I didn't actually follow you, Raef. You were there when I got there. We must have been thinking the same thing. Great minds think alike, huh?"

It was a relief to know that she hadn't followed him. The one thing in life he hated was distrust. If you couldn't trust someone, being around him or her was a waste of time. Even though it was occasionally required in his job to be around the untrustworthy, he did so with prejudice.

"That's good to know. I thought you might be stalking me," Raef joked. "I too found many things of interest. I have even talked to a living relative of Samuel Leeds."

"Seriously?" she asked. "You spoke to a Leeds? I thought they were all dead."

"I didn't say I talked to a Leeds. I talked to an Anderson. She was possibly the last living relative of Samuel and Deborah. In fact, she has been under your nose for years, living on Thirty-Sixth Avenue in the Crystal Springs subdivision."

A light bulb seemed to come on in the head of the woman, and she asked, "You're not talking about old lady Anderson, are you?"

"The one and only, and she was far more than she appeared. What's funny is that the children in the neighborhood were right. She really is a witch, or at least she was. If you have a minute and would like to sit, I will share what I know with you. I am loath to break my promise to your father, but I'm going to need some help, and he isn't volunteering any."

Now he was breaking a promise. It wasn't bad enough that he had taken a life; now he was going back on his word as well.

What's come over you, Raef Lorenz?

She gave him a kiss on the cheek. "Thanks for having faith in me."

Trying hard to keep from blushing, Raef began. He told her all that had transpired from the day before, even his stay at Ms. Anderson's and the unfortunate end that she had come to.

Calling Charlie out from under the table, he introduced the pair. The dog wagged his tail and accepted her gentle petting without growl or complaint. When Raef explained to her that he couldn't just leave the dog there, she nodded her approval, which made him feel better. He was beginning to feel as though he had stolen the dog.

When Raef was done, Kerri went into her tale about finding the document of sale for the property in Bristol and the fact that it had a freshwater spring on it. She told him of the trip with the realtor and the flat tire that had kept her from visiting the property.

Looking into the sky, she noticed that it was getting dark. She still feared the dark, and with good reason.

"Can I buy you dinner to make up for the way I treated you yesterday?" she asked him.

"Only if you'll allow me to tell you what I think I've discovered. Most of it is pure conjecture, but I'm pretty good at conjecture. I've had a lot of practice."

As she pulled her Mercury into the parking lot of a favorite local restaurant, Kerri told Raef to go in and get a table.

She had a call to make. Thirty-five cents was a lot for a telephone call, but what choice did she have?

She became worried when her mother said that her father hadn't come home for dinner. It was 5:17, and he was overdue. Her dad was the sheriff, but he was rarely overdue for dinner, because he had people to stay late for him.

Assuring her mother that she would check up on her father, Kerri hung up the phone and went into the restaurant.

Raef had chosen a table in the non-smoking section in a back corner of the restaurant. He didn't want people overhearing their conversation. They might think he had gone mad.

Taking her seat, Kerri ordered an apple martini. It had been a rough day, and she told herself she deserved it.

Ordering a beer for himself, Raef picked up his menu. He was famished and eager to order from it. He had become so captivated by his study of the diaries and papers that he had carried away from the Anderson home that he hadn't eaten all day.

With drinks in hand and their orders made, the pair began their discussion.

Raef was the first to go, and he had a lot to say.

"I spent a lot of time in the diary of Samuel Leeds. This is what I discovered. I think he bought the property in Bristol because he believed that he could use it to control the devil named Mammon. It was not Satan that he had struck a deal with. It was another devil, one that was far less powerful than the Dark Prince. He was planning on backing out of his deal with Mammon and needed a way to insure himself against the devil's anger. The spring is the reason he wanted the property, and though I know what its purpose is, I don't yet understand how it might have kept the devil from exacting its vengeance upon Leeds. If Leeds discovered a way to control the magical properties of the spring, he never wrote it in his diary."

Kerri was all ears, eating up his story as if it were food. He loved the way she looked at him when he was talking. If only things were different and the shadow of death wasn't hanging over them. Kerri was not only beautiful; she was also smart and attentive. If things were different, she might just be the kind of woman he could have a relationship with.

Shaking the thought from his mind, Raef continued on with his story.

"Believe it or not, Leeds had gotten his oldest daughter pregnant at about the same time that his wife conceived. He was worried that his wife might have complications bearing a child at her age, and he needed insurance just in case something went wrong. It was his daughter who miscarried, and he was forced to send her away, though he vowed to bear another child with her. His wife was unaware of his relationship with their daughter."

The look of disgust on Kerri's face was clear. She hated men who raped, especially pedophiles.

Deciding that it was her time to add something of importance to the conversation, she interjected.

"I think I can help with the importance of the spring, but how did he locate such a piece of property?"

"Unknown to his family or anyone else, Samuel Leeds employed the services of a medium, an old man who could see what others couldn't. It took the old man years to find what Leeds sought out, but he did."

Kerri couldn't hold in the information any longer, so she blurted it out.

"The spring is a gate into hell. At least, I think that's what it is. If Samuel Leeds had such a thing in his possession and the knowledge of how to use it, he could threaten the devil with banishment or reward the creature by bringing it forth from hell. He no longer needed to corrupt his child in order for the devil to enter the world, but when it did, Leeds planned on having control over the fiend. Do you think that Leeds entered into a separate agreement with another devil, possibly even Satan himself?"

Raef squirmed in his seat. He liked the way that Kerri's brain worked. Even if it gave him the creeps, she was on to something.

"If he did, he didn't mention it in his diaries," Raef said. "It was clear that Satan decided to change the deal when Leeds' wife asked that the baby in her womb be born the Antichrist. From what I read in the diary, Samuel was planning on cheating Mammon. I believe that Leeds might have been having second thoughts when the time to change the deal had come. He was wary of Mammon. The devil was cunning and untrustworthy, which should have gone without saying. Leeds was frightened that Mammon might go so far as to murder him when his usefulness to the devil was over."

Allowing Kerri to soak in the information, Raef added some of his own conjecture.

"That isn't surprising. Devils are foul liars. Not a single word from their mouths is ever the truth. That's the mistake that men like Leeds make when they enter into agreements with such creatures. The devils promise them everything and leave them with nothing. There are always excuses for not granting the desires of their earthly business partners. The excuses are endless and unbelievable, but the satin tongue of the devil makes the mortal unaware of the deceit. Men like Leeds will enter into any deal to attain what they desire or what they have lost. They never consider the consequence of their actions.

"Near the end, Leeds began to see the lies for what they were, but it was too late for him to put an end to what he'd started. He had invited the devil into his life, something that could never have ended well for the man. Think about the black spot in the old Whitmore Cemetery. Do you think he or she was aware that he or she was going to get more than he or she had bargained for?"

Though she was beginning to feel cold again, Kerri wasn't about to let Raef know it. She was back in on the investigation and didn't want anything to change it.

"I'm still with you, so far," she said. "But how was Leeds going to control the devil if he didn't know how to use the mystical properties of the spring?"

Though no food had been brought yet, Raef was nervously fooling around with his utensils.

"He must have," Raef said while shaking his head. "The tome of evil we found in the cemetery must have told him how."

Seeing the confusion on her face, Raef elaborated on his words. "The tome was handwritten by a man of evil. Through spell and sacrifice, the evil monk who copied it was able to capture the essence of the book. From reading the diaries of Samuel Leeds, I discovered that the book could never be read the same way twice; it was ever-changing. The words were lies and they changed each time that eyes were laid upon them.

It was the evil in the book that allowed the person in the cemetery to commit the ritual of unbinding, so why not tell Leeds how to use the spring?"

Looking over his shoulder as if he thought someone might be spying on them, Raef offered Kerri a knowing smile.

"There's only one conclusion that makes any sense. The tome allowed Samuel Leeds to understand how to control the spring. From what I read in old newspaper articles, the spring has a deep hole in the center of it. There were news articles in the microfiche at the library that told of divers having lost their lives while trying to explore its depths. Though the name of the place is Blue Hole, divers and locals refer to it as Hell's Hole. The key to ridding the world of the Jersey Devil is to control the spring.

"I don't know that it can be accomplished without the book, so I made a call to Rome this morning. The archbishop said he might have something that would be of service to me. It's on its way here, even as we speak. There is no time to send someone else to force the creature back into the abyss from whence it came. I have the knowledge and time is wasting. If we wait much longer, it may be too late. The devil grows stronger every day, and soon, he will prove unstoppable."

The fear on Kerri's face was evident. She didn't like the idea of Raef taking on the creature alone, and she told him so.

"I'm not alone," Raef said. "I have Charlie." He smiled smugly.

"Great, just great," Kerri exclaimed before excusing herself to the bathroom.

Kerri is truly upset. She must really like me, Raef thought. He still didn't like involving her in his mess. Her father wasn't going to be pleased.

After dinner, the pair headed to the sheriff's department. Kerri's dad had probably been working on something important, which had kept him from calling home.

It didn't take long to realize that something was wrong. Sheriff Wright hadn't been seen or heard from in hours, and no one knew where he was. Deputies had been searching since the late morning for the sheriff with no luck. That's when Raef realized that the sheriff hadn't told anyone where he was going.

Upon discovering where the sheriff had been headed to, Kerri began to cry. She knew why he was going there and if anything had happened to him she was to blame.

The police department in the city of Bristol was contacted, and had promised to send some men to investigate. Kerri wanted desperately to go to Bristol until Raef reminded her that it was after dark.

Promising the deputies that she would go to her mother's house and stay with her mother, Kerri and Raef left. Poking her head back into the office, because she had remembered something important, Kerri told the undersheriff about the burglary to her house. Giving the man the key to the place, she was assured it would be searched and that a report would be completed for her insurance company.

Things were spinning out of control, and Kerri was caught up in them. All of a sudden, she became aware of the devil's influence in everything that had transpired so far. In only a week, the creature had brought about death and destruction, causing fear in the populace of several towns. With its growing power, who knew what it might accomplish if given another week?

As they raced to her mother's house, Kerri and Raef sat in silence. The radio on the car was off and they were both deep in thought. For Raef, it was his future confrontation with the devil that worried him. He had never confronted such a fiend before, and he doubted that any priest had ever confronted such a powerful devil. He wasn't even a priest. How was he supposed to accomplish what needed to be done? He didn't know where to start.

In the morning, a package would arrive from Rome. He would need time to study it before confronting the devil. He wasn't even sure that the creature would waste its time on him. How could he be? What could he possibly do to get the attention of the creature.

Another thought struck him, and he let out an unconscious sigh. If the devil could attack its victims physically, what would protect him from those attacks? The idea of being burned alive wasn't comforting to the man. He had always dreamed that he would die in his sleep, going out peacefully. God was the only answer for him. He would have to trust in the powers of God and Jesus Christ. They would see him through this.

The sheriff would have returned by now if he could have, and Kerri knew it. Something had happened to him. She hoped he was all right. If he didn't come home, her mother would never recover from it. Andy Wright was everything in the world to Kerri's mother. She would die without him.

"Damn," Kerri cursed out loud. Then she silently asked herself, *Why in hell did I get mixed up in this in the first place?*

Even if Raef hadn't come to town, the devil would still be there. Events might have been different, but the outcome would have been the same. Besides, she had a lot of faith in Raef. He might not have been a priest anymore, but she could feel the good in him.

Looking over at the smiling man and the dog sitting on his lap, she knew what she saw in him. He was handsome and honest, things that were rare in this world. The dog sitting on his lap appeared to be lost in thought as well, but that was crazy, dogs didn't think.

The steel-edged scream that echoed above the wind and broke through the silence in the Mercury brought Kerri out of her trance. It was the sound of death and the promise of more to come.

"Holy shit, Raef! Was that what I think it was?"

Rolling down his window, Raef stuck his head out and looked at the sky overhead. He couldn't see the creature, but its scream was its signature. It couldn't have come from anything else.

"I think so, but why can't I see it? I don't know where it's coming from, but it's louder and even more menacing than the last time I heard it. We're running out of time."

"Don't say that," Kerri said. "It scares me."

"Sorry, but I don't know what else to make of it. Somehow, the deaths that the creature is either directly responsible for or indirectly causing are giving it power. There can be no other explanation for it. This comes to an end tomorrow. Either I stop the creature, or it stops me. One of us has to go."

Kerri hated to hear him talk like that, but she couldn't deny his words. Something had to give before the dam broke loose. She had thought about her next question before, but she had forgotten to ask it.

"Why is it that the devil only comes out at night? Is it some kind of vampire or something?"

"I thought about that one too, and I think that the answer lies in Isaiah 59:19. It reads: 'So shall they fear the name of the Lord from the west, and his glory from the rising sun. When the enemy shall come in, like a flood, the spirit of the Lord shall lift up a standard against him.'

"What I think the New Testament is telling us is that God holds the devil powerless during the hours of sunlight. It is in the darkness that the forces of evil may wage their war against what is good.

"If I'm going to confront this creature of evil, it will have to be at night, for there is no other time for the devil. As to why the thing doesn't enter houses and do as it pleases, I'm lost on that one. Something from the past, some kind of decree from the Lord must keep it from doing so. I don't think he remains outside for his own reasons.

"Let's get to your parents' house. We can discuss this further when we get there, but not in front of your mother. I don't want to scare her. She has already been through much, and if the news about your father isn't good, she will have to endure far more before it's over."

Kerri didn't like the sound of that either, but there was nothing she could do about it. When news came about her father she would deal with it then. Until that happened, she would comfort her mother.

The dog beat Kerri and Raef through the front door, wagging his tail and barking to be petted. Mrs. Grace Wright was happy to oblige the strange little dog. She met her daughter with a big hug as tears rolled down her face. Grace was worried sick about her husband, but she was happy that her daughter was home safe and sound. She wasn't as sure about Raef, but she greeted him cordially anyway. She was a lady after all, and ladies weren't rude to guests, even the ones they didn't care for.

Ushering the trio into her house, she sat them down in the kitchen, offering them coffee and tea. Charlie gladly accepted a warm bowl of milk. He was no cat, but he enjoyed it just the same.

As the dog lapped up his treat, Kerri and her mother entered into small talk. Neither of them wanted to talk about the sheriff; they couldn't stand to think that something bad had happened to him.

"How did your day go, dear? Did you like the property in Bristol?" Grace eventually asked.

That was the deal breaker; Kerri couldn't handle the guilt anymore and broke into tears.

"I'm sorry that he went there, mom. I had no idea he would come looking for me," the tortured daughter cried.

"What do you mean, looking for you?" her mother asked. "Why would your father be worried about you in the first place?"

The jig was up, and Kerri felt compelled to fill her mother in on some of what she and Raef had been up to. Explaining what Raef did for the Church of Rome, Kerri hoped her mother wouldn't judge him too harshly. Grace was a Methodist. She had no love for the Catholic Church or its doctrines.

Kerri never allowed the woman a word in edgewise. She explained that Raef was just an investigator and that he had never run into this kind of trouble before. There was no way that he could have known that she would be placed in danger and that people would die while others tried to keep him from discovering the truth of the Jersey Devil.

Raef didn't like that she had to defend him. He would have preferred to do it himself though he didn't understand why he had to.

The world was full of disbelievers, full of people who, if faced with the truth, would rather be lied to. The archbishop and the church were right. The world wasn't ready for the truth; it never would be. In order to keep people from following a false prophet that lied to them and told them what they wanted to hear, the Church of Rome had to keep the true reality of evil hidden from them. It was a daunting task; one that the church took on without complaint.

Grace went to bed before they heard any news about her husband. She was tired. It had been a long day, and she feared what the next might bring for her.

She had never mentioned to her family that she had been short of breath for the past two months. She hadn't wanted to worry her husband and daughter. When she got to the top of the steps, it was worse than ever. She had to stop and catch her breath.

She had a sudden urge to call to her daughter and tell her she loved her. Why she didn't, she didn't know.

Down on her knees at the side of her bed, Grace Wright prayed for the safe return of her husband. She couldn't stand the thought of living without him and asked that God take her too if her husband wasn't coming home. She had lived a good life and raised a fine, loving daughter. She had been through good times and bad, but for the most part she was happy with the way her life had turned out.

Never one to complain about her pain, Grace had kept it all to herself. Her back hurt and her knees popped when she walked, but she never complained.

Crawling into bed, she pulled the covers up over her shoulders and was fast asleep. When her heart stopped beating, she was none the wiser about it. Death had come peacefully for Grace Wright. She would never know the terror that would come over her town that night. She was beyond all of it.

14

After Grace went to bed, the pair's conversation turned serious again. Kerri had been thinking, and she had another important question for Raef. Clearing her throat and setting her coffee down, she looked Raef in the eyes. She took his hands and offered him a smile. He smiled back, and she began.

"I was just thinking to myself, can someone who is not an ordained priest conduct an exorcism?"

"Good question," said the man, the smile falling from his face. "I've been thinking about that one too, and technically it's not an exorcism. It's a binding."

Pulling away from him, she placed her hand over her mouth and wiped at something that wasn't there. "Now I'm really confused," she said. "Do you want to explain this to me, or do I have to read about it?"

Setting down his coffee cup, he grew serious.

"The first thing I need to explain is why it's not an exorcism. Many a man of God, who was not ordained by the Catholic Church, has tried his hands at exorcising evil spirits from those unfortunates who come to be possessed by devils. Though you may have heard different, none of those men has been successful. The danger in doing so is this. By failing when one confronts the devil, he himself may suffer that which afflicts the one he intended to heal. Now that we know of depression and mental illness, the church has pulled away from true exorcism."

Seeing a sliver of understanding in her face, he decided to continue. Kerri was an adept learner, and she was, in some ways, more gifted than he was.

"Medicine is capable of dealing with that which afflicts most of the people in this world, those whom others would call possessed. True possession is a rare thing, but when it happens, only a man of God, one who is trained in the verses of exorcism, can force the spirit of evil from someone. It is something I believe with all of my heart.

"It's like I told you before. I have seen many strange things. Some of them I was able to explain through science and medicine, and some were undoubtedly the works of spirits and devils. There is no one whom I have to make me believe in order for me to feel justified in what I do. I know what I've seen, and it is all that I need to know."

Kerri could feel the power in the voice of the man. He did believe it. He believed everything he said.

"I believe in you, Raef. I don't know what I believed when this started, but I have complete belief in it now. There really are no coincidences in life, are there? I mean, do you think that God put that nail in the tire today? Is it possible that I wasn't meant to go to that property in Bristol?"

"I don't think that you need for me to answer your question, Kerri. In your heart, you already know the answer to what you ask. Can you feel it?"

The woman nodded her head. She could feel it.

"Getting back to exorcism," said Raef as he combed his hair back with his hand. "There is a verse in the scripture that can be found in Acts 19:13–16. It goes like this:

"'Then certain of the vagabond Jews, exorcists took upon them to call over them which had evil spirits the name of the Lord Jesus, saying, "We adjure you by Jesus whom Paul preacheth." And there were seven sons of one Sceva, a Jew, and a chief of the priests, which did so. And the evil spirit answered and said, "Jesus I know, and Paul I know, but who are ye?" And the man in whom the evil spirit was leaped on them, and overcame them, and prevailed against them, so that they fled out of that house naked and wounded.'

"What the verses are saying is that if you don't come in the name of the Lord, with God and Jesus your savior by your side, you cannot hope to win out against the forces of evil. Only those who are ordained by God and Jesus Christ may exorcise the Devil and his minions. All others who try to accomplish the feat shall fall prey to the devil."

Never taking her eyes off of him, Kerri motioned with her hand for him to continue. She was engrossed in what he was telling her, and she wanted to know the whole of it.

Happy that she was following along so well, Raef never broke stride.

"The next thing I need to explain to you is the idea of binding. It was Simon Peter, the one God called his rock, who was tasked with binding things in this world. When Christ said to Peter, 'I will give unto thee the keys of the kingdom of heaven: and whatsoever though shalt bind on earth shall be bound in heaven,' he meant just that. Christ went on to say, 'And whatsoever thou shalt loose on earth shall already be loosed in heaven.'

"What it all means is that Christ gave Simon Peter the power to bind the Devil and all of his minions to hell. For when they are unbound and brought back into the world of men, they shall also be unleashed in heaven.

"Believe it or not, that didn't come to me until now. Sitting here in your parents' kitchen, reciting the verse, I understand what it is that Mammon seeks. He has been unbound. His power is both here and in heaven. If he brings forth an army of devils and demons, it is within the realm of possibility that he could wage war against heaven."

Getting up because he was still coming to terms with what he'd discovered, Raef went to the cabinet for a glass. Filling it at the sink, he sat down and continued.

"As bad as that would be, it gets worse. That war wouldn't take place in heaven. It would take place on earth. When archangels and devils wage war upon each other it is a devastating thing, something that the earth might not survive. Samuel Leeds' diary hints at just such a thing."

Sitting back in his chair and smacking himself on the forehead, Raef exclaimed, "I can't believe it didn't come to me until now. Mammon wants more than just to be unleashed upon the earth. It's not enough for him to do mischief and commit murder in the world of men. Though it is not Satan himself that has come into the world of men, it is just as bad. If Mammon gets what he seeks, the world may not survive it."

Tears were rolling down from the eyes of the woman seated across from him. He hadn't wanted to frighten her, but when his revelation had come to him, he had felt compelled to speak of it. There would be no time for an explanation.

Knowing that it had to be hard on Kerri, Raef reached across the table to take her hand. Her hand was warm and soft, and it felt good in his. She was cold, and it had nothing to do with the temperature in the house. Opening his mouth to say something that might ease her mind, he was interrupted by the ringing of the phone.

When the phone rang, both man and woman froze. Even the dog, which had been licking himself, stopped.

Kerri answered the phone, and was silent as someone on the other end spoke to her. Whatever was happening, it couldn't be good. Raef could see that Kerri was beginning to tremble, her lips quivering as she listened. Kerri began to sob, though she didn't hang up the phone. Her acknowledgements were little more than moans, but their meanings were clear.

Raef knew what she was hearing. Even before the call ended, he had somehow known what was being said.

When the conversation was over, Kerri couldn't move. Her world was falling apart around her and she didn't know how to handle it. Never hanging up the phone, Kerri sort of slid down the wall onto her bottom. Then she put her face in her hands and wailed. If the Jersey Devil were there right now, the wails of the woman would have overpowered its unholy scream.

Raef sat down beside her and wrapped her in his arms. There were no words that might comfort her. She was inconsolable. The loss of a parent was hard when it happened in an ordinary way. To find out that your dad had been murdered was devastating.

"Get my mother up, will you please," said the woman through her tears and sobs. "I need her right now. Can you get her for me?"

Raef went to the bedroom and what he found almost stopped his heart. Grace Wright was in bed and she was blue. A heart attack had apparently taken her while she slept. *What more could happen to Kerri tonight?* thought the man as he took the hand of the dead woman and prayed over her body.

After finding a phone in the bedroom, Raef called the archbishop. The conversation was short. Raef had things that he had to attend to.

When the investigator had relayed his revelation to the archbishop, Wells found his conjecture to be sound. Normally, Raef would have been called back to Rome at once, but this time it was different. Archbishop Wells knew his investigator well and he knew that if Raef felt so strongly about Mammon's growing power, then more than likely, it was true. It was the biggest decision that the archbishop had ever made and he prayed to God that it was the right one. Raef was a great theologian, but as a priest, he had failed. If all were as Raef told it to be, Rome and the rest of the world couldn't afford to have him fail again.

Whether Raef won or lost, the Catholic Church was sending men that could handle such things to Burlington. Raef might be the only hope of the church and possibly the world, but if he failed, others would come to take up the fight.

Hanging up the phone, the words of the archbishop didn't make Raef feel any better. It almost sounded as if the man expected him to fail. Raef hoped to disappoint the man. He was a winner; the alternative wasn't to his liking.

When he returned to the kitchen, Raef held Kerri in his arms again. He waited as long as he could to tell Kerri that her mother had passed on as well. It didn't make the news any easier for the girl in his arms. Her sobs turned to loud wails that filled the house with sadness. The night was long and many tears were shed.

When morning came and Kerri was still asleep on the couch, Raef left a note for her telling her that he'd gone to the park to meet his courier.

While wiping another tear from his eye as he left the house, Raef walked with Charlie to Kerri's car, with the keys he borrowed from the sleeping woman hanging from his finger.

His destiny was close at hand.

15

As was usual when dealings with the couriers who the church sent to him, the meeting didn't leave a pleasant feeling with Raef. The one who delivered his package that day looked like a homeless man. The agents of the church were as mysterious as they were plentiful.

The box he had received was flat and square. Whatever was in it, it wasn't a weapon. Of course, he hadn't expected the Church of Rome to send him a holy gun or a knife that was used by the archangels, but he needed something to combat the devil with. If God meant for him to fight the devil with just his hands and feet, he would gladly oblige, but he didn't see what good that would do against the creature from hell.

When the agent from the church had seen the dog sitting at Raef's feet, Raef saw a slight smile come to the agent's face before he winked at the dog. The dog had acknowledged him with a look, but the look was hardly telling.

"All right, Charlie, spill it. What do you and the old man know that I don't?"

The dog never answered. Raef wasn't surprised.

Tearing the paper off of the box, Raef could see the holy seal of the Vatican on its cover. When he opened the box and removed the Bible from within it, he froze, unsure of the meaning behind the item.

The book was old, and its cover was creased, some of its pages torn. The crucifix on the front was drawn by hand and so were the words, "The Holy Bible, copied by Simon Peter." *No way* Raef thought, *it can't be, can it? Can it actually be a copy of the Holy Bible, penned by the apostle, Simon Peter?*

Such a gift was unheard of. That which the Church of Rome had come by during the crusades had been locked away in the vaults of the Vatican. It was priceless, no, it went beyond that, it was holy. So why had the archbishop sent it to him?

There was only one way to find out, so he opened up the book.

Raef's hands shook as he opened the holy book. He feared that the pages would be old and brittle and that, if he handled them too roughly they would fall apart. None of that happened and he began to turn the pages without fear.

He stole a quick look around the park. He was satisfied that he wasn't being watched. One fight against an assassin was enough. If he was going to learn anything from the book, he would need peace and quiet.

Other than the sounds of children playing, Raef wasn't disturbed. The squeals of delight coming from the future of the world didn't bother him in the least. Though he didn't think that he would ever come to have any of his own, he loved children. They were innocent, and perfect in every way.

Lost in the pages of the Bible, Raef had no idea what time it was. If he was hungry, he didn't know it. Only the words in the book held any interest for him. The words he read seemed to flood his mind, and he could recite them by heart. Scripture that he had struggled to understand before was perfectly clear to him now.

There was magic in the Bible he held, not witchcraft magic, but the magic of spiritualism, magic that was holy in nature. It was as if his body had been filled with the Holy Spirit and his mind had been set free. Possessions had meant nothing to him before; they meant even less now. All he needed was the word of the Lord Jesus Christ and the love of the angels and saints. The foe before him was mighty, but the hand that would guide him through his battle with the evil one was ever the stronger.

By the time he was through reading what needed to be read, it was nearly dark. Raef had spent almost ten hours in the park, never once looking up from the Bible in his hands.

Kerri's timing couldn't have been more perfect, though Raef was concerned when she appeared at the park. She had used the spare set of keys in her purse to collect her car from the parking lot.

She was still in the clothes she had worn the night before, and until fifteen minutes before, she thought she would never climb off of her parents' couch again.

While she had slept, dreams had come to her, dreams that had both scared and comforted her. She had never been very religious, but all of that had changed with the events of one evening. Wearing a crucifix that her mother had kept in the kitchen, Kerri was determined to be of help to the ex-priest from Ireland.

Charlie had come alive when Kerri showed up. The dog's tail wagged furiously. He was glad to see the woman and hopped into the car the minute Kerri opened her door for the mutt.

Raef was still reluctant to drag Kerri any further into the nightmare. He stood unmoving for a time at the side of the road.

With his paws on the door of the now open passenger's window, Charlie barked and growled at the man as if chastising him for wasting time. The dog was something else.

How did I ever get along without him before? Raef asked himself.

As he got into the car, Raef had to push the dog away from his face. Charlie was licking him like crazy; the excitement of the canine reaching new heights. Raef knew that including Kerri wouldn't matter. If he failed, she would probably die that night anyway, and if not that night, certainly in the coming weeks as the war between heaven and hell raged on earth.

Raef didn't ask any questions or tell Kerri where to drive. They both knew where they had to go. Words weren't necessary.

On the way to Bristol, Pennsylvania, Kerri told Raef what had been said to her over the phone the night before. The police from Bristol had found her father in the Pine Barrens around the property that included the spring. He had killed three of his attackers before succumbing to a gunshot wound in his back. The police had left out the fact that his pants were around his ankles and that he'd probably been raped. The deceased was a law enforcement officer. His dignity would be preserved.

The men who had attacked the sheriff and had been killed by him were bikers. They had been covered in tattoos. A check with the National Crime Database showed them to belong to an outlaw motorcycle gang called the Diablos. They were not well-known in Pennsylvania, as they were normally found in West Virginia and Ohio. They were known for devil worship and running prostitutes, and they were as bad as bikers came. Most of the members had had warrants out for their arrests, some of them for killing cops.

The police had told her that her father must have been a strong and brave man to have taken out three of them by himself. They had left her with the knowledge that they had said a prayer for the sheriff and that their thoughts were with her and her mother.

November 10, 1984, 6:20 p.m.

In the woods by the property in Bristol was a statue. It was a statue that no one had ever seen before. Hidden from the eyes of men in the pine forests, the Jersey Devil lay in wait for the barriers of the Heavenly King to be torn down. The statue that was the devil in a state of suspended animation, waiting for darkness to fall on the land, was alabaster white, and it was as terrifying as the real thing was.

When light found the world of mortals, the devil was forced to return to a state of hibernation. Such were the terms of the covenant between the Father of Lies and the Heavenly King. No devil could roam the world of mortals during the light of day. It was forbidden to them.

The devil was awakened by the coming of night, changing from white to a rusty color. Its powers had increased tenfold from when it had been brought forth into the world. It was ready.

Mammon knew that the priest was coming. Lucifer had let it be known to him.

Though Lucifer declined to take part in the schemes of the devil called Mammon, the evil entity praised what the horse-faced devil attempted.

Let the ex-priest come; Mammon had been counting on it. He needed the man to open up the gate to hell. Turning the man to his side would be entertaining. He had done it to greater men before.

The first thing the devil would do was break down the faith of the man and show him the hypocrisy of the Heavenly King and his bastard son. He had something planned for the man, and he had no doubt that the man would do as he wished. Whether the man did his bidding consciously or unconsciously, it would be done.

Mammon was the most cunning of the devils. His penchant for deceit and corruption was unparalleled. He had brought kings and men of the cloth to ruin. The ex-priest would prove as unworthy as the rest of them.

Samuel Leeds had been a worthy foe. Because he failed to realize that Mammon was on to him, he had been undone, and so too would the priest.

On the night that the Leed's baby was to be born, Mammon was in the room just as he had been when Samuel Leeds had penned his deceit into his diary. Once a devil had been invited into a person's house or home, the covenant between the Heavenly King and the Father of Lies didn't apply any more. As long as the devil remained in the house with the Leeds, he was free to move about as he pleased.

For two years, the devil that had gone without a name had been in the house with the family. It was he who had convinced the girl, Abigail, to seduce her father and bring a child of evil into the world for Mammon. It was not Samuel Leeds who was ensuring that a child would be born so that Mammon could take possession of the child and be brought back into the world of men. It was Mammon who had ensured it.

The devil had laughed as the man sweated over the naked body of his twelve-year-old daughter. Every time the man released his seed into the girl, the devil had rejoiced. Samuel had become obsessed with the flesh of his oldest daughter, and it was almost nightly that he corrupted her body with his own.

Mammon was the first to know when Abigail became pregnant. It was he who assured Samuel Leeds that it was so. Every time that Samuel took his daughter, the devil Mammon took her as well. When Leeds was done, the spirit of the devil ravished her, and she knew ecstasy. No physical intercourse took place between them. It was purely spiritual, but the devil could please her still.

Coming down from his perch, Mammon alighted on the hard soil of Bristol. Stretching its tiny wings, the devil began to mentally prepare itself for what was to come. Everything would come down to that night, and it was ready. Let the ex-priest come, and let the angels from heaven follow him. The devil wanted a fight and when his minions were unbound from this world, he would get one. Even if he had to take the fight to the gates of heaven itself, he would do it. It had been eons since he had stared in marvel at the Heavenly King, and Mammon hoped to go back to that place where he would curse the Father and spit on the son.

Mammon wasn't the only devil preparing for what was to come. Though Lucifer had praised the cunning devil openly, secretly he wished for his failure. Lucifer had no desire for a war with God. The time wasn't right. If Mammon somehow succeeded in his war against God, he might find power to rival that of the Prince of Darkness. That, above all else, had to be stopped.

It was Lucifer who had sent the assassin to the hotel room of the ex-priest, not Mammon. The Devil didn't want the copy of *Groban's Tome of Demons and Devils* in the possession of the holy man. Mammon was not familiar with the priestly scholar. He underestimated the man's closeness to God and the Christ child.

The failure of his assassin meant that the unholy tome was in the possession of the Church of Rome. Without some strange twist of fate, the book of evil would never cause pain in the world of men again.

Lucifer found that unpalatable. Such tomes of evil were necessary for him to continue his battle against the forces of good.

There was still another chance. Another agent of evil had been sent to deal with the man before he could reach the spring. Mammon would be sorely disappointed when the ex-priest didn't arrive for the epic battle that the devil had planned.

November 10, 1984, 7:36 p.m.

When the shot rang out, both Kerri and Raef were shocked by it. Everything happened so fast that they couldn't react to it. The ball of brown fur, which climbed up Raef's chest at the same time as the window next to him shattered, was a blur to Raef.

Raef heard the thud and the cry of the dog as blood sprayed over him and the windshield on the passenger's side of the car. Charlie had just saved his life, but he didn't have time to grasp what had happened.

What the devil hadn't counted on was that Raef wouldn't be alone. Charlie had played his part in the scenario and the angel in the guise of a dog was already on its way back to heaven.

The shot scared Kerri so badly that she lost control of her car. The vehicle fishtailed and careened out of control, jumping over the narrow ditch on the side of the road. The front end of the Mercury slammed into the trunk of a large pine tree; the impact nearly knocked out its passengers.

Kerri had struck her chest on the wheel and her face on the dashboard. Blood trickled down her face from a cut on her forehead. The pain was bad, but she would survive. Raef had been virtually unscathed by the crash. His neck had a kink in it, but otherwise he had been left unharmed.

Wasting no time, Raef leaned over and pulled the handle on Kerri's side of the car. Using his shoulder, the man forced the woman out of the open door where she fell hard on her side.

Cursing she shouted, "What in the …?"

The rest of the words never came out. Her breath was knocked from her again as Raef landed on her stomach.

"Hush," he whispered as he put his hand over her mouth.

"Be quiet and remain still. Someone wants us dead."

The bullet had been meant for Raef and he knew it. The devil must have been frightened if it was attacking him so far from the property in Bristol. Raef had no gun, and as far as he knew, a Bible couldn't fire bullets at someone.

Crouching behind the rear tire on the driver's side of the vehicle, Raef listened for any sign that the gunman might be approaching. He couldn't hear a sound. If the gunman was approaching them, he was good at what he did.

The former priest was trapped on the side of the car with no way out; what he needed was a miracle. He could try moving from tree to tree, using the trunks of the pines for cover, but the gunman would have those covered.

Damn, Raef thought as he tried to find an exit or some avenue they could use to escape the gunman. There was no time to worry about getting to Bristol. If the two of them didn't find a way out from there, the point was moot.

The silence was maddening. It was as if the assassin had all night, like he didn't want them to get to Bristol.

The road the pair had run off was well traveled, and it wouldn't be long before a car or truck came by. When the first car went by, Raef realized two things. The car didn't stop to check on them, but it was probable that the next one would. Raef also realized that the assassin had to be on the move. A lone gunman, if that was the case, couldn't afford to have someone stop and render aid to the pair. He was on the move.

The thinking of the ex-priest was sound. The assassin realized the same thing. His time was running out. He had to end this now. It was amazing that such a large figure could move so quietly, but he did. Crashing from his hiding place in the forest, the gunman bounded across the roadway and in a single, athletic leap, he was over the ditch on his way to the car. His gun had been left in the forest. If he needed to make a quick escape, he didn't want the cumbersome weapon slowing him down.

Raef came charging out from behind the car at the same time as the assassin's feet returned to the ground after jumping the ditch. The ex-priest was in good shape, but he didn't look like a fighter. Never one to underestimate a foe, the assassin slowed his charge as the impact neared.

From the time that the agent of evil was three, he had been studying how to kill and maim men. He was nothing but an instrument, a well-honed killing machine.

His leaping front kick was aimed at the ex-priest's throat. The execution of the attack was flawless. Using his left arm, the former priest was barely able to get enough of his hand up in time to divert the full impact of the blow away from himself. Even though it wasn't a killing stroke, the attack caught enough of Raef's neck to cause pain. Spinning and ducking away from the assassin, Raef dodged a roundhouse kick that would have sent him to his knees had it connected.

It was pitch dark. Clouds covered the moon and stars, making the assassin, who was dressed all in black, almost impossible to see. It also helped to mask his blows.

Kerri was up and on her feet. Though she hurt all over, she held her Berretta in both hands, trying to get a shot at the assassin. The agent of evil and Raef were blurs of movement as they continued their deadly dance of kicks and punches, neither of them gaining the upper hand yet.

Even when the assassin turned her way, she couldn't get a shot. The dark suit he wore made it nearly impossible to set her sights on him. Every time she thought she had him, she lost her sight picture and had to hold back from pulling the trigger. Any mistake and she might just as soon shoot Raef.

She was frightened of the man in the black suit and was hesitant to get too close to him. After what Raef had told her about the last agent of evil he had faced, she knew that she would never surprise the assassin.

Raef allowed the straight punch to go by his face, but he was surprised when the assassin bent his elbow and sent it into the former priest's nose. A sunburst of pain went off in Raef's eyes, and he couldn't focus. His nose had been broken. He could feel the blood running into his mouth.

A low block kept the agent of evil from crushing his private parts, but the right cross that followed nearly took Raef's head off. Now he could add a fat lip to his bloody nose.

It pissed Raef off. He wasn't used to getting the shit kicked out of him.

When the spinning back axe kick came down toward his shoulder, Raef turned to the outside and let it harmlessly pass by him.

Raef was a quick study. The assassin didn't throw a punch or a kick without following up immediately.

Allowing the momentum of his turn to take him out wide, to the right side of his attacker, Raef avoided the straight knife hand strike that had been aimed at his solar plexus. The attack could have caused internal bleeding. The man trying to kill him was good at what he did.

With his foe overextended, Raef punched the dark-clad man of evil in the right kidney with his left fist. The assassin let out a light grunt and then delivered a hard right backhand, which Raef ducked.

Too late, Raef realized his error. The attack from his foe wasn't meant to hit him, it was meant to throw him off of his own attack. The assassin had succeeded. Raef had ducked, which was a big mistake, placing his chin at the belt level of his attacker.

Kicking backward and up like a mule, the assassin caught Raef on the chin, sending him back on his heels. His teeth clicked together and at least one of them broke because of the powerful kick. If Raef could find a way to overcome his opponent, he was going to need the services of a dentist.

Seeing Raef go stumbling backwards on his heels, Kerri knew she had to help him. She couldn't see the blood that was splayed across his face like the veins on an old man's hands. If she had, she probably wouldn't have had the courage to rush to his aid. The world was a mass of confusion and she wasn't cognizant of any sound coming from her feet as she ran toward the agent of evil, her gun out in front of her.

In the darkness of night and because she never took her eyes off of the assassin, she tripped over a root that was above the ground and went sprawling face-first onto a mass of pine needles and pine cones. She dropped the gun when her chin struck the ground, and she cried out as her breath was stolen from her again. Christ, she thought as she rolled over, searching for the gun that she'd lost. On her knees, Kerri was frantic to find the weapon. Without it, she couldn't hope to help Raef.

The woman who had shed so many tears that she couldn't possibly have any left, found more, and she wept. Her eyes hurt from crying, and she fought against the drops of salty liquid, but still they came. A feeling of helplessness came over her when her hand wrapped around another pine cone. The ground around her was filled with them and she was likely to find a hundred more of them before she found the gun.

Throughout her search, she could hear the grunts and cries of pain that escaped from Raef as the assassin continued to pummel him. If any of the cries came from the agent of evil, she couldn't tell. But from where she was kneeling, she believed that they all belonged to her friend.

No more than a second had passed from between when he stopped moving backward and when the next attack from his foe came at him. Crossing his forearms in front of his face like the letter *X*, Raef was fortunate to block the sidekick that had been aimed at his throat.

How was it possible that the man could see so well in the dark? Was it something that was just inherent in those who were evil, or did the man have some kind of help?

Raef's thoughts were forming more slowly than before, and he thought he might have suffered a concussion.

His opponent still seemed fresh. He was kicking Raef's ass. The assassin launched a second kick for Raef's throat, and he sidestepped the attack. He didn't think about what he was doing; he let his instincts take over. Only pure, unfiltered thought would get him back into the fight. He put Kerri and the devil out of his mind and focused wholly on the assassin.

When a foot went by his face, Raef could feel the air it cut move by him as well. *Damn, that one would have hurt*, Raef thought as he sent a roundhouse kick into the head of the assassin.

The agent of evil saw the kick coming, but he couldn't get an arm up in time to block it. Taking the side of the former priest's right foot against the left side of his head, the assassin made no noise. He was hurt, but he had been trained not to show injury. He had been no more than a child when he had been beaten for showing such weakness.

Still, the force behind the kick sent the assassin reeling to his right. His eyes went out of focus for a millisecond, but he recovered. His opponent was good. When Lucifer had contacted him, the Devil had told the assassin that he would be.

When a second roundhouse kick came for his head, the assassin expected it. He would have done the same. It was a game of inches, but the agent of evil managed to yank his face away from the attack. The foot of the man of God whizzed by his ear and then he realized he had been duped. No sooner had the foot touched the ground than it came back at him bending, before its heel caught him on the chin and his teeth clicked together.

Under his black mask, the assassin began to bleed, his teeth having come through his lips on both the top and bottom. Now it was the assassin who was stumbling back on his heels.

Raef pressed the attack, hoping to put an end to the fight. As he moved forward, meaning to send a kick into the gut of his opponent, he was surprised by the cunning assassin. The agent of the Devil stopped his backward momentum abruptly and punched straight out with an open hand. Raef tried to turn his face from the blow, but it was fast and unexpected. When the side of the open hand struck Raef on his cheekbone, he heard it crack. It was a brutal attack that hurt like a bitch, but at least it hadn't caught him in the nose. His nose was already broken, but an attack like the one he had just partly dodged could send bone back into his brain. Taking the punch full on was something that could ruin his day, and that was if it didn't kill him.

Reacting to the attack, Raef sent a straight punch of his own into the face of his attacker. It glanced off the assassin's forehead as the man dodged, but it put him off his next attack. The strike was a good one, but it wasn't enough to bring such a tough opponent down.

When the foot of his attacker caught him on the outside of his knee, Raef knew he was undone. Game over. The kick bent his knee involuntarily, and he fell to it. He was in possibly the worst position he could have been in; one that when faced with a skilled opponent, there would be no recovery from.

Closing his eyes, Raef gave a quick prayer to God, waiting for the blow that would kill him.

The blow never came.

Instead, Raef heard a feminine voice say, "Stop right there." Who was he to disobey her?

With the barrel of a gun pressed against his head, the agent of evil stopped. He could hear the breathing of the woman; it was coming fast and furious. She was both exhausted and frightened, and if he played it right she would soon be lying dead on the ground next to him. The man on his knee wasn't going to stay there for long. If he was going to finish the woman, he would have to act fast.

Even though he had been locked in battle against the man of God, the agent of evil had heard the woman as she had run and then fallen, frantically feeling around for something that she couldn't find. The assassin had never guessed it was a gun. He hadn't thought her capable of it. No matter; she was a novice.

Spinning with the speed born of thousands of hours of practice, the agent of evil grabbed the gun hand of the woman and twisted.

Only moments before, when she had finally laid her hand on the gun, Kerri had given out a sigh of relief. It had been difficult to see through the tears in her eyes, but she managed to locate the two men, locked in mortal combat. It had been hard for her not to hear their shouts and grunts as they attacked and injured one another.

After getting to her feet, she had stumbled yet again and fallen to the ground. That time, she had held onto the gun with a death grip, refusing to let it go. Moving from a crawling position to a full-out charge, she cried out in denial against her body's desire to rest. She had been out of breath, but she didn't care. The man she was falling in love with had been fighting for his life. She had had to get to him.

Feeling as though she was moving in slow motion, Kerri had desperately tried to reach Raef. It had been as if time had slowed; she could see her every footfall and feel every breath that came from her chest. She was never going to get there. She was going to be too late.

Bullshit, her brain had screamed out. She was going to get there, and she was going to save Raef.

By the time she had gotten to the pair she had been nearly spent. When she saw Raef go down to one knee, she knew if she would had been a second later in getting to him, he would have been dead. She had shouted at the man to stop, and he had.

She had made it. Raef was saved. If the assassin moved a single muscle, she would pull the trigger; they had won.

Taking her eyes off of the man for just a split second was a mistake. She had wanted to see if Raef was all right, and it was going to cost the woman her life. The assassin turned on a dime and was faster than lightning. He grabbed the gun from her hand and pointed it at her. It was so fast it almost didn't register in her mind, almost.

The assassin was pulling back on the trigger when something struck him in the genitals. No matter how tough the man, it was the one place that made all fighters equal. The blow was powerful, and the assassin bent over.

Raef jumped to his feet and slammed down hard against the back of the assassin's neck with his right forearm, sending the man to the ground like a sack of grain. Snatching the gun out of the assassin's hand, Raef didn't think. He aimed the barrel at the man's head and pulled the trigger. The sound split the silence of the night, deafening Raef and Kerri.

Unfortunately for the agent of evil, he was more than deaf; he was dead. His head splattered on the ground next to where his body had slumped. It happened so fast that Raef was just then beginning to realize what he'd done.

Disgusted with himself and the weapon, he reared his arm back and threw the gun into the forest.

Falling to his knees, the former priest folded his hands in prayer and offered God an apology. He felt unclean. How was he supposed to act as an agent of God and fight the devil when he felt so unclean?

Overcome with emotion, Kerri wrapped her arms around Raef and held him tightly.

Kerri's arms felt good around him. They brought him comfort.

Raef needed something real to hold onto. His faith was shaken. Not only that, he was feeling unworthy of God and that was dangerous when he had to face the devil. Raef knew that the devil would look into his heart, his very soul, and find what the man feared most.

At that moment, Raef was wearing his guilt on his sleeve. One look at him and Mammon would know. If Raef didn't find a way to clear his conscience, he was going to die. No one who suffered a guilty conscience could face-off against the devil and hope to win. Better men than he had done so, only to end up losing the battle. It was not enough to just come in the name of the Lord. If he was to have any hope of succeeding against the devil, Raef had to be of sound mind and clear conscience.

Great, he thought to himself. *I'm of neither.*

The pair remained there, holding one another for long minutes before necessity forced them apart, and they began to walk down a long, dark road that might very well lead to their deaths.

16

The night was dark, and now that Raef's adrenaline was gone, it was cold as well. Refusing to take turns wearing the coat that Kerri had brought, Raef allowed his discomfort to carry him forward. He was wasted, both physically and mentally. His head hurt like hell, and he wanted to lie down and rest. But just like the millions who marched during Ramadan, he couldn't allow himself any rest. He feared that if he sat down, he might never get back up.

The woman by his side was no better off. God bless her, she continued to lift one foot after the other. Whenever a car passed, they took refuge in the forest. Whether it was driven by a Good Samaritan or another agent of the Devil, they didn't have time for the interruption. There was no time for a trip to the hospital or another fight against an assassin.

The last thought made Raef sorry that he had thrown the gun away. He hadn't been thinking when he had done it. Raef's soul had been in pain, and he reacted to that pain, the only way he knew how at the time. His face was swelling, and his cheekbone hurt, but Raef knew where his destiny lay and he was ready to meet it head on. It was hard to breathe through his nose due to all the dried blood in it, so he allowed his mouth to take his air in and out of his body.

No ordinary man could still be standing, she told herself. Kerri had seen the punishment that Raef had suffered at the hands of the assassin, and it was great.

It wasn't as if she hadn't been through a great deal herself. Her father had been killed, and her mother had died of worry, leaving her all alone in this world. Live or die, she would be facing a lot of changes in her life after that night.

Would Raef ever be the same? Was she really falling in love with the man, and could there be anything between them? Their lives were very different, and they lived on separate continents. There were a lot of questions to be answered, and she was sure that they would be, if she and Raef survived the night.

Taking Raef by the hand, Kerri asked, "Where's Charlie? I heard him yelp, but haven't seen him since."

The man never looked at her; it hurt too much to do so. Charlie had become special to him in such a short amount of time, and he had not had the proper amount of time to grieve for the mutt.

"He died saving my life," answered the man, his sorrow plain in his voice. "He took the bullet that was meant for me, the bullet that shattered the glass and sent you careening off the road."

The dog had given its life to save Raef. She knew that Charlie's sacrifice was worth it. Raef was their only hope and possibly the only hope for the world as well.

Kerri couldn't believe that she was willingly walking to where the man would confront a devil. It was an actual devil, one that had once been an archangel. She had no business being there, but to abandon Raef was no longer a possibility. They had been through a lot together, and it was coming down to one last confrontation with evil, a confrontation that had to be won.

The pair had walked for a little more than an hour. Raef changed course once or twice without the use of a map. It was as if the location was programmed within him. He somehow knew where he had to be. The man was quiet, lost in his thoughts, listening to whatever force told him which way to go.

If it was possible for the night to get any darker than it once had been, it had. Not a single star had shined through the clouds since they had arrived. If the moon was out there somewhere, it was hiding. It was as pitch-black as she had ever seen the night. No wind stirred the pine needles on the trees, nor did any insect cut though the silence with its mating call.

When she looked at Raef, Kerri wondered how the man was still standing at all.

Raef wore no coat. He had to be freezing. His fight with the agent of evil had been over an hour before. He couldn't possibly be warm from the adrenaline any longer.

When they had arrived at the property, the front gate on the western-style fence was opened as if someone or something had invited them inside. Raef had moved through the gate without pause. There had been no sign of hesitance in the man.

Kerri could barely differentiate the water of the spring from the grass-covered fields surrounding it. The water was flat; nothing appeared to mar its surface, though Kerri knew her impression was false. The area was as turbulent as any storm, only something held that turbulence back. The serenity of the place was strange. It gave off a false sense of security that the woman wasn't buying into. What they were about to confront was dangerous, and no calm water or gentle breeze could make Kerri forget that.

From the minute they entered the property in Bristol, she knew where they were. The oppressive sense of evil was nearly suffocating. She could almost taste it.

Taking the Bible from his back pocket, Raef opened it to an earmarked page and began reading from it. The verse was one that helped to lift some of the evil in the air, but it didn't seem to bring much comfort to Kerri.

Coming to a point on the side of the spring that left Raef no more than twenty feet between him and the chill water, Raef stopped. His enemy had shown itself.

Sensing a change in the air, Kerri took shelter behind the man's broad shoulders. She was too frightened to look at what Raef faced.

Hiding behind the man, she was surprised that he was so steady on his feet.

They had been through a lot, and now he was facing the enemy without any sign that he was scared. Unwavering, the former priest just stood and stared at something that Kerri was too frightened to look at. When she found the courage to look, she could see what Raef was staring at, and it was hideous.

Standing nearly ten feet tall, the bastion of evil was a mockery of angelic beauty. It had the head of a collie dog, the face of a horse, and tiny, monkey-like ears. A pair of tiny bat wings stood out behind its shoulders, and though she knew that they carried the devil in flight, she couldn't see how it was possible. Swishing back and forth behind the devil was a tail that truly belonged on a devil. It was the only thing that gave the heritage of the creature away, but it was enough.

The torso of the animal was like that of a dog as well. The front legs of the animal were bent as if in prayer, ending in the paws of a dog. The rear legs were long, at least four feet in length, and resembled those of a crane or a stork. The legs ended in the cloven hooves that were responsible for frightening those who lived in the homes that the creature had danced upon.

Craning its neck forward, the devil let out a steely cry that was sent as a challenge to the ex-priest. Raef offered no challenge back to the creature; he simply stared at it, remaining lost in the warmth that the words of the Lord had brought to him.

The mere sight of the creature wouldn't be enough to wither the man in front of it. In the past, such things had been possible for the creature, but this time would be different. If the man of God wanted a test of wills, the devil would oblige him. How could it lose?

The eyes of the creature began to burn like the embers of a campfire, and its nostrils flared and snorted. Saliva poured from the corners of its mouth and stained the ground crimson red where it struck. The devilish tail of the creature began to wave with menace and its wings started a rhythmic flapping that was meant to hypnotize.

Standing firm with the words of the Lord in his head, Raef refused to have his will dominated by the devil. He could feel the heat of the creature's eyes as they bore into him, reaching for his soul, but he was up to the challenge.

Every time the creature screamed at him, it tore a little of his resolve away. There was more to the cry of the beast than met the ear.

It seemed to Kerri like it was hours that the pair remained locked in a battle of wills, but it had merely been minutes. Though Raef stood calmly, she could now feel his arm trembling where her hand touched it. The struggle had to be a mighty one. She had faith that the man was up to the challenge.

Moving her eyes from Raef to the devil, she could see the frustration in the beast's eyes. The creature's hooves had dug large divots in the ground, and its head shook back and forth in denial of Raef. When the creature began to levitate from the ground, Kerri knew it was just another attempt to unnerve Raef. She felt a shiver go through her spine, and her skin went cold. If the display of the devil wasn't frightening Raef, it was doing a good job on her.

Deciding that she couldn't look at the creature for another second, Kerri placed her cheek against Raef's back and took comfort in the man's breathing. His body may have trembled, but his breathing was calm. Through all that must have been going on in his mind, Raef was still in control.

It was Raef who broke the silence with words that stung the devil as if they were physical weapons. "And the Heavenly Father cast them out, banishing them forever from the gates of heaven."

The words were like daggers, each of them more painful than the last. Mammon moved back away from the man of God, until he was up against the spring. The sides of the spring were steep; the layers of pine needles and leaves making them slippery.

The devil roared with fury before it countered the attack of the man, digging its cloven hooves deep into the ground. Its words were not spoken out loud, but Raef and Kerri could hear them. The mental force behind them was powerful.

"Fool of a lost holy man," hissed the voice of Mammon. "It is God who is the great deceiver. He did us a favor when he set us free of his boring home."

Letting the words sink in, the devil watched the face of the man in front of him. Any sign of weakness, and he would have him. *Patience*, the devil told itself. The man would succumb to him. Like all those before him, this one would be turned.

"Do not speak of the Heavenly King as if he means something to you. You forsook him when you left his church. Don't you see the folly of obedience to him," continued the devil as it danced on its hind legs, while its tail continued to whip furiously behind it. "He asks too much of his flock and gives little in return. I know, for I was once one of his most favored."

Testing the man, the monster in the form of a devil was pleased with itself. "Why don't you side with me? Besides saving your life, it would allow you that which your heart most truly desires."

"Still thy tongue, evil one," Raef shouted as he shook the beguiling words of the devil from his head. He had come to terms with his leaving the priesthood long ago. God had had another plan for him. "Turn from thy lies, for it is poison that comes from your mouth. It is you who is the liar, the great deceiver, not God. Through God and his only true son, Jesus Christ, shall I find the might to tear you from this world and send you back to the fiery pits where you belong."

The words hurt, and the devil cried out against the pain.

"What about the girl?" asked the devil. "Wouldn't you like to possess her, heart and soul? I can make that happen. I can give you what you desire."

Seeing that Raef was shaking, the devil pressed its mental attack. "You desire the flesh as strongly as any other man. Why not accept the offer? You deserve her, don't you? What has the whore of a king and his bastard son ever done for you?"

The words were meant to confuse and Raef knew it. He wasn't sure where his feelings for Kerri went, but he knew that he liked her.

Once or twice in his life he had questioned where his devotion to God was taking him. The devil was reading his mind or had found a way to see into his past. It wasn't so much that the promises of the devil were enticing to the man, it was that he felt guilty for ever having had the feelings in the first place. The whole time he'd been a priest in America he had wondered if he had mistaken his calling. It had required long nights of prayer and conversation with the archbishop for him to understand that he had not. There were other callings from God in the world, and he had answered the wrong one. He was where he belonged now, rooting out the evil that would devour the world.

"I reject the words that come from your lying mouth, oh devil from hell. You have no place among men or heaven and you shall be bound by the word of the Lord, Jesus Christ. For it is through him that Simon Peter bound you from this world, and it is through him that you shall be bound once more."

The cry from the devil was both awful and real. Backed by the power of the Holy Spirit, Raef's words affected Mammon greatly. The words dug deep into the creature, and it began to slide down the side of the spring's bank. Its wings flapped, and its tail went straight out as it tried to slow its fall into the water below.

With incredible effort, the devil managed to stop its descent and stand firm.

The man was falling into its trap. All it needed was a little more time and more persuasion. Mammon was the clever one. He didn't misread men. The devil knew that it would never turn the ex-priest away from the bastard son, but it could use the man's arrogance and defiance against him, couldn't it?

Already, the man was shaking with the rage that the devil would use against him. It would prove to be his undoing. The devil would continue to add fuel to that rage, blinding the man to what it truly desired of him. By the time the mortal realized he'd been duped, it would be too late for him.

"In your readings, was it ever revealed to you that Mary was a whore, that she slept with other men for money until she became pregnant with the bastard that you have come to call Christ? Oh, but it's true. Joseph knew it; he even wanted her stoned to death for her adulterous behavior. If not for the true father of lies, the one who sits in a throne over us and judges us as if it were his right, Joseph would have had the woman stoned to death. I can see it in your heart. You know that it's true. Did you also know that Joseph only accepted the baby because your God threatened him with death if he refused?"

The words sent Raef back on his heels and caused his heart to flutter in his chest. The wind suddenly grew strong and it whipped his face like a storm of stinging insects. He knew that the words were false, but the creature had said them with conviction. Above all other women, the Virgin Mother was sacred to Raef. The love he felt for Mary was real, and it was crushing to his soul to hear the devil speak about her in such a manner.

Even now, the devil was climbing back up the steep embankment. Raef's words were failing him, and he still had no idea how to control the gate. Raef's brain raced, looking for an answer to his dilemma.

Kerri was on her knees behind him. The words of the devil had battered her into submission. Without the help of the Lord, no one could hope to stand against the will of the beast

Focusing his thoughts, Raef cried out another denial of the devil, it had to work.

"It is God who commands thee, not you who commands the Lord. Fall back from the world of men, so that they need feel your evil no more. It is you who are the lie. It is you who falsely accuse the Virgin Mother."

Good, the devil thought as spit flew from the mouth of the angry man. Mammon's words had hurt him, but not only that, they had hurt the sense of pride he took in the woman who had been offended. *Pride, oh yes, pride.* It was the one thing that men could not leave behind them, and it was the very thing that would bring this one to his knees. The man was on the verge of losing it; all he needed was a little push.

The devil did something that was as unnatural as it was grotesque. Moving its short, deer-like arms out wide as if asking why, the creature cocked its head to the side. It was as pitiful as it was ugly to behold. Its wings folded neatly behind its back, and the tail looped over the side of its left arm. Looking as defenseless as possible, the devil reached into the mind of the mortal again.

"I am sorry if the truth is painful for you. I only wish for you to see things as they truly are. Come, don't you feel the truth behind my words? You know I'm telling you the truth. Forsake the son and the whore who brought him into the world," the devil suddenly shouted into Raef's mind. "I shall be the new way, the light, the only true light. The crimes of the heavenly king shall be seen for what they are, and I shall rule over this world, and its inhabitants shall call me lord."

The words of the beast sent Raef over the edge, and he lashed out against them. "Lies and false accusations, that's all you offer, Satan's spawn."

Opening up the White Bible, Raef tried to read the words from its pages, but they were blurry in his eyes.

Mammon had used the ex-priest's rage to blur his eyes against the words of the book. He needed the man to become further confused. He needed the man to make the fatal mistake. That mistake was close at hand; the man was desperate.

Raef's words alone could not hope to defeat the devil. He needed the words of Simon Peter. When remembrance struck him, he clung to it. He could see the words clearly in his mind, but he could not understand their meaning. The rite started out with six words and then a pause. In the middle were another six words, followed by a pause, and then six words to finish the rite.

Raef had been desperate for a way to attack the devil, so it never dawned on him that he had just read the rite from *Groban's Tome of Demons and Devils* until after he had done it.

Falling to his knees, Raef looked up into the heavens. He couldn't find the words to apologize. It hurt just to think about them. Redemption was out of reach for the man. He had been tricked into a fatal error, an error that had cost the world and the heavens equally. Why had he been entrusted with such a task? God must surely have known that he would fail.

Defeated, Raef remained on his knees with Kerri sobbing behind him. The woman had been witness to it all. Raef had failed her as well.

The wind continued to assault him, but he didn't care. Thunder and lightning shook the earth and split the sky, lighting the beast and the gate that would bring his army of devils into the world.

Hail fell from the sky, and the trees swayed from side to side, threatening to topple over on him and Kerri. The water in the spring began to boil and then changed into a maelstrom of swirling current. It swirled with fury, threatening to jump over the banks that gave it shape. All the while, the devil cried out with its steely scream, welcoming its minions into the world of men.

Already, Raef could hear the screams and howls of the devils that answered the beast. They got louder and grew closer with each passing second. They were legion. They were as one. It was more than his mind could take. He had lost the fight that he'd been tasked with. It was a fight that was more meaningful than any he'd had in the past. There would be no future for him or for mankind. The growls and howls of the coming army seemed to promise as much.

The devil drew pleasure from the recognition in the mortal's eyes. The sweet satisfaction that he had duped the man into opening the gate for him was all consuming. All of it had been planned, and the man of God had fallen for it.

Neither the priest nor Leeds realized that Mammon required one of them to open the gate. The devils that lay in wait for the gate to be opened had been bound by man, and it was only through man that they could be unbound. Mammon hadn't the ability to do it, though he had bragged otherwise.

If the mortal had only refused to play his game, he might yet have succeeded in turning him from his plan. No, the mortal couldn't send him from the earth. Only an exorcist could do that. But it was possible that the man of God could bind him to a place, such as the Pine Barrens. It had been done in the past.

Pride and anger had been the tools of the devil. Men were always proud and quick to anger. The ex-priest wasn't the first to have been undone by it.

The devil's attention was pulled away from the man and sweet victory when it heard the call of its minions. Turning its back on the defeated mortal, Mammon watched the water and the glow that grew brighter as his army drew nearer. They were so close. It was only a matter of time before they began to stream forth from the spring.

Mammon was so busy watching the swirling water and welcoming his horde of devils, that he never saw Raef get to his feet. Tears rolled down Raef's cheeks, and a fire burned in his eyes. His anger was still with him, but his pride had faded. It was he who had been the tool of the devil, and it made him sick to his stomach. How could he have been so stupid? How could he have been so blind?

The archbishop had warned Raef that the devil would be cunning, using his own feelings against him. He had allowed his own feelings and doubts to get in the way of the job at hand, and it had cost him everything.

Turning around, Raef looked at Kerri. She was sitting on her backside, stunned by what she'd witnessed. Raising the White Bible to his lips, Raef kissed it, and placed it in her hands. Without thought, Kerri accepted the book, grasping it tightly as if it were a lifeline.

Turning his attention back to the devil, Raef could see the spring glowing. Then it burst into flames.

There would be no more thinking. He'd had enough thinking for one night.

Lowering his head and shoulders, Raef ran the twenty yards to the edge of the spring and dove headfirst. When his shoulder struck the giant creature in the hips, his shoulder shattered, which sent a current of agony through Raef's body. He grunted with the impact that sent both him and Mammon falling into the spring.

The hot water stole the breath from Raef, who clung with all of his might to the shaggy waist of the beast. It was all he could do not to let go of the monster.

Mammon cried out in denial. The ex-priest was close to undoing what it had taken the devil so long to bring about, but it wasn't over yet.

The swirling water caught the devil and the man clutching to it and sucked them into the flaming maelstrom that it had become. The flames licked at Raef, burning his flesh wherever they touched. He screamed as his flesh burned away from his bones, but still he held onto the creature.

Though the flames didn't burn Mammon, the beast was equally terrified. The swirling waters, which promised to bring forth his army, were sucking him down into the hole, which led straight to hell.

Only when the gateway had been activated did it open onto the fiery realm of devils and demons, but now was one of those times. The mystic spring only had the power to pull. No matter which direction a creature entered from, it would pull it to the opposite end.

Faced with the possibility of being drawn back into hell, the devil opened up its tiny wings and began to beat them furiously. If Mammon could free himself of the priest, he could still win the day. It wasn't the weight of the man alone that defeated the attempts of the devil to be free of the water. It was the added weight of the man and the pull of the maelstrom. Under normal circumstances, the devil would have been able to pull free of the spring, but the added weight of the mortal made it impossible for the tiny wings of the creature to accomplish the feat.

The wind raged, and the maelstrom continued. Raef was little more than a skeleton from the waist down and his bones showed in many other places. How he could still be alive was beyond mortal reckoning, but he was. Mammon fought against the raging water and the pull of the gate, crying out for his master to help. There would be no help from the Prince of Darkness. Lucifer had hoped for his failure from the outset. As the water pulled the pair of screaming entities under and began to suck them into the hole, Raef screamed out six words that came rushing to his mind. They too were from *Groban's Tome of Demons and Devils*. They were the words that would close the gate behind him.

Mammon and the host of devils became tangled in one another as the gate closed, and once again, they were blocked off from the world of men. Their screams of protest and curses, promising pain and suffering to the world of men, died as they were drawn back into the fiery pits of hell.

The cries of the devils weren't the only ones to be drowned out by the closing of the gate. The cries of the man named Raef Lorenz died along with them.

Through it all, Kerri had been screaming, and her throat was sore. Her voice was gone and she had no more tears left to cry. Though she had wailed against it, the whirlpool of water and flames had taken Raef along with the devil.

All alone, the woman fell into a fetal position. Grief overtook her, and she slept.

That night, the temperature in the Northeast grew twenty degrees warmer. The miracle saved her life, keeping her from freezing to death.

When she awoke, she carefully went to the edge of the spring, hoping that Raef would miraculously appear. There was no such miracle to be had. The man was gone.

Kerri offered a silent prayer for the soul of her friend. She hoped he would find peace. Never before had there been a man like Raef Lorenz in Burlington, New Jersey, and there never would be again.

17

Returning to the main highway, Kerri thumbed a ride into Burlington. She had reported the death of her mother before she had gone to find Raef earlier that day. Kerri was alone in her parents' house. Why she had come back there instead of going to her own house, she didn't know. It just felt right to her. Wandering the hallways of the home, she romanticized the pictures that hung on the walls. They were fond remembrances of her childhood, and they brought some good feelings back into her life.

When she closed and locked the door behind her, Kerri knew that it would be months before she would return there. Too much pain was locked behind that door, and she couldn't face it.

After catching a ride home with a neighbor, Kerri entered her house. It was still a mess from having been ransacked, but at least it was familiar to her. She was hungry, but she couldn't bring herself to eat. What she had just been through was far too awful for her to do anything but close her eyes and try to make it go away.

Getting on her knees, the woman offered God the first prayer that she had said in years. She prayed for Raef, her father, and her mother. Even Charlie received a prayer from the woman.

After crossing herself the way she'd seen Raef do it, Kerri climbed into bed and closed her eyes. Somehow she was at peace, and the horrors of the past week left her alone.

November 13, 1984, 11:30 a.m.

The wind blew fiercely as the two coffins were placed into the open hole in the ground. One on top of another, Andy and Grace Wright were laid to rest.

Snow flurries blew through the air, and the wind howled as if crying out for the husband and wife who had joined the ranks of the dead far too early.

Holding two roses in her hand, Kerri walked to the edge of the hole. She tossed the flowers on top of the caskets belonging to those she loved.

She had made a decision to take a job at the Smithsonian Institution as a history researcher. In the last week, she had learned enough about history research to fulfill a four-year degree. Her diploma from Brown University didn't hurt either.

Though she would never broach the subject again, Kerri Wright would often think of the ex-priest and his sacrifice. She had witnessed a battle between the forces of good and evil and seen good win. That was the way it was supposed to happen, but she knew better. In life, there were no guarantees. You got out of it what you put into it, and still, sometimes it was only the sacrifice of others that made any difference whatsoever.

Kerri never noticed the man taking in the funeral service from behind the iron fence of the cemetery. He wore a black pea coat and blue jeans, his long dark hair blowing in the wind to reveal an earring in the shape of a crucifix hanging from his left ear.

When Raef had awakened on the far side of the spring, he had been amazed. All of his burns and other injuries had been healed. Touched by the hand of God, he was just thankful to be taking another breath of air. His suffering in the burning whirlpool had been real, and he would never forget it. He was happy to have served God, but he took no pride in it. Pride had almost led to his undoing. From then on, he would only praise the Lord for what he was able to accomplish.

Raef offered a prayer for the souls of Andy and Grace Wright. Kerri received one too, but she would never know of it. Staying in a hotel in Bristol until today, Raef had decided that it was best if Kerri believed him gone. Chasing down the supernatural wasn't for Kerri, and he knew it. She had played a vital part in his investigation, but her place was elsewhere now.

In just a few short hours, Raef would be onboard a flight to Florida. Something had come to the attention of the church that needed Raef's immediate attention. He might have preferred some rest after saving the world, but such was the life of a man of God.

As he walked away from the cemetery, it began to snow in earnest. He had a plane to catch and another assignment to take on.

At least he wouldn't have to wear a coat when he got there.

THE END